11-14

DATE DUE

QUICKSILVER

QUICKSILVER

R.J. ANDERSON

carolrhoda LAB
MINNEAPOLIS

Carolrhoda Lab™
An imprint of Carolrhoda Books
A division of Lerner Publishing Group, Inc.
241 First Avenue North
Minneapolis, MN 55401 U.S.A.

Website address: www.lernerbooks.com

The definition of "inductive kickback" on pg. 8 is copyright © Maxim Integrated
Products (http://www.maxim-ic.com). Used by permission.

Cover photography © Sandy Honig 2013.

Main body text set in Janson Text 10/14.
Typeface provided by Linotype.

Library of Congress Cataloging-in-Publication Data

Anderson, R. J. (Rebecca J.)
    Quicksilver / by R.J. Anderson.
      pages cm
      Summary: To prevent the public from learning about Tori's unusual DNA,
technology "geek" Tori and her adoptive parents move to a new town and change
their names.
      ISBN 978–0–7613–8799–2 (trade hard cover : alk. paper)
      [1. Identity—Fiction. 2. Technology—Fiction. 3. Extraterrestrial beings—
Fiction. 4. Science fiction.] I. Title.
    PZ7.A54885Qu 2013
    [Fic]—dc23   2012027062

Manufactured in the United States of America
1 – SB – 12/31/12

FOR NICK, WHO LIKES TO MAKE THINGS

PROLOGUE: Aliasing

(The distortion that results when a reconstructed signal is different from the original)

On June 7, the year I turned sixteen, I vanished without a trace.

On September 28 of the same year I came back, with a story so bizarre that only my parents would ever believe it and a secret I couldn't share even with them.

And four weeks later I woke up in my hometown on Saturday morning as Victoria Beaugrand and went to bed that night in another city as a completely different person.

That last part wasn't as bad as you might think. There's something exciting about reinventing yourself, even if it means leaving all your friends and the only life you've ever known behind.

My only fear was that I might not have made myself different enough.

The move was the first step. My mom and I loaded our last two boxes into the rental van, latched the doors, and watched my dad drive off with the few pieces of furniture and clothing we still owned. Then we got into the car and backed down the driveway of our house on Ridgeview Court for the last time ever.

We drove through the city and out onto the highway, rock cuts boxing us in on either side. At first the landscape was rugged and wild, but as the kilometers ticked by—one hundred, two hundred, three—the pine trees and swampy lakes gave way to leafy woods and rolling hillsides. By the time we took our first rest stop, the horizon was wide open, and the air so mild I didn't even need a jacket.

I stuffed my long hair under a baseball cap and walked around the parking lot to stretch my legs, while my mom went into Shoppers' Drug Mart and bought the stuff we needed. Cash, not credit, so there'd be no paper trail. Then she handed me the bag and we drove off again.

Seven minutes later we squeezed ourselves into a tiny restroom that stank of gas and old urine. The drain was rusty, the sink barely larger than my head. My mom taped a garbage bag around my shoulders and worked the brown dye into my scalp, while I took shallow breaths and tried not to think about all the brain cells I was losing. After twenty minutes and a rinse my hair looked duller, even mousy in parts. But it was still mostly blonde, with a few stubborn gold strands sneaking through it, and when my mother bit her lip, I knew what she was thinking.

"Cut it short," I said. "Like yours was at my age." I'd seen her first modeling shots, all pouty lips and sultry eyes under the feathers of her pixie cut. People said we looked alike, but I'd never looked like that.

"Oh, but that's so—"

"It's different," I said, and with tears clumping her lashes, my mother picked up the scissors and cut.

At four thirty we stopped and bought more dye, for her this time. The auburn looked good on her, but it also made her look older and less like my biological mother. Still, it wasn't like I was the only adopted teenager in the world, so there was no point panicking. We'd done the best we could.

The 401 at rush hour was as busy as I'd always been warned, eight lanes crammed solid with traffic and all of it moving at the speed of toffee. It took us an hour and a half just to get through Toronto, but after that the congestion started to clear, and by seven fifteen we were pulling into the driveway of our new house.

It was a shoebox-shaped bungalow with a brick front and peeling aluminum sides, and it couldn't have been more than a thousand square feet. The houses around it were no bigger, and there were plenty of them, crowding both sides of the road and twinkling in the street-lit distance. A scattering of mature trees gave the neighborhood some dignity, but we definitely weren't living on Snob Hill anymore.

"Hey, Gorgeous One and Gorgeous Two," said Dad as he bounded down the front steps to meet us. His chin was prickly with stubble, and in a few more days, he'd have a beard, which would take some getting used to. "You look fantastic. Want to order pizza?"

His cheerfulness was too much for my mother. Her face crumpled and she fled inside, the screen door slamming behind her.

"She's just tired," said my dad, into the uncomfortable silence. "She'll be fine in a minute."

Ron Beaugrand: former semipro hockey player, current salesman, and perpetual optimist. Not that I disbelieved him—my mom's emotions could be stormy, but in the past few months she'd weathered a lot worse than this. Still, my chest tightened at the reminder of what I was putting her through. Both of them.

Dad must have seen the shadow on my face, because he tweaked my nose and said, "Hey, none of that. This is an adventure, remember? New life. Fresh start." He handed me his phone. "One extra-large Hawaiian, delivery. Then we can start unloading."

Which made me feel worse, because I was the only one who liked pineapple on my pizza. Still, I knew better than to argue with Dad once he'd made up his mind, so I made the call.

000010

My new bedroom was half the size of my old one—58.7 percent smaller, to be exact. I didn't mind not having a walk-in closet anymore, but I did wonder where I was going to put my workbench and all my tools. Maybe I could take over a corner of the basement, once we finished unpacking.

I sat on the naked mattress and hauled a box onto my lap, my newly shortened nails picking at the tape. It was hard to believe that I was moving into a new house for the first time in my life; even harder to fathom that it was 475 kilometers from the house I'd left that morning. Until last summer I'd always been the girl who spent her holidays camping half an hour away, who had to fake being sick the year her hockey team went to provincials, who'd never been to Disney World or even Canada's Wonderland, because I couldn't travel more than fifty kilometers from my hometown without having a seizure. But that problem was solved now—one of the few good things that had come out of my disappearance—and I could go anywhere I wanted.

Except back to my old life, because that would be far too dangerous. Not that there was a lot about being Tori Beaugrand that I was going to miss, especially not after that ugly breakup with Brendan just before I went missing and the way Lara had reacted afterward when I didn't want to talk about where I'd been. The only real friend I had left in Sudbury now was Alison, and she'd be safer and probably saner without me.

Or at least I hoped so. Because the alternative was more guilt than I could deal with right now.

I shook off the thought and ripped the cardboard box open, tossing aside my soldering iron, multimeter, and other familiar tools until I found what I'd been looking for. A metal spheroid the size of an orange, featureless except for a circular socket at one end, a tiny aperture at the other, and a thin, dimpled seam running around its equator.

The relay device. The mechanical angel that had followed me all the days of my life, though until recently I'd never suspected its existence. If the liquid-metal chip in my arm was the shackle binding me to my hometown, the relay had been the ball at the end of that invisible chain. But the chip was neutralized now, its programming wiped and its quicksilver sensors disintegrated. And the relay hadn't shown a flicker of interest in me since.

The device felt cold in my palm, dead as a fossilized egg. But there was still one taunting little light glowing deep inside. And though I'd spent my last two days in Sudbury trying to get rid of the thing, it had resisted all my attempts to destroy it. The hammer had bounced off without leaving a dent; the bonfire hadn't even scorched its surface; and when I tried dropping it into the middle of Ramsey Lake, it simply hovered beside the canoe, dodging every swipe I aimed at it with my paddle, until I gave up in frustration and retrieved it again.

My last idea had been to lock the relay in a metal box and bury it somewhere deep. But you couldn't dig far in Sudbury without hitting rock, and I had a bad feeling it'd Houdini itself out of there in a few minutes anyway. And as long as the relay still worked, I couldn't just leave it behind, because if anyone stumbled across it and set it off, Alison would be the first one to suffer. So I'd given up and brought the relay with me, because if it ever woke up again, I wanted to be the first to know. I pulled out the early-warning monitor I'd kludged together from an electromagnetic field detector and my old Nokia phone, and clamped the relay into it.

"Tor— I mean, Niki!" came my dad's muffled shout. "Pizza's here!"

Niki. My new name was going to take some getting used to, even though I'd picked it myself. After ruling out all my favorite female engineers and inventors—*Mildred* was out of the question, and *Marie, Grace,* and *Elizabeth* were too old-fashioned for my taste—I'd taken a different tack and settled on *Nicola.* After Nikola Tesla, of course, but a little less Serbian. Or male.

With the new name came a new identity, but I hadn't yet figured out who Niki was. I knew how she looked on the surface, but how she dressed and behaved, who her friends were, and what she did with her spare time were still a mystery. Would she be more like the real me than Tori had been or less? Which was safer?

Or was I fooling myself to think I could ever be safe again?

I understand, said Sebastian Faraday's deep, rich voice in my memory, *that the data you've collected from her is extremely important to your research.* And suddenly I was back in that cold grey place with Sebastian and Alison by my side, confronting the man who'd abducted me . . .

I gave myself a mental slap, and the memory dissolved. Why was I thinking about Mathis and his stupid experiment? He was out of my life now, and I had other things to worry about.

"Niki!" yelled my father.

"Be there in a sec!" I called as I headed for the washroom. "Just putting my contacts in!"

It was the final step in my transformation—grey-tinted lenses, to dull my turquoise eyes to a more ordinary shade of blue. From Tori Beaugrand, the girl everybody wanted, to Nicola Johnson, a new and unknown element in the universe.

I told myself it felt like freedom, and it did. But deep down, it also felt like death.

I eased the contacts into my eyes, wiping the saline from my cheeks and squeezing my lids shut until the sting went away. Then I took a deep breath, forced my shoulders back, and strode out to begin my new life.

INTERLUDE: Inductive Kickback

(The rapid change in voltage across an inductor when current flow is interrupted)

(1 . 1)

The day I got back to Sudbury, I'd been missing for fifteen weeks and awake for thirty-five hours straight. I was filthy, exhausted, and longing for home, but I had to take care of Alison first—the relay had overloaded her synesthesia, and she was barely holding herself together. Once I'd seen her safely down the hill and off in the ambulance, I had no strength left, and all I wanted to do was lie on the scrubby grass and breathe cool, fresh air until my parents came to get me. But the rescue workers and the police had their own ideas about what I owed them, and soon a van from the local TV station was circling the scene as well. By the time Mom and Dad arrived, I was a mess of tears and helpless rage.

Guests at my parents' house parties often compared my mom to a butterfly, because she was beautiful, charming, and had a knack for being everywhere at once. They didn't realize that behind the gracious smile and light, ripping laugh were sharp teeth and a will of titanium, and that anyone who messed with her family would regret it. Her eyes misted up at the sight of me, but she didn't break down. She greeted the police officers with a frosty little speech that sent them skulking back to their cruiser, dismissed the paramedics with the assurance that my family doctor was on his way, and with one arm tight around my waist and my father lumbering ahead of us like a human shield, she hurried me past the cameras into our waiting car.

The next two days were a recurring nightmare of examinations and interviews and conversations I'd have given anything to avoid—especially the talk with my parents, when I told them how Mathis had taken me and why. Lying to them, even partially, was one of the hardest things I'd ever done. But they were so relieved to have their only daughter back alive and whole and so anxious not to hurt me any more than I'd been hurt already that they didn't ask nearly as many questions as they could have. Their biggest fear was of losing me again, and once I'd assured them—truthfully—that Mathis had been dealt with and the chip he'd put in my arm was gone forever, they were satisfied.

And then, in true Beaugrand parental fashion, they closed ranks to protect me from the world. They shielded me from the journalists camped out at the end of our driveway, they kept the police at arm's length until we'd worked out a statement about my tragic memory loss and inability to identify my kidnapper, and they made polite excuses to all the friends and neighbors who called to find out how I was doing. Lara came to visit on the second day, but only after promising my mother not to ask questions or say anything that might upset me, which made our conversation stilted and uncomfortable. Not quite as stilted as when I'd tried to explain to Lara why I wasn't interested in Brendan and definitely not as uncomfortable as when she found out I was going out with him anyway, but it would be hard to top either of those.

By the third day the media were losing interest and the flood of phone calls had tapered to a trickle. Lara sent me a rambling, semi-apologetic e-mail about how she and Brendan had got together in my absence, which explained why she'd looked so uncomfortable around me. Not because she'd given me up for dead—she knew I wouldn't blame her for that—but because I'd told her that Brendan was a manipulative dirtbag who didn't deserve to touch anything female for the rest of his life, and obviously she'd decided that I was wrong. I was hesitating over the keyboard, wondering how to say "good luck with that" without sounding bitchy, when the house phone rang.

Mom usually answered it, but right now she was out in the backyard, raking leaves. Gardening was one of the few things that relaxed her, and when she got into the zone, she didn't like being interrupted. So I let it ring and waited for the answering system to pick it up.

"Good afternoon, Mrs. Beaugrand," said a tinny female voice over the speaker. "This is Dr. Gervais from GeneSystem Laboratories. I'm sorry to intrude, but we have a few concerns about your daughter's sample . . ."

I snapped upright, shoving my laptop aside. Sample? Laboratory? The only one who had any business asking about my health, let alone knowing anything about it, was Dr. Bowman—that was what my parents paid him the big money for. Thanks to him, I'd never done a blood or urine test, never been vaccinated, and never set foot in a hospital except as a visitor. My rare visits to the doctor's office were recorded on paper, my file kept separate from the usual patient database. No one was allowed to touch it except Dr. Bowman's personal secretary, and Leah had been a close friend of my mom's for twenty years.

And besides all that, our number was unlisted. So if a strange doctor was calling, something in the system had gone badly, even disastrously wrong. I leaped off the sofa, hurtled into the kitchen, and grabbed the phone.

"Dr. Gervais?" I said breathlessly. "I'm sorry, I was outside. This is Gisele Beaugrand." I'd always had a talent for mimicry, and when I imitated my mother's voice on the phone, even Dad couldn't tell the difference. So there was no reason Dr. Gervais should suspect anything—but my heart was oscillating in my rib cage, just the same. "What were you saying about Tori?"

"Oh, hello," said the woman. Was I paranoid, or did she sound excited? "I apologize for catching you at what must be a very emotional time. But when I heard that Tori was back home, I wanted to contact you as soon as possible. Do you have a moment?"

"Yes, of course," I said, gripping the phone tighter. "Go on. What findings?"

"Well, back in August our forensic technicians compared the follicles we'd found on your daughter's hairbrush to the blood and tissue samples the police had given us, and as you know, they were a match. But when we did the PCR on the tissue, we found some abnormalities, so we sent a few genes for sequencing . . ."

My knees buckled. I clutched the edge of the sink, nausea spiraling in my stomach.

The police had my DNA.

I should have seen it coming. When I was missing, they'd needed a way to identify my body, if they ever found it, and to help bring my supposed murderer to justice. And at that point, all the evidence pointed to Alison, the strange and possibly schizophrenic girl I'd been fighting with just before I disappeared. They'd found blood on her hands and bits of tissue stuck in the ring she'd been wearing—of course they'd wanted to know if the blood and tissue were mine.

"The results were extraordinary," Dr. Gervais went on rapidly. "None of us have seen anything like your daughter's gene sequence before, and we can't account for the discrepancies between her DNA and that of an average young woman. We believe . . . " She checked herself and continued in a graver tone, "We're concerned that Tori may have a rare genetic disorder. One that could be harmful, or even fatal, if not treated."

Genetic disorder—so that was what they were calling it. Maybe they even thought it was true. Maybe they were sincerely concerned for my well-being and wanted to help me out, even though it wasn't part of their job.

Or more likely they'd known for weeks that they were sitting on the biggest scientific discovery of their careers, and now that they'd found out I was alive, they'd say anything, do anything, to get me under their microscope again.

Well, screw the advancement of science. I'd just escaped from one man who thought he owned me, and it had been the most terrifying experience of my life. I wasn't about to become anybody else's lab rat. Not ever.

"I'm sure you're mistaken," I said coldly. "Tori is perfectly normal, and we've never had the least concern about her health. Obviously your results were compromised, or tampered with in some way."

"That's a possibility, yes," said Dr. Gervais, not missing a beat. "And we're looking into it. But the easiest solution would be to take a scraping of cells from your daughter's cheek or get a blood sample for comparison purposes. If you'd be willing to cooperate—"

"No," I snapped, and slammed down the phone. With trembling fingers I erased the message and added Dr. Gervais's number to our Blocked Callers list.

But I knew that wasn't the end of it. Now that she and the other scientists at GeneSystem had seen how unusual my DNA was, they'd never be satisfied until they knew why. No matter how many times I said no or how hard I tried to avoid them, they'd keep hounding me until I gave in. Or until they got impatient enough to stop asking and start looking for some legal—or not so legal—way to force my hand.

And then all my dreams of living a free and happy life and becoming a successful engineer one day would be over. Because once Dr. Gervais and her people realized just how extraordinary I was, they'd never let me go.

As if to prove the point, the phone started ringing again. This time I didn't wait for the message or even look to see who it was. I ripped the plug out of the wall and ran to find my mother.

The worst of it was, there was nothing *good* about my weird biology. Sure, I didn't get sick often and when I did, the symptoms were usually mild, but Lara rarely got sick either, so I didn't put much stock in that. I had a knack for figuring out how machines worked and making them work better, but there were plenty of engineering prodigies in the world. It wasn't like I'd been gifted with super-hearing or X-ray vision—nothing like Alison and her synesthesia.

Yet as far as our DNA was concerned, Alison was perfectly normal. I was the freak.

"We always knew something like this might happen," Dad told me, as we held our conference around the dining room table. He patted my mother's shoulder—as usual she'd been calm and decisive while the crisis was fresh, but now that the shock had hit her, she was shaking. "And since Tori doesn't have that chip in her arm anymore, there's no reason not to use our emergency backup plan. I'd hoped it'd never come to this, but . . ." He opened the file folder in front of him and leafed through the stack of notes, letters, and printouts inside. "Maybe it's time."

"There's no *maybe* about it," Mom said thickly through a fistful of tissues and fumbled across the table to grip my hand. "I'm so sorry, sweetheart. When they said they needed your hairbrush for the investigation, I should have guessed . . . but I was so afraid we'd never see you again . . ."

"I don't blame you, Mom," I said. "You didn't know, and you couldn't have done anything else." Not without obstructing the cause of justice and ending up as a murder suspect, anyway.

I turned to my dad. "So what's the plan?"

"If the people at GeneSystem can't find you, they'll give up," he said. "They'll have to. There's no murder investigation anymore, so they can't ask the police to help. And they're supposed to destroy all the DNA evidence, now it's no longer needed. If they want an exception, they'll have to fight for it in court, and by the time they get it, we'll be long gone."

"But . . . where?" Mom asked. "And what are we going to tell everyone? All our friends . . ."

This was the problem with being so community-minded, as both my parents were. If there was a charity event to run or a local festival to promote, Gisele and Ron Beaugrand were bound to be involved at some point. They threw a massive house party every New Year's Eve and an outdoor pig roast every August, with plenty of smaller dinners and cocktail parties in between. Once the news got out that we were selling our house, the shock waves would ripple across the whole city.

"Tori needs a fresh start," said my father. "We all do, after everything that's happened. We'll tell them we're moving to Vancouver."

Clear across the country, right on the Pacific Ocean. I'd always wanted to see more of the world, but this was so far away I might as well be moving to another planet. I was about to beg him to reconsider when my mother said, "We aren't, though," and I realized I'd misunderstood.

"No," Dad replied. "There are a few places in southern Ontario that should suit us fine, and we can move faster if we don't have to go out of the province." The chair creaked as he shifted his weight. "It's going to be a big change, I know. But now Tori's secret is out. I don't see that we have a choice."

I clenched my hands together, fingers latticed tight. Four days ago, I'd despaired of ever seeing my parents or my hometown again. When Alison and Sebastian turned up to help me escape, it had seemed like such a miracle that I'd almost believed my troubles were over. That I could go back to my old life, piece myself back together, and carry on.

I should have known it wouldn't be that easy.

"I'm sorry, pumpkin," said my dad, sounding tired. "I know it isn't fair, especially after all you've been through. You have a right to be angry. Even if it's with us."

How could I be? All they'd ever wanted was a child to love and raise as their own. Even after Dr. Bowman found the chip in my arm and told them he'd never seen anything like it, they'd refused to give up on me. When it became clear that I had a natural affinity for machines but no instincts whatsoever when it came to people, they'd poured all their energy into teaching me how to relate, how to connect, how to care. My dad had coached me through girls' hockey until I understood what it meant to be part of a team, and my mom had shown me how to read people's facial expressions and turn their frowns into smiles. All the awards I'd won, all the popularity I'd gained at school, I owed to them.

And now they were ready to sacrifice their house, their jobs, and their reputations, just to give me a chance at a normal life. I knew there was no point trying to talk them out of it; like Dad had said, they'd anticipated this all along, and they were ready. But I hated Dr. Gervais for forcing their hand. And I hated whoever had given GeneSystem our name and phone number even more.

I straightened up in my chair. "I'm okay," I said firmly. "Just tell me what you want me to do."

"You're kidding me," said Lara, sweeping her hair back behind her ear. "Vancouver?"

We were sitting together in the food court at the mall, sharing an order of poutine—our traditional after-shopping indulgence. I'd told her I wasn't going to come between her and Brendan or say anything more about him, so we were on friendly terms again. My parents and I had just spent a week in the Caribbean, and by the time we got back, the house had sold, so that was a load off my mind as well.

But while we were gone, Dr. Gervais had called from a different number, confirming that my abnormal DNA results were accurate and urging my parents to bring me in for more testing before it was too late. And that same week our neighbor had seen a pair of neatly dressed strangers, a man and a woman, standing on our front step. She'd thought they were Mormons or Jehovah's Witnesses at first, but they'd parked right outside our house and driven away without visiting anyone else on the street.

I was past feeling wistful about the life I'd lived in this town. Now all I wanted was to get out of here while I still had the chance.

"I know," I said to Lara, picking at a stray cheese curd with my plastic fork. The gravy had gone cold, and the two remaining french fries were limp and soggy. "It's a long way. But after everything that happened and the way people look at me now . . . I think it's for the best."

Lara reached for the container and scooped up the last bite, making a little face that told me she regretted it. Then she said in a carefully casual tone, "So . . . what did happen? Or would you rather not talk about it?"

She'd been my best friend since I was twelve. We'd had a few misunderstandings and the occasional fight, but she knew more about me than anyone except my parents—and a few things even they didn't know. If I was going to tell anyone the truth about where I'd been, what had been done to me, it should be Lara.

But I knew how she'd react if I told her. First, she'd be confused. Then she'd laugh nervously because she thought I was joking, and after a while, she'd get upset because it wasn't funny anymore. And then I'd have to apologize and make up a story she'd find easier to believe, which would be worse than if I'd just lied to her in the first place.

So I bit my lip with what I hoped was convincing uncertainty, and I said, "I don't really remember much of anything. And frankly, I don't want to. After what the doctor said . . ." I let the sentence trail off, so Lara's imagination could fill in the rest. In my experience, people usually told themselves more convincing lies than I ever could.

Lara reddened and looked down, and I thought I'd embarrassed her. But when she raised her head again, her lips trembled as though she were about to cry. "That's it?" she asked. "The same thing you told the police? That's all you're going to tell me, really?"

I was taken aback. It wasn't like Lara to want all the gruesome details, especially from me. "Why do you want to know?"

"You have to ask." She gave a shaky laugh. "Because I care about you, maybe? Because I'm your friend? Because I thought it might help you to talk about it to somebody you could trust?

You were gone for *three and a half months,* Tori. I cried myself to sleep so many nights, imagining what you were going through. And then Alison disappeared too, and the police were looking for some guy named Faraday that they thought might have kidnapped you both, and I felt sick knowing he was out there and I could be next—"

"Lara—"

"Don't. Let me finish." She took a deep breath. "And then you came back, and I was so happy. Scared too, because I didn't know what he'd done to you or how much you'd changed. But I wanted to be there for you when you needed me. Only...you didn't. You still don't."

I was silent.

"You know, you could have said you weren't ready, and I would have understood. You didn't have to lie about it."

"I didn't—"

"Yes, you did. I *know* you, Tori." She crumpled the empty poutine cup and dropped it onto the tray. "But okay, if that's what you want. I won't ask you again." She paused and added in a bitter undertone, "He told me you'd lie to me, just like you'd lied to everyone else. And I didn't believe him."

"Who said that?" I was getting angry now. "Brendan?"

Lara jumped up, grabbing her purse and swinging it across her body like a shield. "That's what this is about, isn't it? Just because you didn't want Brendan, you think he's no good for me either. And now you don't trust me anymore." A tear trickled down her cheek, a thread of mascara running with it. "You'd rather hang around in the psych ward with *Alison Jeffries.*"

How she'd found out about me visiting Alison I had no idea, but I wasn't going to get into that now. "What's she got to do with anything?" I demanded. "Just because I don't blame her for what happened—"

"I thought you didn't remember what happened. So how do you know she's not to blame?"

Logic wasn't usually Lara's strong point, especially when she was upset. Something was definitely wrong here. "I just know, okay?" I said between my teeth. People were turning to look at us, and I could tell from their expressions that some of them recognized me. "And if you're going to yell at me, can we do this somewhere else?"

Lara swiped her fingers across her eyes, smearing makeup in all directions. "There's nothing to do," she said thickly. "You're leaving soon, and we're never going to see each other again. And like you said, it's probably for the best. So have a nice trip. Have a nice *life*."

She turned her back on me, but her shoulders were hunched, and I knew she didn't mean to walk away. She was hoping I'd call out to her, with the catch in my breath that would tell her I was crying too. And then we'd hug and murmur apologies to each other and go somewhere to talk it out.

But she was right. I was leaving, and there was nothing to be done about it. So I stared down at the table, silently counting the dots patterned across its surface. I had to stop at eighty-seven because my eyes stung too much to focus, and when I looked up, Lara was gone.

(1.4)

The next day I was upstairs in my bedroom, packing up my old hockey medals and a few other mementos I couldn't bear to throw out, when the doorbell rang. I heard my mother's steps click slowly across the tile, then speed up as she hurried to answer it.

Which meant the visitor was someone she trusted. Probably a friend or a neighbor dropping by to tell us they were sorry we were moving. I was reaching for another box when Mom's voice echoed up from the front hall below:

"Oh, hello, Constable. What can we do for you?"

I froze, not quite believing what I'd heard, then backed out into the hallway for confirmation. When I leaned over the railing, I could see him standing on the step—a compact, sandy-haired man in uniform, his policeman's cap tucked beneath his arm.

"Good day, ma'am," he said. "I'm following up on some details of your daughter's case, and if you don't mind, I'd like to ask her a couple of questions."

Constable Deckard. We'd only met once, when I came into the station to give the police my statement. But I knew that when I disappeared, he'd taken a special interest in my case. So special, in fact, that my mom had made a point of seeking him out and thanking him personally before we left.

"He was so *thorough*," she'd reminisced as we were driving away. "And he never gave up, even when the other officers seemed to have lost hope and moved on. He spent hours interviewing us and your teachers and all your friends—anyone who might know even the tiniest detail about what had happened to you."

"That's what police officers do, Mom," I said, but she shook her head.

"Not like this. I ran into one of the dispatchers at the Blueberry Festival, and she told me that he'd been putting in fifteen or twenty hours of overtime a week on your case alone. She said he'd always been a hard worker, but she'd never seen him so determined—you'd think it was his own daughter who had gone missing."

I found that idea a little disturbing, but my mother obviously didn't see it that way. "And he was always so easy to talk to," she went on dreamily. "So patient and kind. I really felt like he understood."

"Is there something I should know, Gisele?" my dad had asked in a mock-jealous tone, and she'd swatted him. But beneath the teasing, I could tell Dad felt the same way about Deckard as she did.

So when Mom opened the door and showed Deckard into the parlor, I wasn't surprised. Though if I'd had the chance, I'd have warned her that the last thing we needed right now was a policeman who'd taken a personal interest in my case and was trying to wrap up all the loose ends.

Still, there wasn't any easy way to get rid of him now. So when my mom called me, I came downstairs and took a seat on the sofa across from Deckard. But I kept my eyes lowered and my shoulders slumped, hoping he'd take pity on me and keep it brief.

"As I told your mother," Deckard began with a nod in her direction, "I'm looking into a couple of matters related to your case. I'd appreciate any help or information you can give." He slid a picture across the coffee table for me to look at. "Do you recognize this man?"

It wasn't a mug shot, just an ordinary photo of a young man with a lean face and shaggy brown hair—the underfed graduate-student type. I studied it for exactly three seconds, and then I handed it back. "No. Who is he?"

"He calls himself Sebastian Faraday. You've never met this man or spoken with him?"

Thanks to Lara, I knew what this was about. The police still thought Sebastian might have been responsible for kidnapping me. But they were never going to find him now, no matter what I told them. And I didn't want to talk to Deckard one millisecond longer than I had to. "No," I said.

Deckard gave me a steady look. Then he said to my mother, "Mrs. Beaugrand, would you mind stepping out of the room for two minutes? I think Tori might find it easier to answer my questions if you weren't here."

Mom looked troubled, but she didn't protest. She touched my shoulder reassuringly and walked out, shutting the French doors behind her.

Deckard waited until she was gone. Then he said in his soft, measured voice, "Tori, it's important that you answer me honestly. Because if you tell the truth, I may be able to help you. But if you lie, there could be serious consequences. Not just for you but for your family as well."

No doubt that was supposed to encourage me to do the right thing, but to me it sounded more like a threat. I licked my dry lips and nodded.

"Did Sebastian Faraday threaten to hurt you or your parents or your friends, if you talked about him?"

My heartbeat quickened, but I didn't hesitate. "No," I said.

"Are you afraid that you'll get in trouble for making a false statement to the police?"

An unfair question by any standard. I made my expression puzzled and slightly hurt, though inside I was seething. "No."

"So you stand by your original statement? You still claim to have no recollection of who abducted you or where you were taken?"

I could see the trap coming, but it was too late to escape it now. "Yes."

"That's interesting," said Deckard, leaning forward and taking a notebook out of his pocket. "Because I happen to know that when you visited Alison Jeffries at Pine Hills Psychiatric Hospital two weeks ago, you told her psychiatrist a different story."

Stupid, stupid, stupid. I'd assumed my interview with Dr. Minta would be confidential, but I should have known better. Especially since I'd left him with the impression that the police already knew everything. "Oh?" I said, stalling for time. "What story?"

Deckard flipped the notebook open. "According to Dr. Minta, you told him that you and Alison were arguing outside your high school when a team of masked men drove up in an unmarked van. You claimed that these men injected Alison with an unknown substance, then left her lying on the ground while they dragged you into their vehicle. You were subsequently driven to a secret facility where you were held captive, beaten, and used in scientific experiments against your will . . ."

"Enough," I said sharply. I didn't want to hear all that again. "All right, yes, I lied. Alison's a good person, and what happened to me wasn't her fault. I wanted him to let her go."

"I see." He put the notebook away. "So when you told Dr. Minta that Sebastian Faraday had played a part in your escape, where did you get that idea from? Since you've never seen or met Mr. Faraday yourself."

It was bad enough falling into the trap without finding spikes at the bottom of it too. "Alison told me a few things," I said. "And I knew she liked him, so I thought . . ."

"Ms. Beaugrand," interrupted Deckard, "you were assaulted. You were abducted. For nearly four months you were missing, and your family and friends believed you to be dead. When you came back, your nose had been broken and reset, there was severe bruising around both your eyes, and your clothes were covered in dried blood—the same clothes you'd been wearing when you disappeared. You had obviously been through an extremely traumatic experience. Don't you think that whoever did this to you should be punished?"

His tone was level, even reasonable. But his jaw was set, and his eyes bored into mine without the slightest trace of pity. And that was when I realized that my mother, who taught me to read people, had been wrong about this man. It wasn't concern for my safety or sympathy for my parents that had made Deckard so determined to solve my case.

It was obsession.

Not with me personally, but with the mystery I represented. The sheer divide-by-zero impossibility of how I'd vanished into nothingness and reappeared out of nowhere, a case unlike anything he'd ever seen. He'd done everything he could to solve the puzzle, but the pieces refused to match up. So he'd come here today to intimidate me into telling him what had really happened.

I stood up. "I'm sorry," I said. "I can't help you." I turned to leave—

Deckard's hand shot out and grabbed my wrist. Not hard enough to hurt me, just enough to let me know who was in charge. "I'm not finished," he said.

I'd been wary before, but not really frightened. After all, Deckard couldn't prove that I was lying. And if he tried to lay charges against a sixteen-year-old kidnapping victim just because she didn't want to talk about what she'd been through, he'd have a hard time getting the courts to back him up.

But I was scared now. Because I could see the pent-up emotion sizzling behind every line of that square face, the muscles twitching beneath his sun-roughened skin. This wasn't just a policeman doing his job anymore. This was personal.

"Let go," I said hoarsely. "Or I'll scream."

He must have realized his mistake, because he released me and sat back. "If that's how you want it," he said. "But you don't seem to understand the seriousness of what you're doing. You're protecting someone who doesn't deserve to be protected. And as long as you keep lying to the people who care about you, you're going to be on your own."

The French doors rattled and Mom stormed into the room. "I saw that," she snapped at Deckard. "How dare you touch her! Get out."

For a moment Deckard didn't move. Then with casual calm he picked up his hat and put it back on his head. "You've misunderstood the situation, ma'am," he said as he rose. "I'm just looking out for your daughter's best interests."

He delivered the cliché so blandly that it made me want to spit. I backed away, fists clenched, as he strode past me and into the front hall. He went to the door, opened it—then paused and turned back.

"One more thing you might want to consider," he said to my mother. "I've had a call from one of the senior scientists at our genetic testing facility. She's concerned you're not answering her messages. I'd suggest you get in touch with her before you leave town, just to keep things simple. It'd be a shame if you had to bring Tori all the way back here from Vancouver." With an ironic smile he tipped his hat to us and left.

My mom locked the door behind him, then put an arm around me and pulled me close. "I'm so sorry," she said. "I should never have left you alone with him. Did he hurt you?"

I shook my head mutely, but I couldn't stop shaking. Because I understood now who had given Dr. Gervais our unlisted phone number. Who had told Lara I'd visited Alison in the hospital and warned her that I'd lie to her the same way I'd lied to everyone else. Deckard was determined to get the truth out of me by any means necessary, and he wasn't going to give up on this investigation without a fight.

"Call Dad," I said. "Tell him we can't wait until next Saturday. Tell him we need to get out of here as fast as we can."

PART ONE: Demand Load

(The power required by all equipment in a receiver or transmitter facility to ensure full continuity of communications)

000011

"Hey, Niki, do you know the code for juniper berries? I can't find it on my spinner."

I didn't even pause to think about it. "4922," I called back, stacking cans into my customer's bag and swinging it onto the counter. "That'll be $257.29," I said brightly to the harried-looking woman before me, who appeared to be shopping for a family of eight or possibly just a couple of teenaged boys. "Do you have a Points Club card?"

She didn't have one, and she didn't want one either, though I had to mention it anyway because that was part of my job. Like always remembering to check the bottom of the cart for large items and watching out for broken eggs or leaky milk. After a month of working the cash register for twenty-five hours a week, it had become automatic.

Remembering produce codes was part of the job too, though nobody expected me to know *all* of them. But numbers had a way of sticking in my head. So I didn't realize I'd done anything unusual until the woman moved on, and I saw Jon Van Beek goggling at me from the next register.

"How'd you know that?" he asked. "I don't even know what juniper berries *are.*"

"My mom bought some last week," I said with a shrug. It was a tiny slip and probably not worth the trouble of lying about. But even after five months in this town, I wasn't taking any chances. There was still a chance that someone from my old life might be searching for me, and anything that made me exceptional, or memorable, could be dangerous.

"Oh," Jon said. "Huh." He turned to greet his next customer, and the tension eased out of my muscles. No reputation as Amazing Memory Girl: mission accomplished. Now if only I could get Jon to stop quizzing me about my plans for the weekend.

It wasn't that he was bad-looking. It wasn't even that he was a jerk or at least not that I'd noticed. But his blond hair and farm-boy good looks reminded me of my ex-boyfriend, and I had enough memories of Brendan groping me and slobbering down my neck to last a lifetime.

I glanced at the clock. Five minutes left and only two more shoppers in sight, neither of whom looked ready to hit the checkout right away. I propped the "Next Register Please" sign at the end of the conveyor, switched off the overhead sign, and started spraying and wiping down my lane.

I'd finished tidying the coupon drawer and was stepping back to let Shandra close out my till, when Jon waved to me. "Hey, I'm done in a couple minutes too. Want a ride home?"

The offer was tempting, especially since it was freezing rain outside. But I wasn't the type to waver once I'd made up my mind, and I'd already decided not to encourage Jon if I could help it.

"No, thanks," I said. "I'm good."

0 0 0 1 0 0

I was heading across the parking lot with hands deep in the pockets of my thrift-store coat, collar turned up against the March sleet, when one of the stock boys came sprinting out to join me. "The Regina bus?" he panted, skidding to my side. "Has it come yet?"

He had feathery black hair, cat's eyes behind rectangular glasses, and a pair of earbuds tucked into the collar of his jacket. Like Jon and most of the other part-timers he was around my age, and I was pretty sure he'd been at the store at least as long as I had. But our breaks were at different times, so I didn't know much about him beyond his name: Milo Hwang.

"Yeah," I said. "It went by a couple of minutes ago."

"Do you know when the next one is?"

"At this hour? Forty-five minutes."

He swore softly and turned to head back inside. I called after him, "But the bus I take runs parallel to yours, and they overlap in a couple of places. You could take that one, if you don't mind walking a couple of blocks."

"Oh. Okay." He reversed direction and fell into step with me again. "Thanks."

When we reached the bus shelter, there was a trio of girls huddled together inside, passing a cigarette around and giggling. Milo and I stood beneath the glare of the streetlight, icy rain needling our faces.

"Well, this sucks," he said after a moment. "You take the bus all the time?"

"Pretty much," I said. "We've only got one car, and I don't have my license yet."

"I used to ride with my mom," he said, "but then she switched over to the night shift—oh, finally." The bus had eased itself around the corner and was trundling toward us. It squeaked to a stop and the door rotated open, letting out a blast of warmth.

"Go ahead," Milo told me, rummaging in his pocket for change. I took the steps two at a time, flashed my pass at the stoic-looking driver, and dropped into a seat, shaking ice from the bangs of my pixie cut.

Milo was still standing by the fare box when the three girls squeezed past him, caromed off each other, and landed en masse on the bench seat along the left side, whooping with hilarity. I could see the driver's grimace in the mirror, but he didn't speak. He closed the doors, and as the bus pulled out from the curb, Milo stumbled down the aisle to me.

"OK if I sit here?" he asked.

Usually I kept my eyes closed all the way home, building prototypes in my head. But I supposed a bit of company wouldn't hurt. "Sure," I said.

He swung himself in beside me, stretching out his legs and unzipping his jacket to reveal the green store polo beneath. "Nicola, right?" he said. "I'm Milo."

"Niki," I said. "And I know." Remembering people's names was an old habit my mother had drilled into me—her number one tip for making a good impression. "So are you going to take the bus from now on?"

Milo took off his sleet-speckled glasses and wiped them on the hem of his shirt. "Probably bike it, once the weather uncraps itself. I thought about getting a car, but that'd put a major dent in my university fund."

There was a rhythm to small talk, once you got into it. It had taken me a few years to master, but now I barely had to think about it. "Which university?"

"Haven't decided yet." He pushed his glasses back onto his nose. "You?"

"I've got another year of high school first," I said.

"Oh yeah? I thought you were older."

I felt older. Actually, watching the girls across from us gleefully snapping duck-faced pictures of each other with their cell phones, I just felt old. I gave a faint smile and left it at that.

"So," said Milo after a moment, "what school are you at, then? Cartier?"

"I'm not," I replied. "I'm taking my courses online."

He nodded, as though it made sense. But he shot me a sidelong glance from behind his lenses, and I knew he was trying to figure me out. Nothing about me screamed *shy* or *bullied*, and I didn't look like I came from a super-religious family. None of the usual reasons that a girl of sixteen—no, seventeen—might be finishing up high school on the Internet seemed to apply.

"And how do you like that?" he asked.

I liked it a lot, actually. Before I went missing I'd been one of the most popular girls at my high school, but all that social stuff had taken a lot of energy. Now I didn't have to worry about anyone else's expectations, I could take as many math and science courses as I wanted and get top marks in all of them.

"It's not bad," I said.

"So what made you do it?" he asked.

This was why I didn't go out of my way to talk to people anymore. Because they got curious, and they asked questions. I was debating how to answer when a horn blared suddenly from the darkness, and I heard the screech of spinning tires.

Black ice, I thought numbly, as headlights swept the front of the bus. Somebody's lost control, there's going to be an accident—

And then I realized that the driver had slumped onto the wheel, his foot still on the accelerator, and that the bus was drifting into the oncoming lane.

The girls screamed and clung to each other. Milo started to his feet, but it was obvious he'd never make it in time. Caution vanished and instinct took over: I leaped to the front of the bus, shoved the unconscious driver aside, and grabbed the steering wheel.

The road was slick, and I could feel the back end skidding sideways even as I wrestled the front back on course. If I didn't do this right, we'd spin out across all four lanes of traffic. But even as my heart hammered against my rib cage, my mind sharpened to a crystal point. The bus was a machine. I knew machines. I could do this. I made myself turn back into the skid, feeling the tires like an extension of my own body, until the bus stopped fishtailing and we were on the right side of the road again.

I barely registered Milo hauling the driver out from behind me, but at least those big feet weren't blocking the pedals anymore. Was that the brake? No, it was the accelerator (another scream from the girls in the back). Okay, *that* was the brake. I practically had to stand to reach it, the seat was cranked up so high. But a slow, steady pressure did the trick, and in a few more seconds I'd lined us up beside the curb. I killed the engine, yanked out the key, and turned to Milo.

"How is he?" I asked.

Milo crouched beside the man, feeling for a pulse. "There's no heartbeat," he said.

My dad had had a heart attack four years ago. He'd nearly died. "Do you know CPR?" I asked, and when Milo hesitated, I tilted the driver's chin up and blew a couple of breaths into his mouth. "Start with that," I said. Then I grabbed Milo's hands and put them on the man's chest, laying mine over them. "Now do this," I said, showing him how far to press down. "Keep doing it for a count of thirty. Then do the breaths again."

I was afraid he'd ask why I wasn't doing it, but he didn't. His head was down, his whole concentration on the man. Reassured that he'd got it, I was pulling myself to my feet when I heard a tiny *click*. One of the girls had raised her pink, glittery cell phone and snapped a picture of me.

Blind fury took over. I marched down the aisle, snatched the phone from the girl's hand, and erased the pic with a few savage swipes of my finger. "Don't you *dare*," I snapped, and her two friends hastily shoved their own phones back into their pockets.

I dialed 911 and thrust the pink cell back at its owner. "Tell them we're on the 25 bus just past the corner of Huntington and Caledonia," I ordered. "Tell them to send an ambulance." She clutched the phone with both hands and began to gabble into it, while I went back to Milo and the driver.

"I have to go," I said quietly. "Right away."

"What?" His head snapped up. "You can't leave now! The police'll want to know what happened, they'll need to talk to us—"

"I know," I said. "But I can't stay." Now that the adrenaline was wearing off, I was starting to shake. I'd just done exactly what I wasn't supposed to do—something extraordinary, something that would get people's attention. I crouched beside Milo, bringing myself down to his level, and put a hand on his shoulder.

"Please," I whispered. I didn't hide the tremor in my voice. I needed him to *feel* my desperation. "Milo, you can't tell the police or the media anything about me. Not my name, not that we work together, none of it. It's incredibly important."

He recoiled. "Why? Are you in trouble?"

"No, but if you don't help me out, I will be. I'll explain later. But *please*, Milo. Promise me you won't tell."

For a moment Milo's eyes were as blank as his glasses, and I thought I'd failed. But then he sighed. "All right. I'll handle it. Go."

"Thank you," I breathed. Then I ran to the back doors, shoved them open, and leapt out into the freezing rain.

"Hey!" yelled a voice behind me, but I didn't look back. I skidded across the sidewalk, flung myself over somebody's box hedge, and vanished into the anonymous night.

000101

By the time I got the front door open, I was soaked and my teeth were chattering.

"Niki?" called my mom faintly. "Is that you?"

Crackers frolicked around my ankles, delighted to see me. I swore under my breath as I hopped around, trying to get my boots off without squashing him. "I'm home!" I yelled. "I'm fine!"

"Oh, thank God." Mom hurried out of the bathroom, wrapping her robe around her. "When I called the store and they said you'd left forty minutes ago, I was so—" She stopped, aghast. "What happened?"

It had been hard convincing my parents to let me take this job at Value Foods in the first place, even harder to persuade them that I could get around the city safely on my own. If they so much as suspected that I'd been in serious danger tonight, it would be the end of my independence.

"It's no big deal." I let out a *silly-me* laugh. "I got on the wrong bus, so I had to walk a couple extra blocks, and a truck splashed me on the way."

"You should have called!" She brushed ice pellets from my hair and shoulders, her brow creased in distress. "It's too dangerous for you to walk in this weather. What if you slipped and broke your leg? What if we had to take you to hospital?"

For anyone else, the worst part of that scenario would have

36

been the broken leg. But for me, it was the hospital. Doctors poking and prodding me, nurses giving me drugs that could cause violent reactions or no reaction at all. And if anyone decided to take a blood sample, we might as well call up Dr. Gervais and be done with it.

But I couldn't spend my life encased in bubble wrap either. And when I'd jumped off that bus tonight, wiping out on an icy sidewalk had seemed a lot less scary than ending up on the eleven o'clock news.

Not that I planned to tell Mom about that if I could help it. It had taken six weeks in our new house before she'd stopped being wary of the neighbors and nearly four months before she felt secure enough to start redecorating. She'd even been reluctant to adopt Crackers at first, afraid of getting attached to a dog she might have to leave behind. Now that she was finally starting to settle in, the last thing I wanted to do was unsettle her all over again.

"It wasn't that bad out," I said, as I wriggled out of my coat and hung it up to dry. "More wet than slippery. Did you know you have paint on your face?"

"Oh." She touched the white smear on her cheek self-consciously. "I was just getting into the shower. But you should go first—you must be freezing—"

I shook my head. "I'm just going to change and make some hot chocolate. Go ahead."

She gave me a doubtful look. I returned my brightest smile, and finally, she sighed and retreated into the bathroom. I waited until I heard the water running, then peeled out of my jeans, put on a pair of flannel pajama pants, and headed downstairs.

"You're pretty wet," said my dad, glancing up from the

sofa with the TV remote in hand. "What'd you do, fall into the lobster tank?"

"Caught the wrong bus." I spoke lightly, knowing he wouldn't make a big deal out of it if I didn't. Especially since he could see for himself that I was okay. "Who's playing?"

"Montreal and Toronto. Habs are winning 3–1. Want some popcorn?"

So I grabbed a blanket, wrapped it around me, and cuddled up next to him to watch the hockey game. By the time it went to commercials, I'd warmed up and was starting to relax. But then Dad started channel-flipping, and halfway through the second lap we hit a local news bulletin.

"—taken to hospital. Police are at the scene . . ."

The reporter stood by the curb, with the bus behind her. By the flashing lights of the police cruiser I could just make out the girl with the pink cell phone, gesturing and pointing as the officers listened to her story.

Dad's finger hesitated over the button. "Isn't that . . . ?"

My thoughts flashed ahead, anticipating all the ways this conversation could go. Then I sat up abruptly, the blanket dropping from my shoulders. "Whoa! That's *my* bus!"

He gave me a sharp look. "The one you were on tonight?"

"No, the one I was supposed to be on." I leaned forward, staring at the screen as though mesmerized. "Did you catch what she said? Was there an accident?"

Please don't let the bus driver be dead. Please don't let it be my fault.

". . . Further details at eleven."

The darkened roadside vanished, and a model bounced across the screen with a bottle of shampoo in hand. Dad switched back to the hockey. "Well," he said. "I guess we'll find out in a few minutes."

I groaned and dropped my head into my hands. "Great. Now Mom's never going to let me ride the bus again."

But all the while, I was watching between my fingers to see if he'd bought it. Because if he saw through my act and ordered me to tell him the truth, I'd be doomed.

"Ah." Dad cleared his throat. "Good point. Maybe we'll just finish the game and call it a night."

Relief washed over me. My gamble had paid off—if only because Dad was even more reluctant to worry Mom than I was. For the moment at least, I was safe.

"Yeah," I said, tucking my legs beneath me and reaching for another handful of popcorn. "Sounds like a good idea."

000110

When the hockey game ended my dad went upstairs, but I stayed in the basement. My nerves were still fizzing, and I knew it'd be a while before I could unwind enough to sleep. So I turned on the ventilator, sat down at my workbench, and plugged in my soldering iron.

I'd always found it relaxing to work with solder, applying precise drops of molten metal to anchor diodes, resistors, and other small components into their proper places—or even better, squeezing a thin line of gel flux along the edge of an integrated circuit and gliding a hoof tip over it to seal the tabs flawlessly in a matter of seconds. There was a warm satisfaction in populating a circuit board that was nearly as good as the afterglow of finishing the project I'd designed it for, and when

I was soldering, all my worries seemed far away.

Most people would probably think it was strange for a teenage girl to take such pleasure in building machines, but I'd gotten used to being different a long time ago. And though I'd spent years hiding my passion for electronics, it wasn't because I was embarrassed by it. It was more because my parents had warned me that showing off my technical skills would make people curious about where I'd learned them, and I had no easy answer to that.

My current project was a Geiger counter, to replace my old one, which had become touchy and unreliable with age. I cleaned the board, soldered the remaining diodes and then the resistors, my tension gradually melting away. By the time I started yawning, it was 12:36 A.M.

Well, at least I was tired enough to sleep now. I stretched, turned off the soldering iron, and headed upstairs. But the pleasant feeling of distraction vanished as soon as I started down the hallway to my bedroom and remembered the bus driver lying grey-lipped and motionless in the aisle. He could be dead now, for all I knew. And when I thought about Milo and those three girls talking to the police, I felt icy all over again. He'd promised not to say anything about me, but could I trust him? And even if I could, what about them?

In the end I went to bed anyway, because I couldn't think of anything else to do. But sleep was a long time coming, and when it arrived, I wished it hadn't. Deckard was chasing me through the corridors of my old high school, his boots pounding like drumbeats against the tile. He had his pistol out of the holster, and I knew that if he saw me, I was dead, so I ducked into the music room to hide. But when I opened the equipment closet, Brendan jumped out, laughing at the shock on my face. He dragged me inside and put his hands and his mouth all over me, and I couldn't make him stop until I grabbed a microphone off the shelf and hit him in the head with it. He crumpled, and when I turned, Alison was standing in the doorway, looking so sad and disappointed that it made me want to cry.

"You've killed him," she said. "It's all your fault."

"No, I haven't," I protested. "He's only bleeding a little." I turned Brendan over to show her, but when I looked at his face, I realized it wasn't Brendan after all.

It was Mathis, and he was smiling.

I tried to shout for help, but no sound came out. Alison had vanished, and I was alone with Mathis in a cold grey space with no windows, no doors, no escape at all. He grabbed my upper arm so hard I could feel his thumb grinding against the bone, pulled my face close to his, and said in his thick accent, "You can't get away from me. *It's still there.*"

Repulsed, I pushed myself free and backed away. But he only smiled wider and pointed to my arm. I looked down—and saw the chip, bright as a bead of fresh solder, gleaming on the surface of my skin.

I choked on a scream, and woke.

The room was dark, the house silent. Only Crackers's whine from the foot of the bed and the thump of his tail against the covers as he toddled up to lick my hand told me that I'd made any sound at all.

I touched on the bedside light and ran my finger over the tiny scar above my elbow—the place Dr. Bowman had tried to cut the chip out when I was little, right before I went into a seizure and he had to stop. I couldn't see anything there now, but then, I never had. Still, Sebastian and Alison had both told me the chip was gone, and I believed them.

I lay back, breathing out slowly to calm my jittering heart. It wasn't the first nightmare I'd had since I got away from Mathis, but it was the first one I'd had in a long while with him in it. These days it was usually Deckard who stalked me in my dreams, and occasionally some brittle-looking middle-aged actress stood in for Dr. Gervais. Which made sense, because both of them were still a potential danger if I got careless. But I'd escaped from Mathis, and as far as I knew, he shouldn't be able to touch me or threaten me ever again.

So why was I still dreaming about him?

000111

When I came down to breakfast the next morning and saw the newspaper lying on the table, I braced myself for the worst. But my mom passed me the croissants and went on reading the classifieds without even glancing up. And once I'd unfolded the front section and flipped to the local headlines, I understood why.

"TEENS STOP RUNAWAY BUS, SAVE DRIVER," the article began, and beneath it were two school pictures. One was of Milo, minus the glasses and wearing an artificial smile.

The other was the girl with the pink cell phone.

Disbelieving, I skimmed the rest of the story. The details were pretty much what had actually happened, except with the other girl—Breanna Gingerich, apparently—taking charge of the wheel. One of her friends claimed to have helped Milo with the CPR until the ambulance arrived, while the other took responsibility for making the 911 call. Thanks to their quick thinking and courageous teamwork, said the article, the driver had made it to hospital alive, with a good chance of recovery.

I stared at the page, the croissant crumbling forgotten in my hand. I didn't mind Breanna and her friends taking credit for what I'd done: if anything, I was grateful. I was just surprised they'd had the nerve to pull it off.

No, more than surprised. I didn't believe it. There was no reason three total strangers, let alone a bunch of giggly girls who couldn't be more than fourteen, would lie to the police and the media for my sake. Not unless there was something in it for them, and they could be sure of getting away with it.

Which meant that Milo hadn't just covered for me. Somehow he'd talked the girls into covering for me too.

001000

"Hey there, hero!" called Jon heartily as Milo came through the sliding doors. "Nice picture in the paper!"

Milo pulled the earbuds out of his ears. "Thanks," he said without enthusiasm. He stuffed the headphones into his pocket and headed for the stockroom, not even glancing at me.

I was glad he was playing it cool, but it didn't make my job any easier. I still owed him an explanation for last night.

Halfway through the shift, I switched off with Kayleigh and was heading to the break room when Milo slipped into the corridor behind me. "I feel like a secret agent," he said. "Do you have the documents, comrade Nikita?"

Nikita was actually a boy's name in Russian, but I wasn't going to make myself obnoxious by saying so. "It's a long story," I said. "What about later, on the bus? Or have you sworn off public transit?"

"Have you?"

"Not really. What are the odds of anything like that happening again?"

"Zero, I hope," he said fervently. "But my brother's home for the weekend and we're going out for pizza, so the bus is out. Can you give me the short version?"

The break room was empty. No more excuses. I shoved coins into the coffee dispenser and fished a couple of creamers out of the fridge while I waited for the cup to fill. Then I took a deep breath and said, "First, I need to thank you for what you did last night. That was pretty brilliant of you, bringing the girls in on it."

I wasn't just flattering him, either: it really had been a genius move. Not only did it give Breanna and her friends good reason to keep their mouths shut, it also guaranteed that any other pictures they'd taken of me would be long gone by now. The only possible glitch was that I'd probably been caught on video, since all the city buses had cameras these days. But how likely were the police to even look at the tape, let alone make an issue of it?

"Yeah, well." Milo took the coffee out of the dispenser and handed it to me, then started plugging in his own change. "I'm just glad they decided to play along."

I glanced at the door, half hoping one of the other employees would come in and interrupt us. But nobody did, so I took the plunge. "So. You're probably wondering why I took off like that."

Idiot. Of course he was; that was why we were here. "Look, this is really private and personal, so please don't tell anybody. But a few months ago, before I moved here, something happened to me. Something . . . bad."

Milo kept his head down, watching the cup as it filled. But his shoulders tensed, and I knew I'd got his attention.

"It wasn't my fault," I went on in a low voice. "I couldn't have done anything to stop it—I know that now. But there was an investigation, and it was all over the news, and everybody in my school was talking about it. It was like I wasn't even a person to them anymore, just a story. The kind of story that follows you around for the rest of your life."

Carefully, Milo pulled his hot chocolate out of the dispenser and fitted a lid onto it. He still didn't look at me.

"So my parents and I decided to move," I said. "We even changed our names, so we could start over." It was a risk, telling him that. But if he tried to look up Nicola Johnson online and couldn't find her, I wanted him to know why. "Nobody from my old life knows where I am now, and I want to keep it that way."

"And that's why you ran off and left me doing CPR on that guy by myself," he said.

"Yeah," I said. "I felt bad, but you were doing all right. And . . . this isn't just about me." I laced my fingers around my cup, watching the steam coil and vanish in the air. "My parents left their jobs and their friends and everything, just to give me a chance at a normal life. I don't want them to have to go through that again."

We stood in silence a moment, listening to the tinny pop music from the loudspeaker. Then Milo said, "Okay."

Which could mean any number of things—*okay, I understand*

what you're saying; *okay, I forgive you for ditching me*; *okay, I'm on your side.* I was hoping for the last one, but I couldn't be certain until he turned his head, and his dark eyes locked onto mine.

He looked serious. He also looked slightly nauseated, but the disgust wasn't aimed at me. He held my gaze steadily, and then one corner of his mouth turned up in a rueful smile.

"Wow," he said. "Life can be pretty complicated, eh?"

I knew, then, what he thought had happened to me. He was wrong, but I wasn't about to tell him so. At least it was the kind of tragedy that would make sense to someone like Milo, something he wouldn't find hard to believe.

If only it were half so easy to explain the truth.

0 0 1 0 0 1

March made one last halfhearted attempt at snow, but it melted as soon as it hit the ground. Then April arrived in force, stealing the chill from the air and washing the grit-dulled streets to a sheen. I took my mom's umbrella to work three days in a row, until a freak gust turned it inside out and I had to huddle inside my coat instead.

Jon kept offering me rides, and I kept declining them. Milo and I didn't see much of each other, but whenever our paths crossed, he gave me a nod as if to say, *Don't worry. I've got your back.* Mom pulled up the carpet in the living room and refinished the old wooden floor, which turned out to be gorgeous. Dad coaxed her into going out for dinner and a movie every Friday, and after their first couple of dates, she stopped worrying about leaving me alone in the house. All seemed well, except for one thing.

I was restless. Worse than restless, I was *itchy*. Frustrated, short-tempered, and increasingly depressed, because I couldn't find enough to do with my hands. My mother's new decorating theme was cozy and organic, the opposite of the airy modern look she'd always gone for before, and the more our house looked like a feature in *Country Living* magazine, the less use she had for even the most practical devices I could build. I'd already automated my entire room from light switch to curtains, and I'd been warned against piling up too much electronics junk in the basement. So right now I was building a couple of laptops from parts I'd got cheap off the Internet, with a vague idea of selling them and making a profit when I was done.

But I wanted more. I always had, but now I wanted it worse than ever. A chance to build something new and challenging and exciting, something other people could see and use, something that actually *mattered*. How I could do that without getting noticed by the media was a question I hadn't resolved yet, but I couldn't bear to hide my LED under a bushel for much longer. Because six months ago, in a desperate all-or-nothing effort to escape from Mathis, I'd tackled the greatest technological challenge of my life. My synapses had sizzled like white lightning; my body had thrown itself completely into the task; and when I finished the machine and turned it on, the surge of exhilaration was like nothing I'd ever felt before. It was like a dam had burst inside me, and my whole mental landscape had changed.

Ever since then, I'd been constantly bombarded by ideas, and I couldn't look at the simplest machine without thinking about how to improve it. As I swiped groceries over the scanner and keyed in produce codes, I was envisioning the technology that would make both those tasks unnecessary. When I watched a news report about a mechanical exoskeleton that could help people with spinal cord injuries, I started brainstorming ways to make the device stronger, lighter, and cheaper. At night I lay awake calculating equations to the last decimal point, designing and testing prototypes in my head until they worked without a hitch.

But that was where it stopped. Because my workspace was limited, and even if I could afford the parts, the tools I needed were beyond my budget. My urge to create had never been so strong, yet there seemed no way to satisfy it.

But then I saw an interview in the paper with an artisan who made clocks out of recycled coffee cans, and he mentioned the local makerspace.

"It's a place where engineers and woodworkers and artists—basically anybody who likes to make things—can get together and work on shared equipment," I told Dad that evening, as I got up to pull my dinner out of the microwave. "If I go to a few of their events and Open House nights, I could apply to become a member—*ow!*"

I stifled the gasp, but too late. My mother zipped across the kitchen at the speed of light, turning on the cold tap and dragging me over to the sink. "Honey, it's hot! Be more careful."

"Mom, I'm fine." I pulled free, shaking water from my hands. "It was just a little steam." I grabbed a potholder and carried the plate to the table, where my dad was looking over the brochure I'd printed out from the makerspace website. "But seriously, it's perfect. I could make all kinds of stuff there. I could collaborate with other makers, work on bigger projects. And it's not just for tech geeks either, they've got sculptors and musicians and people making jewelry. I wouldn't even be the only girl."

I might have spoken too quickly. I might have been a little flushed. I knew I ought to stay calm so my parents would see I'd thought this through and wasn't just asking on impulse, but I couldn't. I wanted it *that* badly.

Dad sighed. "Pumpkin," he said, "it sounds great. But it's fifty dollars a month. And if they see the things you can do, it's going to attract attention—"

"I'm not going to show off," I interrupted. "I know better than that. I can stick to easier projects when the others are around and do the more complicated parts on my own."

"But you'll be going to university in another year anyway," Mom pleaded. "Can't you wait until you're a little older? Until you've taken a few courses, and it won't look so . . . unusual?"

"Girls in engineering are always unusual, Mom." Which, I realized a millisecond later, was pretty much the worst argument I could have used with her. In desperation I turned to my father. "I can't stand playing around with old junk in the basement anymore. I can do so much better. I *need* this, Dad."

Dad went quiet, and for a moment I thought I'd won him over. But then he glanced at Mom's anxious face and shook his head. "I'm going to have to say no, sweetie. It's not that we don't trust you, but they've got some pretty dangerous equipment in that place. And there are too many things that could go wrong."

"Like what?" I asked incredulously. "I'm not stupid, Dad. I'm not going to cut my hand off or blow anything up, and I'm not going to let anybody take pictures of me either. And besides, when I go into engineering, I'm going to be working with all kinds of stuff like this anyway. I know you're scared of losing me again, but you can't protect me forever."

Mom got up and hurried out. I could hear her blowing her nose in the next room as Dad said heavily, "I know it's hard, Tori. When I was your age—"

"Niki, Dad. My name is Niki, remember?" I was furious, but I kept my tone civil. My parents were all I had in the world now, and I couldn't afford to alienate them. Literally. "And no, you don't know how hard it is. You have no idea what it's like to be me."

Dad said nothing. I picked up my fork and tried to eat some lasagna, but it tasted like old plastic. I shoved the plate away. "I'm going to be late for work," I said and left.

001010

My phone clanked at me halfway to the bus stop. I pulled it out and read:

−Sorry, honey. Talk when you get back?

I knew what that meant: Mom was planning to cancel her night out with Dad so they could wait up for me, sit me down, and explain their decision all over again, in the most loving and guilt-inducing possible way.

What it *didn't* mean was that their decision was going to change. I texted back with the last of my remaining patience:

−Nothing to talk about. I get it. It's OK.

I sent it off, then added another:

−Working late. Home at 11. Kayleigh's giving
me a ride.

Which was a total lie, since Kayleigh wasn't even on my shift tonight. But if Mom thought I'd be gone all evening anyway and that I was in good company, there'd be no point in her staying home.

Value Foods was quiet, since most people had better things to do on a Friday night than buy groceries. Between customers I swapped out last week's gossip mags for the new issues, listened to Sarah complain about her ex-boyfriend, and watched Milo stack flats of store-brand soda in the bargain aisle. I was counting the cases and calculating the total volume of liquid in my head when Jon piped up that he'd bought an awesome new stereo for his truck, adding a few seconds later that it was raining like Noah outside. I smiled vaguely at the first comment and nodded at the other, while pretending not to notice the hint.

At eight thirty I was sitting in the break room leafing through an old issue of *Chatelaine* when Milo poked his head in the doorway. "Hey," he said. "You okay?"

I looked up, surprised. "I'm fine. Why?"

"Just wondering," he said. "You seem kind of . . . off somehow. Uptight."

Was it that obvious? I rubbed a hand across my forehead, trying to massage away the tension. Either Milo had some pretty impressive emotional radar, or I wasn't as good at hiding my feelings as I'd thought.

"It's nothing big," I said. "Just some stuff with my parents. You know how it is."

Milo nodded slowly, but he didn't say anything more. I picked at an uncut corner of the magazine, feeling self-conscious under that steady gaze. But when I looked up again, he'd disappeared.

I finished my coffee and headed back to my station just in time to keep the lineup at Jon's register from turning ugly. But my customer-greeting smile felt more fake than ever, and my attempts at small talk fell flat. It was a relief when the unexpected crush moved on and the store was quiet again.

There had to be a way to convince my parents they were wrong about the makerspace being too dangerous. But though I spent the rest of the shift arguing with them in my head, it was no use. I'd already done my best to convince them—it just hadn't worked. I rang through my last customer, closed down, and stalked off to the office.

Milo was sweeping the corridor as I came in, dark head bobbing to the rhythm of his music player. He hailed me with a lift of his eyebrows. "Heading out?" he asked, a little too loudly.

"Yeah," I said. I pulled my coat off the hook, thrust one arm into the sleeve, and was reaching for the other when my phone vibrated in my pocket.

Now what? Irritated, I pulled it out and turned it over. There were twenty-three messages.

It couldn't be Mom or Dad. They knew I couldn't answer when I was on shift, and anyway they'd have called the store line if it were that important. It had to be someone drunk-texting the wrong number. I opened the message window, hoping it would at least be funny—and the bottom dropped out of my stomach.

–20:35:23 RELAY ACTIVATED

My leg muscles locked, my whole body trembling with the urge to fight or flee. I forced my stiff finger to move, scrolling through one message after another. Activated. Deactivated. Activated again . . .

"Whoa," said Milo, leaning the broom against the wall and pulling his earbuds out. "What's the matter?"

I breathed in through my nose, telling myself not to panic.

Something was interfering with the relay's signal, or it wouldn't be cutting in and out like that. So nothing major had happened yet. My parents were still out of the house, so if I got home fast and dealt with this, there'd be no reason for them to suspect that anything had gone wrong at all.

There was only one problem. I had no idea why the relay had come online or what it was doing. For all I knew, it might just blow up in my face.

"What is it?" Milo asked again.

"It's nothing," I replied, stuffing the phone back into my pocket. "But I need to get home. Right away."

001011

"Thanks for this," I told Jon, climbing into the passenger seat of his rusty 1990 Ford F-150 pickup. Drops speckled the windshield, but the worst of the storm had subsided. "Sorry I didn't take you up on the offer before."

"No problem." He turned the key, and the truck revved to life. Judging by the growling noise it needed a new water pump, but that was the least of my worries right now. "So what's the hurry? Sure you can't stop for a coffee on the way?"

I was trying to think of a plausible lie when Milo popped up in the headlights, waving both arms above his head. "Hey," he said breathlessly as Jon rolled the window down. "Can I grab a ride too? I'm just a couple streets over from Niki."

"Yeah, I guess," said Jon, giving me a *what-can-you-do* glance that I pretended not to notice. Milo climbed in beside me and we started off, splashing through the puddles toward the main road.

Jon switched on the radio, and some country singer began to wail about the hardworkin' boy who loved her and the hard-drinkin' man she loved. I hoped he'd change the station, but Jon seemed perfectly happy, tapping his fingers against the steering wheel as we waited for the light to turn. "Which way?" he asked.

"Ross Street," I told him. "Off Hilliard, just south of Caledonia." I kept my tone casual, though my fists were balled and my foot pressed hard against the floor. Getting home fast might be all I cared about, but I didn't want Jon getting too curious about why.

"Oh yeah? My grandma lives around there. So how long have you . . ."

"Hey, Jon," interrupted Milo, "that arrow's not gonna get any greener."

Jon's mouth puckered, but he pressed the accelerator and swung into a left turn. We drove a few blocks before he spoke again. "You don't have to keep taking the bus unless you want to," he said. "Most nights I've got the truck anyway, so if we're on shift together, give me a call and I'll pick you up."

"Awesome," Milo said brightly. "You're the man."

I knew and Jon knew and probably Jon suspected Milo knew that the offer had been meant for me. But Jon could hardly say so without being rude, so he forced a smile. "Nah, not really. Like I said, it's not a problem."

I almost felt sorry, then, about the way I'd blown him off before. But then Jon edged closer, his thigh pressing mine, and my charitable thoughts vanished in a surge of revulsion. I jerked to the right, crushing Milo against the door. But Milo didn't protest, or even make a sound. He angled his legs until not even a millimeter of our bodies were touching and kept his eyes on the road.

Jon stiffened, and I knew he'd got the message. I was half afraid he'd stop the truck and tell us both to get out, but he must have decided it wasn't worth the drama. A sharp turn flung me into Milo again, who let out a barely audible "oof." Then with a roar we swung onto Ross Street, and I saw the lights of number 28 glowing in the near distance.

"Right here," I blurted, and the Ford jerked to a halt. I scrambled over Milo and popped the door open. "Thanks, Jon. Night, Milo. See you—" I jumped down onto the driveway and took off, fumbling for my key as I went.

The porch was lit, but the front window was dark, and when I wrestled the key into the lock and shouldered the door open, no one answered my call. Only the light above the kitchen sink and the soft murmur of CBC Radio hinted that anyone might be home, but those were just my mom's usual antiburglar tactics. I sprinted down the corridor to my bedroom and waved on the light.

At first glance everything seemed normal, from the pile of laundry on my unmade bed to Crackers whining hopefully from his crate in the corner. He didn't seem upset, just eager to get out, which made me breathe easier. If anything strange had happened in my absence, he'd have been yelping and scratching like crazy.

"Hang on," I told him, flinging open my closet door and digging through the heap inside. Two pairs of dress boots, a sweater that had fallen off its hanger, a library book on cybernetics that was six weeks overdue . . . and shoved into the back corner, a cardboard box marked THIS END UP with an arrow pointing sternly at the floor.

Was it safe to look inside? Or was I about to make a fatal mistake?

Yet I couldn't ignore the danger, and I certainly couldn't run away and leave my parents to deal with it. There was nobody in the world who could handle this right now, except me.

Don't panic, I reminded myself. Then I picked up my old hockey stick, slid it under the bottom corner of the box, and flipped it aside.

There sat the relay, a silver egg on a nest of multicolored wiring. But no light came through the aperture, and the seam around its perimeter was intact.

It wasn't active. In fact, it didn't look as if it had powered on recently at all.

I exhaled, my tension draining away. There'd been a lightning storm not that long ago, and the monitoring device was plugged in to my old phone charger. Maybe a power surge had triggered a false alarm? I unplugged the charger and picked up the base, relay and all, for a closer look.

Sure enough, that was the answer. One of the capacitors had melted—my own fault for not using a surge protector. I was inspecting the scorched circuits to see how much I'd have to replace when Crackers started to whimper pathetically.

"Oh, all right, you," I said, setting the relay down on the nightstand and crouching to unlock his crate. He trotted out, tail wagging, and pushed his cold nose into my hand. "I'll take you outside in a—"

The lights flickered. The clock radio snapped on, blaring, and the remote-controlled curtains whirred open as the room went into its wake-up routine. I dived for the radio and was smacking it silent when a low hum vibrated the air behind me. "Oh *crap*," I breathed and spun around—just in time to be blinded by an explosion of white, scintillating light.

Sparks danced across my retinas as I staggered back, tripped over the laundry basket, and fell, cracking my head against the wall. For three vital seconds I lay there in a daze, and by the time I scrambled to my feet, it was too late.

It hadn't been a power surge that pinged my phone after all. Someone had been signaling the relay, trying to send a transmission through—and now that unwanted packet of information had finally arrived. All six foot three, 185 pounds of him, stretched across my bedroom carpet with his back arched in agony and the roots of his dyed brown hair glinting like gunmetal in the light. For an instant, his body glowed and flickered, and I could see the nightstand through it. Then he solidified and collapsed with a thud onto the floor.

Crackers yelped and scuttled behind me. But I stood riveted, staring at the new arrival. His dark grey uniform shirt was wrinkled and half untucked, one shoulder ripped at the seam as though he'd been fighting. His eyes were closed, and his lips were pulled back from his teeth in a grimace. But he didn't move, and he didn't appear to be breathing. Misgiving flashed inside me, and I was stooping to check his pulse when he stirred, groaned, and slowly opened his eyes.

The look on his face when he saw me was extraordinary— but the dismay turned quickly to resignation. "Tori," he murmured, struggling up onto his elbows. "Your hair's different. How long . . . ?"

Even in my half-stupefied state, I knew what he was asking. "Since I saw you last? About six months."

His brow creased in dismay. "Six . . . *no*. Is that all, really?"

Some people might have been charmed by the absent-minded professor routine, but I had no patience with it. "You just scared the crap out of me, Faraday!" I snapped. "If you were planning to come after Alison all along, you could at least have let one of us know!"

He was silent.

"Is it safe?" I demanded. "Is it over now? Or do we still have to worry about—"

But Sebastian wasn't listening. He had gone absolutely still, staring at something behind me.

Dread zapped into me, lighting up every nerve in my body. I whirled—

And there stood Milo in the doorway, my phone clutched in one hand.

"Um," he said in a voice that cracked over two octaves, "you dropped this."

0 0 1 1 0 0

I was so furious I couldn't even be scared. I grabbed Milo by the collar—he was still wearing his green polo from work—and twisted my fist up under his chin. "What are you doing here?" I demanded. "What makes you think you can just walk into my house?"

"Tori," said Sebastian Faraday in his deep, smooth voice, but I shot him a glare and he fell silent. He had no idea what was going on here, and I was *not* going to let him pull that Wise Older Brother act on me.

"Your phone fell out of your pocket when you got out of the truck," gasped Milo, his Adam's apple bobbing against my knuckles. He had seven inches and sixty pounds on me, but it didn't seem to have occurred to him to free himself by force. "I only noticed after we drove away. And I knew you'd want it back, so I got Jon to let me off at the corner, but when I got to your place the door was open, and I remembered how upset you'd looked before and I thought . . ."

He didn't finish the sentence, but he didn't need to. Reluctantly I opened my hand and let him go.

"All right," I said, trying to regain my calm. Maybe Milo hadn't seen anything, or at least nothing extraordinary. Maybe he just thought he'd walked in on me arguing with my secret university-aged boyfriend. The idea of me and Faraday soured my stomach, but I could fake it if I had to. "So you walked in. Then what?"

Milo blew out his breath and tugged his shirt back into shape. He glanced at Sebastian, at the relay, and a slow grin spread across his face. "That was the most amazing thing I've ever seen in my *entire life.* What is that thing? Some kind of tele-port device?"

So he'd seen the whole thing. The relay going off, Sebastian beaming in, all of it. I sank onto the bed and put my head in my hands.

Crackers leaped up beside me, burrowing under my elbow for comfort. I was tousling his ears, wishing we'd adopted a proper guard dog instead of the sweetest miniature dachshund in the universe, when Sebastian struggled to his feet and came to join me.

"This is my fault," he said. "I apologize. I should have double-checked the readings before I came through, but I never expected—"

"The readings," echoed Milo, quavering with glee. "He said *readings*."

I snatched up a cushion and flung it at him. "This is not funny!" I shouted.

He caught the pillow and lowered it slowly, eyes wide behind his skewed glasses. "Sorry. I guess I'm a little overexcited."

"Of course," Sebastian said, with a gentleness that made me want to kick him. It had taken me years to learn how to talk to strangers as though they were friends, and he made it look as natural as breathing. "It's not every day you see somebody materialize out of nowhere, and I won't insult your intelligence by claiming that it's magic or some kind of hoax. But if you care about Tori even a little—"

"Niki," I moaned. "My name's Niki. Sebastian, shut up. Please."

He looked slightly hurt, but he obeyed. I turned to Milo. "Look," I said, "I'm sure you're dying to know what this is all about. But it's way too complicated to explain. And if I tried, you wouldn't believe me."

Milo's brows lifted. "You think so?"

Never talk down to people, my mother had taught me. *If you can't make them believe that you like them, at least make them feel that you respect them.* "It's not that I don't think you're smart enough," I added quickly. "And I know you're a good guy. I really appreciated you running interference for me with Jon back there."

"But?" Milo asked. His guard was up now: he was realizing that I might not be as fragile or vulnerable as he'd thought. And if I didn't win back his sympathy fast, he might even start to resent me for it.

Time to amp up the emotional voltage, then. I got up and walked to Milo, stopping just inside his personal space so he'd feel his own vulnerability—and mine. "But I'm asking you," I said in a low voice, "I'm begging you, to stay out of this. To walk away and forget everything you just saw. Because if anyone finds out about this, even my parents, it's going to ruin my life all over again."

I held Milo's gaze as I spoke, silently counting seconds until he shifted and looked away. Good: I'd made him feel guilty. But then he said, "Why should I cover for you and this guy, whoever he is? I don't know him, and I barely know you. And wherever the two of you got this relay thing, I'm pretty sure you're not supposed to have it."

I opened my mouth to deny it, to tell him he had it all wrong—and then, in a flash, I realized what a fool I'd been. Why bother wasting time on persuasion, when the real solution was far more simple?

"Go ahead, then," I said coolly, stepping back. "Talk to your friends or the media or anyone you want. Tell them the girl you work with at the grocery store has a teleportation device, and you saw a guy beam right into her bedroom. Nobody's going to believe it."

"Not even when they see the video I took on your phone?" asked Milo.

My stomach twisted like a Möbius strip. I made a grab for the phone, but he held it out of reach. "Not yet, Niki. Or is it Tori?"

I wanted to body check him into the doorframe just for saying that, but I held myself back. "Fine," I said between my teeth. "What do you want? Money?"

He looked startled. "No! I only meant—"

"He didn't take any video," said Sebastian calmly. "He was too surprised, and it happened too fast. Give her the phone, Milo."

Milo blanched at the sound of his name. His upraised arm wilted—and I snatched the phone from his grip. A scroll through the contents assured me that Sebastian had been right: no video, no pictures, no evidence of any kind. He'd been bluffing.

"You're still wearing your name tag, by the way," Sebastian told him and flopped backward onto the mattress with his hands folded serenely across his chest. "Niki, can I borrow your laptop? I need to check a few things."

Unbelievable. He had no idea what a disaster he'd caused just by showing up, and I had no idea what he was doing here, and for all I knew that relay could go off and beam us both back to Mathis any minute. Milo looked apprehensive; there was no telling what he'd do next. And yet Faraday was acting as though it was one big happy pajama party, and all we needed was a couple of movies and some popcorn to make everything perfect.

"Absolutely not," I told him. "My parents'll be home any minute, and if they find me talking to a couple of strange guys in my bedroom, it's going to be awkward for everybody involved."

"Ah. Yes, good point." Sebastian sat up again and took his wallet out of his back pocket, thumbing past several different bank cards to peer into the empty billfold. "Well, then, we'll go elsewhere. I just need to stop at an ATM first."

"No, we won't," I said. "I have to be here when my parents get in, or they'll panic." I pulled my old cell phone out of the monitoring device and tossed it to him. "My number's in there. Call me tomorrow."

"All right," said Faraday, putting the phone and the wallet away. "Do you want me to take the relay as well?"

The offer surprised me, but it was also reassuring: it meant he didn't think it was dangerous, at least not at the moment. "Okay," I said.

"What about your friend here?" Sebastian asked. "Is anyone expecting him home?"

"Not likely," I said, before Milo could answer. "His mom works the night shift, and his brother's at university."

"Good. Then I'll take care of him too." Sebastian picked up the relay and headed out into the corridor. "Come on, Milo."

"Please tell me he's not going to snap my neck and hide my body in a Dumpster," said Milo, and I could tell he was only half joking.

"No," I replied, "but the last person who tried to get the relay away from him ended up beaming themselves into space. So I wouldn't try anything, if I were you."

He gave me an exasperated look. "I'm not a thief, okay? And I'm not an idiot either. I wasn't trying to threaten you. I just wanted to find out what was going on."

"Well, it looks like you're about to," I said. "Tell Sebastian he can borrow the green jacket out of the hall closet, if he needs one. Have a nice walk."

Without waiting for an answer, I pushed Milo out into the corridor and slammed the door behind him. Then I pressed my forehead against the wood, closed my eyes, and clenched my teeth until I no longer felt like screaming.

It was midnight before my parents got home—they'd gone out for drinks after the movie. I could tell because my mother was giggling as the two of them came through the front door, and they both became very straight and solemn when they saw me.

"Hi, pumpkin," said my dad. He smelled of beer, but I could tell he wasn't drunk, only mellow. He propped my mom against the wall and stooped to peer at me, looking more like a tame bear than ever. "You all right? Something bad happen at work?"

He'd forgotten about the makerspace already—that was how little it meant to him. How little he understood. And yet I knew he didn't mean to hurt me. He was only trying to protect me—and despite everything that had happened last summer, part of him still believed that he could.

He was wrong, but I didn't want to be the one to tell him so. If things went bad with Sebastian and the relay, he'd find out soon enough.

"It's okay," I said. "Just—this guy at work keeps hitting on me. Not harassing me," I added as Dad started to bristle, "but he's been hinting around, hoping I'll go out with him. And I don't want to."

"Which one?" asked Mom, struggling out of her coat. She knew most of my regular coworkers by sight, since she shopped at Value Foods every weekend. "That Chinese boy?"

Actually, Milo's family was Korean, but I wasn't going to get into that now. "No, Mom. Jon. The blond guy who works the express lane."

"The cute one?" She gave an owlish blink. "What's wrong with him?"

She'd liked Brendan too. "I'm not interested, Mom. That's all."

"You're too picky," she told me with a shake of her head. "You're seventeen and you've only had one proper boyfriend! I'll never be a grandmother at this rate."

She spoke lightly, smiling all the while so I'd know she was only teasing. She didn't really expect me to be thinking about marriage and children at this age. But I knew enough Latin to remember *in vino veritas,* too. I wanted to tell her not to get her hopes up, but if there was ever going to be a good time for that discussion, it wasn't now.

"So you're saying I shouldn't hold out for a guy like Dad?" I said, and the flush in Mom's cheeks deepened as Dad kissed her temple.

"Oh, no," she told me with a hiccup of laughter in her voice. "You absolutely should."

0 0 1 1 1 0

When I woke up the next morning, there were two texts waiting for me. The first one came from my old cell number and read:

    –Sunrise Café. 11 am. Pancakes?

Trust Sebastian to tell me nothing that I actually wanted to know. I texted back:

    –Pancakes first. Then I kill you. WHAT
    HAPPENED???

While I was waiting for his answer, I opened the second message, from a number I didn't recognize. It said:

    –U OK? GET UR PHONE ALRITE?

Great. Jon had made Milo give him my number before he let him out of the truck. I was trying to think of a polite way to ask him never to text me again when Faraday's reply came through.

—Milo says French toast is better. Also, no need
for violence. It's all fine.

Which didn't tell me much either, except that Milo was there and that Sebastian thought he'd solved the problem somehow. Probably by telling him my entire life story and trusting to Milo's inner goodness, which wasn't my idea of a workable solution at all. Muttering a few swear words, I kicked off the duvet and headed for the shower.

"I'm meeting some friends downtown for breakfast," I called over my shoulder twenty minutes later, ruffling my still-damp pixie cut with one hand. "I'll be back in a few hours, okay?"

"Friends? You mean some of the people from—" Mom came out of the kitchen and stopped dead in dismay. "Oh, Niki. Are you really going to wear that?"

I looked down at myself automatically, though I already knew what I was wearing. Dark tights under frayed jean shorts, a long-sleeved tee with a barely visible pattern of sine waves across the chest, and a brown suede jacket I'd nabbed from Goodwill last week. Tori Beaugrand would never have worn anything like it, but that was kind of the point. "Why not?" I asked. "It's clean, and it fits."

She gave a little sigh. "Yes, I suppose. Never mind."

As I headed outside, I was still puzzling over her reaction, and then it clicked. Back in my old life, I'd always left the shopping to my mom—not only because I didn't particularly care what I wore but because she had such definite ideas about what clothes would suit me and help me fit in. But now I was Niki, the rules were different, and this outfit was all my doing.

It wasn't that I looked bad. It was just that I didn't look like her daughter.

A brisk walk and an eighteen-minute bus ride later, I walked into the Sunrise Café to find Milo and Faraday sitting in the booth at the back corner, building a tower out of coffee cups, cutlery, and packets of peanut butter and jam. They were so absorbed in the task that neither one looked up until I sat down next to Milo, who jumped, swore, and dropped his fork under the table.

"Good morning to you too," I said, and he looked sheepish.

"Sorry. I just wasn't expecting you yet." He shuffled over to give me more room and began disassembling the pyramid into its component place settings. "So, Sebastian invited me along. Hope that's okay."

I shot a *this-had-better-be-good* look at Sebastian, who met my gaze mildly and slid a menu across the table. "Milo and I had quite a talk last night," he said. "About the top secret research facility I work for—excuse me, *used* to work for. A place called Meridian."

My breath stalled in my throat. I stared at him, mouth frozen in an *O* of disbelief.

"Would you rather I lied?" said Sebastian.

There was no answer to that, at least not that I could think of. I pulled a serviette out of the dispenser and unfolded it with deliberate care. "Go on," I said. "What else did you tell him?"

As it turned out, Sebastian had told Milo pretty much everything. How he'd grown restless with his employers' restrictive policies and decided to take a sabbatical and do some research on his own. How he'd discovered that one of his fellow scientists was doing experiments with far-ranging effects on civilians—particularly a young woman named Alison Jeffries, who had ended up in a psychiatric hospital after exposure to one of their devices. How he'd talked to Alison and learned that another girl had been with her at the time—a girl named Tori Beaugrand, who had since vanished without a trace . . .

"Do you want me to stop?" Sebastian asked, and I realized I'd shredded the paper napkin into confetti.

"No," I said, brushing the pieces away. "I want to know everything he knows."

"Look," said Milo uneasily. "We don't have to get into this. He told me they kidnapped you with that relay thing and that they were doing experiments on you. I didn't ask for details."

I gave a little, dry laugh. "Did he tell you they'd been experimenting on me my *whole life?*" That had been one of the worst moments of the whole ordeal, when I found out who'd put the chip in my arm and what it meant. That, and realizing I was never going to see my parents or my friends again.

"Actually, no," said Sebastian. "That's your story, not mine. All I told Milo was that when I realized what they'd done to you, I went back to Meridian. I found where you were being held, released you, and sent you back home against my colleague's protests. Then I stayed to make a full report of his unethical behavior to the senior staff. But . . . things didn't turn out quite as planned."

Even I hadn't heard this part. "Why not?"

"I'd rather not go into that now. Let's say I decided it would be prudent to get out while I still had the chance. And that I have no desire to work for Meridian or anyone associated with it ever again." He ran a long finger down one edge of the menu and flipped it open. "Ready to order?"

Milo and I traded glances, and I could see he was as unsettled by the gaps in Sebastian's story as I was. "So what now?" Milo asked him. "You're just going to hide out here and let it happen? Let them go on doing to other people what they did to Niki?"

"No," said Sebastian, not looking up from the menu. "And I have no intention of letting them do it to Niki again, either. But she's perfectly safe at the moment, as are you. If there's any threat of that changing, I'll look after it."

I had my doubts, but I wasn't going to argue. Not in front of Milo, anyway. "So," I said slowly, "Milo's on board with all this? You trust him?"

"He's also sitting right here," said Milo, "and getting tired of being talked about in the third person." He flicked a creamer, and it flipped 180 degrees and landed neatly in its original spot. "Anyway, I let Sebastian couch-surf at my place last night and I didn't even touch your precious relay, so give me a little credit—oh, hi."

This last was to the waitress, who was standing by the table with order pad in hand. Hastily I skimmed the menu and handed it back to her. "Pancakes and back bacon," I said. "Oh, and coffee." I waited until she marched off again, then turned to Milo.

"Sorry," I said. "But after what I went through, it's hard for me to trust anybody. It's nothing personal." Then I pulled out the tiny, tentative smile that meant *I know I screwed up, but I'm cute, forgive me?*—and it worked. Milo smiled back.

"Good," said Sebastian. "Milo, I think you're in. But could

Niki and I have a private word? Just for a minute?"

"Uh . . . yeah, sure," said Milo, looking taken aback. "I was going to the washroom anyway." He slid around the curve of the bench, and Sebastian got up to let him out.

When he'd disappeared, I leaned across the table and hissed, "Why is he here? We need to talk. Alone."

"I know," said Sebastian. "But I owed him a favor for letting me sleep on his sofa. And after what he saw last night, I don't see how we can keep him out of it."

There was a faint reproach in his voice, and it annoyed me. "Well, it's not my fault," I said. "I only kept the relay because I couldn't find a way to destroy it, and I was afraid to leave it behind. How was I supposed to know you were going to show up? Especially after what you said to Alison—"

"I didn't think I'd get the chance," he said. "You'd only been gone a few seconds when Mathis came in."

Heavily armed, no doubt. After the way Sebastian had double-crossed him to help Alison and me escape, he must have been furious. "Then what happened?" I asked.

"The negotiations were delicate," Sebastian said. "They included a brief standoff with weapons, a message he really didn't want me to send, and a long and tedious argument about ethics. But eventually we worked it out." He took a sip from his mug and folded his hands around it, inhaling the steam. "This is excellent coffee."

I didn't find Sebastian as easy to read as some people, but hiding behind a coffee cup was a bad sign. There was more to this story that he wasn't telling me, and I had a suspicion I knew what it was about.

"Does Alison know you're back?" I asked.

The cup froze on his lips. He lowered it to the table, a slow and deliberate motion. "No," he said and then more cheerfully, "Oh look. Pancakes."

I gave the waitress a tight smile as she began setting out the plates, silently willing her to hurry up and go away. But she'd only been gone two seconds when Milo returned from the washroom, so I had to admit defeat.

I wasn't out of ammunition yet, though. I waited until Milo was happily distracted pouring syrup over his French toast, and then I caught Sebastian's eye and mouthed, "Coward."

He kept his expression bland, as though he hadn't noticed. But I saw his jaw tighten, and I knew the shot had gone home.

0 0 1 1 1 1

By the time Sebastian, Milo, and I had finished our breakfast and about three cups of coffee each, we'd come to an agreement. Milo promised to keep his mouth shut about what he'd seen in my bedroom last night, as well as everything we'd just told him, and that he wouldn't mention the names "Sebastian Faraday" or "Tori Beaugrand" to anybody ever. And in return, since Milo was so curious, Sebastian pulled the relay out of the old camera case he'd brought with him and explained a few things about how it worked.

I'd heard the "matter is information" speech before, and I already knew about the relay's built-in propulsion system, as well as its camouflage and self-defense capabilities. So I propped my chin on my hand and counted the wall tiles until Sebastian said, "Niki, would you mind opening it up for us? Milo wants to see inside."

Until last night I hadn't worried about touching the relay, because I'd thought it couldn't send or receive transmissions anymore. Now that Sebastian had proven me wrong, I wasn't nearly so comfortable with it. "Is it safe?" I asked.

He gave me an odd look. "Would I ask if it wasn't?"

It was hard not to wonder what the restaurant staff and other patrons were making of all this. But at the moment nobody was even looking our way. I sighed, and Sebastian dropped the relay into my outstretched palm. I let my fingertips rest on its brushed metal surface for a moment, then gripped the top half and turned it.

The casing opened, revealing a lattice of gleaming filaments and a bubble of silvery liquid. "Wow," Milo said, leaning closer. "What is that stuff in the middle? Mercury?"

"It looks similar, doesn't it?" said Sebastian. "And since the best translation I can give you for its scientific name is *quicksilver*, it's an understandable mistake. But it's no substance you've seen before. It's a form of programmable matter: a superfast information processing and transfer medium that makes the most sophisticated modern computers look like an abacus. And no, before you ask, I don't have the recipe. It's classified."

What Sebastian didn't say and I didn't feel like saying either was that the chip in my arm had been made from the same substance. I'd seen it used for other purposes as well. But when Milo reached over to poke the gleaming liquid, I slapped the fork out of his hand. "Are you trying to get yourself fried?" I demanded, then closed up the relay and pushed it back to Sebastian.

"So what are you going to do with it now?" Milo asked, as Sebastian tucked the relay back into its case. "If it came from

Meridian and you're not working for them anymore, aren't they going to want it back?"

"If they do, they'll be disappointed," said Sebastian evenly. "Because as soon as I get the chance, I'm going to destroy it."

Good, I thought, but Milo recoiled. "What? Why?"

"Because it's experimental technology, and it's dangerous," said Sebastian. "Now if you'll excuse me . . ." He got up and whisked the bill off the table.

"Wait," I protested, but he cut me off with a shake of his head.

"Don't worry about it," he said. "It's on me."

"I still don't get it," Milo said, while I watched Sebastian walk to the register and tried not to cringe with guilt. "So what if the relay's experimental? It obviously works fine, or Sebastian wouldn't have used it to get here."

"Trust me," I said distractedly, "you'd have to be either desperate or a masochist to put yourself through that thing. It might only take a couple of seconds in real time, but it feels like you're being fed through a quantum sausage grinder for about eight million years." Just thinking about my last trip made me feel queasy. And Sebastian had done it *three times.*

"Okay," said Milo, though I could tell he wasn't convinced. "But you could still use it to send other things, right? You could revolutionize the shipping industry—"

"No, we couldn't," said Sebastian as he rejoined us, shrugging my dad's old jacket back onto his shoulders. "Because to make it work, we'd need a second relay and a computer fast enough to process all the information, and we don't have access to either of those since I left my job. Believe me, Milo, it's better this way."

Milo nodded reluctantly, and the three of us headed out onto the street. But we'd only taken a few steps before Sebastian made an exasperated noise and started patting down his pockets.

"I've dropped my phone," he said. "Or rather, I should say, your phone, Niki. Go on, I'll be right with you—" and he dashed back inside the café.

So much for my hopes of getting Sebastian alone for a real conversation. Not only did he show no signs of wanting to send Milo away, but it almost seemed like he was avoiding me. Was it Alison he didn't want to talk about? Was this his way of keeping me from asking about her?

If so, it wasn't going to work. Milo couldn't stick around forever, and the minute he left, I'd confront Sebastian and get the truth out of him, whether he liked it or not. I leaned against the café window, watching a gaunt old man with a mustache feeding the pigeons in front of City Hall, until Milo said abruptly, "I looked you up on the Internet last night."

If anybody but Milo had said that, I would have taken off like a rabbit. But he'd heard Sebastian call me Tori, and he knew I'd been through a bad time last summer. Given those two clues, it wouldn't have been hard for him to sleuth out the rest. "And?"

"The articles said you couldn't remember where you'd been or who'd taken you. That the police had no leads, so the investigation had been closed." He sat down on the narrow windowsill beside me. "Why didn't you tell them about Meridian?"

I watched the old man stoop to let a snow-white pigeon peck grain from his outstretched palm. There was something sweet and sad about the way he craned toward her, as though he were the one begging and not the other way around. "Because I knew nobody would believe it."

"Why not? I did."

"Oh, come on, Milo. If you hadn't seen Sebastian come through the relay with your own eyes, would you have believed there was a device that could reduce people to subatomic particles and beam them halfway across the—the planet? Let alone that some wacked-out scientist at a top secret research base had used it to kidnap a teenage girl?"

"Point," said Milo. "But there's another thing I don't get. Why you? What was so special about—"

"Stop right there," I said. Earlier this morning I'd told Milo more about my past than even Sebastian thought he needed to know. I wasn't going to make that mistake again. "What they did to me and why is none of your business. But it wasn't because I was special, believe me. It was because I was *disposable.*"

Milo was silent. Then he said, "I don't believe that."

Anger sparked through me. "You think I'm lying?"

"No. I think they are." He drew breath to explain—then glanced at the window behind us and frowned. "Where's Sebastian?"

"Probably in the washroom," I said, but Milo had already pulled open the café door and ducked inside. With a sigh, I dusted myself off and followed.

I was standing by the table we'd left behind, idly drawing patterns in my spilled orange juice, when Milo reappeared from the back corridor. "He's not in there."

I gave him a blank look. "Then where is he?"

"You tell me," he said.

Apprehension tingled inside me. I pushed the swinging door open and walked through.

Milo was right; the washrooms were empty. But there was a fire door leading out into the back lot, where the smell of grease and rancid potato peelings mingled with the exhaust fumes from a truck idling nearby. I stepped onto the pavement and looked around. Aside from the truck driver, there was no one in sight.

This was crazy. There had to be some mistake. As a last resort, I pulled out my phone, called my old cell number, and let it ring, listening for an echo in the distance.

No sound. No answer.

Sebastian Faraday had vanished.

010000

"I don't get it," Milo said as the two of us sprinted across the diner's back lot, heading for the street. "Why would he ditch us like that?"

I had no answer. Until now Sebastian had seemed so calm, so perfectly in control. He'd befriended Milo, made a deal with him—and as soon as everything was settled, he'd panicked and run off? It made no sense. Skidding to the curb, I shaded my eyes and scanned the pavement in both directions. No telltale flash of green from my dad's borrowed coat, no scarecrow figure loping away into the distance. He'd disappeared so completely, it was almost as though . . .

I spun back to Milo, whose bleak expression told me he'd been thinking the same thing. "Maybe he was wrong about the relay," he said. "Maybe it wasn't safe after all."

Could Sebastian have made such a careless mistake? Assumed the relay was dormant, only to have it activate and beam him back to Mathis against his will? The idea was chilling, but the more I thought about it, the less plausible it seemed.

"No," I said. "That's not what happened."

"How do you know?"

"Because it's too neat. If it was an accident, it could have happened any time, not just when he was alone. Why would he leave us and go back in the café unless he—"

My phone buzzed in my pocket. With a startled glance at Milo, I raised it to my ear.

"Hello?" The voice was young, female, and unfamiliar.

"Hi," I said warily. "Who is this?"

"It's Lindsey, from the Science Museum. Have you lost a phone? Because a guy just dropped one off at the front counter, and this was the only number in it."

The last of my doubts melted in a gush of molten fury. The next time I saw Sebastian Faraday, I was going to strangle him.

"Yeah, it's mine," I told the girl. "Thanks. I'll be right there."

0 1 0 0 0 1

The Science Museum was three blocks down from the café, on the other side of the street. As Milo and I raced up to the doors, we barreled into a family coming out. I exchanged breathless apologies with the mother, Milo caught the toddler and plopped him safely back in the stroller, and the two of us plunged inside.

Coming out of the sunshine, it took my eyes a good five seconds to adjust. But once I'd blinked away the dazzle, I spotted Lindsey at once. She was leaning over the front desk, pressing an admission stamp onto a little girl's hand, while her parents waited by the entrance gate for her to buzz them through.

"Hi," I said. "I'm Niki. You have my phone? It's an old Nokia, black with a silver keypad."

"Oh—yes—wait a second. I'll be right with you." She pressed a button and waved the family through, then stooped and retrieved a bundle from beneath the counter. "Is this jacket yours as well?"

Green cotton canvas, folded into a neat square. "It's my dad's," I said. "Thanks." I dropped the old cell into my purse and shook out the coat, feeling its slight weight. "There wasn't . . . a bag with it or anything?"

Lindsey shook her head. "Just what you have."

I'd figured as much. So not only was Faraday gone, he'd taken the relay with him.

"Now what?" asked Milo, as I turned away. "You want to keep looking for him?"

I draped the coat over my arm, slowly smoothing out the folds. I didn't really care who had the relay, as long as it didn't fall into the wrong hands. And I trusted Sebastian, even if he was annoying. If he said he was going to destroy the relay, then that was what he would do.

"There's no point," I said. "He knows what he's doing, or at least he thinks he does. He'll come back when he's ready."

"Or maybe he won't," said Milo, watching me sidelong. "Are you okay with that?"

"Why wouldn't I be?" I asked, and then I realized what he

was implying. "Oh, no. No *way*. And also, ew."

"Well, you seemed to know each other pretty well . . ."

"Ew," I repeated fervently.

Milo grinned. "Okay, okay. Just checking—" He broke off, staring at something in the air behind me. "What is that?"

I turned, following the line of his gaze past the front desk and into the atrium, where a crowd was watching a demonstration. The children bounced and squealed, while the adults gazed up toward the ceiling, heads swiveling in unison . . .

Then I saw it. A miniature flying machine, small enough to fit in my two hands. It hummed low over the audience, flipped over, and shot straight upward, out of sight.

All thought of Sebastian Faraday evaporated from my mind. I dug into my purse for the admission fee, shoved it across the counter to Lindsey, and slapped my hand down for the stamp.

"Hey, wait for me!" said Milo. The gate buzzed open and the two of us shot through, straining for a view of the little machine. It paused in midair and executed a triple flip, then dropped six feet before pulling up to another hovering stop.

"That is so cool," Milo murmured. "I want one."

I did too, but I was pretty sure it hadn't come from the gift shop. X-shaped, with a propeller on all four spokes and a microprocessor wired into a superlight body, it had the unpolished look of a home electronics project rather than some prepackaged kit. As the machine went through its radio-controlled paces, I looked around for the maker.

And there he was on the far side of the atrium, a stocky, bespectacled man with thinning hair and a goatee. An LED name tag that said "Make!" was clipped to his shirt pocket, and he clutched a control box in both hands. I slipped around the edge of the circle and came up behind him.

"Hi," I said to the man. "That's a quadrotor drone, right?"

"Yep," he said absently, thumbing the controls. The drone flipped over again.

"And you built it yourself?"

The quadrotor's battery was draining, and the propellers had begun to sputter. The man scurried forward and caught it as the crowd broke into applause. "Thanks for watching!" he called. "Check out our information table before you go!" Then he ambled off, my question apparently forgotten.

Annoyed by the dismissal, I watched as he packed the quadrotor away in its case and carried it toward the exit. There beneath a poster reading GET EXCITED AND MAKE THINGS stood a table covered with refrigerator magnets and brochures—all bearing a logo I recognized.

My heart did a 180. I chased after the man and tapped his elbow. "Wait a minute," I said. "You're from the makerspace?"

"That's right," he said, thick brows rising. "You've heard of us?"

"There was an article in the newspaper," I said, as Milo strolled to join us. "It sounds fantastic. Is that where you built the quadrotor?"

"Uh, yeah." His poise seemed to have deserted him. His eyes skittered past mine and focused on Milo, as if looking for reassurance.

"How long did it take you to build?" asked Milo.

That opened the floodgates. Immediately the man relaxed and started expounding on the schematics he'd used and all the challenges he'd had to overcome in the construction process, popping the case back open and pointing to one part of the machine after another as he talked. By the time he'd finished, Milo looked slightly dazed, but I'd seen as much as I needed to know.

"You should see what the guys down at the University of Pennsylvania are doing with these things," the man went on eagerly, still talking to Milo. "They've got 'em flying in formation, building towers, even playing instruments. They make great surveillance cameras too. Totally the next big thing in military tech."

"So if I wanted to visit the makerspace sometime," I said to the man, "would I be able—"

"Oh, sure, always looking for new members." He fished a brochure out of his back pocket and handed it to Milo. "You should come to one of our Open House nights. We just bought a laser cutter, and we've got some great projects in the works right now."

Never mind that I was the one who knew what a quadrotor was, the one who'd shown all the interest. All it had taken was one not-very-technical question from Milo, and suddenly *he* was the potential recruit? Seething behind my smile, I said in my perkiest tone, "Thanks. That was super interesting," and watched the man trot away.

010010

"Wow," Milo said, as the two of us left the museum. "That was some fine sarcasm back there. Too bad he didn't notice."

I sighed. "Like it would have made a difference if he had. You're the one he was interested in. He probably thinks I liked his quadrotor because it reminded me of a butterfly."

"And he probably thinks I'm going into engineering because I'm Korean," said Milo dryly.

Hope fluttered in my chest. "You are?"

He snorted a laugh. "Are you kidding? I can barely keep my bike from falling apart."

Stupid, to feel disappointed. But for a moment I'd thought that Milo and I might actually have something good in common. "Oh," I said.

"You are, though." He stuffed his hands into his pockets, a smile curling his mouth. "And you're going to blow all the guys in your class away."

"With my beauty and charm?" I said ironically. "Thanks, but I don't think their standards are going to be that high."

Milo's smile inverted to a look of reproach. "I'm not talking about your looks. I mean you're going to be better than they are."

"Oh really?" I kept my tone light, but an uneasy feeling was fizzling in my stomach. I hadn't realized I'd given so much away. "What makes you think so?"

"Well, your bedroom, for one thing. I know there was a lot happening last night, but I did notice you had a pretty sweet automated system there. So you're obviously smart. And I thought that flying machine was cool, but when you saw it, you just—" He spread his fingers in a firework gesture. "I've never seen you so excited about anything."

I could feel a blush sneaking across my face. I pretended to look in a shop window, though I didn't really need any new handbags or shoes. "So what are you going into, then?" I asked.

"Guess," said Milo, and now he sounded resigned, even

faintly bitter. It took me a second to process that, but then I got it: whatever his chosen major was, it wasn't something his family approved of. Either because it wasn't challenging enough, or prestigious enough, or it just wasn't the traditional Korean thing to do.

I stepped back and looked Milo over. Good running shoes—*quality* running shoes, not just the brand everybody else was wearing, and well broken in. Slim jeans in a classic style. Navy T-shirt with a Nike swoosh across the chest, just visible behind the zip of his dark olive windbreaker.

All of which could mean any number of things or nothing in particular. But I'd also seen Milo in short sleeves, effortlessly stacking water cooler refills and 20-kilogram bags of cat litter, and I knew what his arms looked like.

"Something athletic," I began, and his face lit up. I almost said *ballet* or *figure skating* just to see how he'd react, but I'd seen his work schedule and there was no way he had time for lessons. Besides, he didn't move like a dancer.

"Phys ed," I announced. "You're going to be a gym teacher. Or a coach. Or a personal trainer."

"Technically, that was three guesses," said Milo, but now his eyes were smiling along with his mouth, and I knew I'd got it right the first time. "What gave it away?"

"You don't get biceps like that from reading textbooks," I said. "And no offense, but apart from the earbuds, you don't seem like the artsy type."

"Tell that to my grandmother," he said. "She's the reason I had to suffer through ten years of Suzuki violin." He mimed bowing and made a screechy noise. "But yeah, you're right. I'm okay at math and science and business and that other traditional stuff, but I don't want to spend my life in an office. I like running. I like the outdoors. And . . . " He gave a little shrug. "I like kids."

Now that I'd put the pieces together, it made sense. I could see Milo being good with children, and I could see them liking him too. But kids were one of the things I didn't talk about, because I was never going to have any. So I just said, "Well, good for you. I'm sure you'll be great at it."

"Tell that to my mom," he said wryly. "Or better yet don't, because I haven't figured out how to break the news to her yet. She knows I'm into sports, but she thinks that just means I'm going to become an orthopedic surgeon and work on top athletes. The kind of thing that will show everybody how brilliant and hard working I am, and make lots of money." He gazed into the distance, dark eyes wistful behind his glasses. "When she finds out I got accepted at Laurentian, she's going to flip out."

"Laurentian!" I hadn't meant to sound dismayed, but it just slipped out. Laurentian University was in Sudbury, my old hometown. "Why there?"

"They've got a great phys ed program, that's why. I applied to Nipissing and Windsor too, but Laurentian was my first choice." He cocked his head at me. "Why, does it matter?"

"No," I said quickly. "I just—wasn't expecting it."

Milo looked about to say something more, but then a whistle blew shrilly from his pocket. "Probably my mom," he said, taking his phone out. He frowned at the screen for three seconds, then put it away. "Sorry. You were saying?"

I wouldn't have suspected anything if not for the slight catch in his voice. But I'd been reading people too long, and I knew Milo too well by now, not to pick up on it. "What's wrong?" I asked.

"Nothing!" His eyes opened wide. "Why?"

I held out my hand. "Give me the phone, Milo."

"Excuse me?"

"Sebastian just texted you, didn't he? I want to know what he said."

He deflated. "How'd you guess?"

I snatched at his pocket, but he spun away, catching my shoulder and holding me at arm's length. His grip was gentle, but his muscles were like steel. "Hey! What if I told you it was none of your business?"

"It's to do with me. That makes it my business," I snapped, trying to duck under his arm. He grabbed my other shoulder, holding me steady.

"All right, calm down. I didn't want to scare you, okay? And I'm guessing Sebastian didn't either." He let go and pulled out his phone, turning the face toward me. The message read:

–Niki's in danger. You're not. Stay close to her, please. I'll be back as soon as I can.

010011

We texted back right away, of course. I had a million things I wanted to say to Sebastian, most of them rude—what kind of idiotic, useless, high-handed message was that?—but Milo talked me down, pointing out that we'd get more out of him if he thought the conversation was private. So I let him try first:

–What kind of danger? What am I supposed to do?

After we'd waited twenty minutes and sent a couple more messages for good measure, it was obvious we weren't going to get any answer. He'd sent the text from an online service, probably using one of the computers at the library, and moved on without waiting for a reply.

"Maybe he'll get back to us later," said Milo. But he didn't sound optimistic, and I wasn't either. Sebastian's last message hadn't read like the start of a conversation. It was more like a good-bye.

"Jerk," I muttered, but my heart wasn't in it. I kept thinking about the way Sebastian had looked back in the diner when I called him a coward—that flicker of guilt and, for one second, anger . . .

I'd never bothered to turn on the charm for Sebastian; he'd seen too much of the real me to be fooled. Besides, he was already on my side, for reasons that had nothing to do with my winning personality, so I didn't need to tiptoe around him.

Or so I'd thought. But now I was beginning to regret needling him about Alison. Sure, their relationship made no sense to me, but it was also none of my business . . .

Though if Sebastian had decided he'd rather take off and leave me in some unspecified danger than tell me why he hadn't called his girlfriend, then he really was a jerk.

As we walked, the sun disappeared behind the clouds and the wind swirled along the sidewalk, kicking up little tornadoes of grit and paper scraps. The empty storefronts suddenly looked menacing, dark windows staring us down, and the scattered tattoo parlors, bars, and used bookshops were no better. I pulled my dad's coat around my shoulders.

"What now?" Milo asked. "Do you want me to take you home?"

Chivalry was not dead, just totally out of its depth. I sighed. "Milo, you don't have to do this. No matter what Sebastian says, I can look after myself."

"Hey!" He sounded stung. "I may be a jock, but I'm not stupid. Even if I thought you needed a bodyguard, I wouldn't hang around just because some guy I met yesterday told me to."

"Then why are you doing it?" I rounded on him. "I'm not exactly a sparkly ball of fun at the moment, as you've probably noticed. I haven't even been that nice to you—" Oh, crap, my throat had closed up and my eyes were prickling. I had to start walking again, fast, so he wouldn't see.

"Yeah, I'd noticed," he said, matching my pace. "But I kind of like you anyway."

"You *are* a masochist."

"Not really. It's not like you've been nasty, just uptight. And kind of hostile sometimes, but I don't blame you. If I'd been through the kind of stuff you have, I'd probably be in a padded room somewhere—"

"Don't," I said sharply.

"What?" He frowned at me. "I'm not flattering you. I mean it."

"No. I mean, don't joke about that stuff. Straitjackets and padded rooms and—" I closed my eyes, seeing Alison's white, strained face in my mind. "Just don't, okay?"

"Okay." Milo sounded subdued. "Sorry." We walked another block in silence, and then he said, "What I'm trying to say is, you're so . . ." He made a vague gesture. "I don't even know. Just different. But in a good way. I'm trying to figure out how you do it."

"Do what?" I asked warily. He'd said *in a good way,* so I wasn't ready to hit the panic button yet. But I wasn't sure I liked where this was heading.

"How you just throw yourself into things and *deal* with

them. Like that night on the bus. I'd barely tuned in to what was going on when, *bam*, you jumped up there and grabbed the wheel." He huffed a laugh. "It was like all the rest of us were stuck in one of those slow-motion dreams, and you were the only one who was awake. Like it had never even occurred to you to be scared."

"I was scared," I protested, but he cut me off.

"I know you were, afterward. But right then? You were like the perfect athlete. Totally focused."

"Only because I didn't want to die," I said. "And as soon as it was over, I panicked and ran off. You're the one who stayed and made sure the driver was okay."

Milo gave an uncomfortable shrug. "Yeah, but you had to show me CPR first, and the rest was nothing special. I mean, I couldn't have done anything else."

"Sure you could," I pointed out. "You just didn't."

He sighed. "Okay, I get it. You don't want to be a hero. I'm not trying to be one either. But my point is, if there's danger involved . . ." He gave me a sidelong look. "I think the two of us make a pretty good team."

And with that, I finally understood what Milo was offering. This wasn't about pity or duty or morbid curiosity; it wasn't because I'd made some special effort to charm or impress him. He simply liked being around me, and wanted to be friends. A slow warmth spread through me, loosening the knot in my chest. "Together, we fight crime?"

"Something like that." He nudged my shoulder. "Why do you think I started working out? All that stuff about going into phys ed was just the cover story. Really I wanted to look good in the super-suit."

I threw my head back and laughed, the first genuine laugh I'd had in days. And despite the worries still skulking at the fringes of my mind, it felt good.

"Okay, Robin," I said. "Let's hunt down the Batmobile and go home."

0 1 0 1 0 0

"I'm home!" I yelled as I came in the door, then stopped as I realized Mom was in the living room, barely three meters from me. She was standing at the front window with Crackers tucked under her arm, watching Milo as he jogged away.

"Who's that boy, honey?" she asked.

"Milo," I said. "You know, from work. He lives around here, so we got off the bus together."

"He's not bad looking," she mused. "For an Asian."

Oh, wow. And she was a pretty nice mom, for a racist. "He's Korean," I said wearily, hanging Dad's coat back on its hook in the closet. "And he's just good-looking period, okay?" As soon as the words left my mouth I cursed myself. The last thing I needed was my mom thinking I had a crush on Milo Hwang.

"I didn't mean it like that. You know what I mean, honey—"

"Don't explain, Mom. It doesn't help."

Mom didn't answer. She was silent so long that I turned— and saw tears in her eyes.

"I know you're unhappy, Niki," she said, letting Crackers go as he began to squirm and whine. "I know you think we're wrong about everything right now. But we're only trying to keep you safe. And a year isn't so long to wait, is it?"

Oh, no. I did not want to talk about the makerspace. Not after that depressing incident at the science museum, and with so much else on my mind. And now that Milo was gone, the laughter we'd shared seemed to have happened a thousand years ago and a billion miles away. "I already told you, I get it. It's fine." I kicked off my shoes and headed down the corridor to my room.

She followed me. "Sweetheart, please. I don't want this to come between us."

I stopped in the doorway, one hand on the frame. "Mom," I said with all the patience I could muster, "there's nothing to talk about. Really."

"I know you," she persisted. "Do you think I can't tell when you're upset? If we just sit down together, I know we can work this out—"

I shut the door in her face.

In the stillness that followed, the only sound was the catch of my mother's breath. Then the floor creaked, and in a few rapid footsteps she was gone.

I slumped against the wall, pinching the bridge of my nose. Stupid, to think I could hide anything from her. She'd taught me everything I knew about reading people; of course she knew how to read me.

But there was nothing Mom could do to help me right now, and there was no way I could convince her that my being upset wasn't her fault. Not without telling her about Sebastian and the Vague Text Message of Doom, anyway—but if I did that, she and Dad would panic and move the whole family to Inuvik.

Which meant the only way to solve the problem was to

solve the problem, literally. To find the threat to my safety and eliminate it, before it eliminated me.

I only wished I knew how.

010101

That night my parents and I small-talked our way through dinner without anybody bringing up what had happened. But Mom kept giving me pained looks and Dad's jokes were a little too hearty and in the end, I couldn't take it anymore and excused myself without even waiting for dessert. I spent the evening in the basement upgrading my Dad's old PC and was in the process of rebooting when I got a text from Milo.

–Have you seen this? Wonder how long it's going to stay up . . .

He'd included a link to a website, so I checked it out. The title read, in too-large orange letters:

DISCOVER THE TRUTH

And below it were a series of links to articles with titles like "9/11 Conspiracy", "Cell Phone Mind Control", and "CBC Radio — BEWARE!!!"

I was frowning at the page, wondering if Milo had sent me the wrong address, when I noticed the final link:

MERIDIAN—Canada's Dark Secret

For one frozen second my brain refused to process what I was seeing. I stared at the screen, the letters blurring and refocusing before my eyes. Then, with dreamlike slowness, I reached out and clicked.

DID YOU KNOW?

For twenty years the people of Ontario have been unaware of the terrifying experiments being performed every day on them and their families. The truth about the top secret laboratory buried deep within the rock of the Canadian Shield and its covert military-political agenda has been hidden by government collusion and corruption at the highest level. Because of the many mysterious deaths and disappearances ignored by the so-called Canadian "justice" system, the military's deliberate cover-up of incriminating evidence, and our health "care" network's conspiracy to stigmatize and hospitalize those who know and dare to speak the truth, the average Canadian remains completely unaware of their danger. But now thanks to the testimony of a brave survivor known as S., the facts can and will BE REVEALED!!!

The article continued for several more paragraphs, getting more rambling and disjointed as it went on. The quasi-journalistic style vanished halfway through, replaced by a first-person account of the writer's abduction and torture at the hands of Meridian scientists. They had implanted a tracking chip in his arm and taken him to a place with locked doors and no windows, where they performed brainwashing and mind-control experiments on him. They had injected him with hallucinogenic drugs, put a helmet on his head that made him feel as though he were floating in space, and sent him to be interrogated by men in grey uniforms who claimed to be visitors from another galaxy...

I shoved back my chair so hard it nearly tipped over. The room spun around me, my stomach churning with it.

But Milo was still texting:

–Sounds pretty crazy. Maybe that's why they haven't shut it down.

I didn't reply. I was too busy taking slow, shuddering breaths, willing the fury inside me to subside.

I knew he hadn't meant to upset me, much less make me angry. He'd been trying to help, in his own misguided way. But right now, with those words glowing coldly in front of me, I wanted to snatch the phone out of my lap and hurl it through the computer screen. Not just for my sake but for Alison's too.

But I had to say something to Milo, or he'd start to worry. I gave myself five seconds to mutter all the swear words I could think of, and then I picked up my phone again.

–And you wanted me to see this? Why?

–I thought maybe we should get in touch with this guy. See what else he knows.

–Why would we do that?

There was a long pause. Then Milo replied:

–Because it's Meridian that's after you. That's the danger Sebastian was talking about, right?

That was when I knew I had passed beyond fear and anger into some kind of macabre hysteria. Because the first idea that leaped into my mind after Milo said that was to e-mail the address on the contact page and suggest an article called "How Meridian Reads All Your Text Messages, OMG!!!"

I suspected Milo wasn't in the mood for black humor, though, and the website owner would probably appreciate it even less. I had to go back to deep breathing for a while before I felt calm enough to reply.

I'm not sure yet, I began, only to erase the words and start over. I was tired of lies and evasions: I'd spent a lifetime pretending, and sometimes I hardly knew what the truth was anymore.

I hope not, I tried again, but that wasn't right either. So finally, I just gave up and typed:

–Yes.

INTERLUDE: Asynchronicity

(A transmission technique in which timing signals between communicating devices originate within the data stream, and not from a shared timing mechanism)

(2.1)

I'd been alone in this place for what seemed like forever. There was a crust of dried blood down the front of my clothes, my eyes were puffy and bruised, and the bridge of my nose throbbed with every heartbeat. I felt like I'd been torn to pieces and put back together wrong, and I hated it.

Not that it made any difference how I felt. I'd cried out for help, even begged for it. I'd yelled and screamed and pounded the walls. When all else failed, I'd sat in a corner and sobbed myself hoarse. No one answered.

Maybe this was one of those psychological experiments.

Put a scared teenage girl in a half-lit maze of vacant rooms and dead-end corridors, all by herself, and see how long it takes for her to crack. How many hours, days, weeks of isolation before she forgets how to be human and turns into a wild animal, filthy and savage? And after that, how much longer before she stops eating, curls up in a corner, and simply waits to die?

Apparently I was going to find out. I wanted to vomit with the sheer terror of it, but I'd thrown up what was left in my stomach hours ago.

And I still didn't know where I was or how I'd got here. There were no signs on the walls, no posters or pictures, not a single word in any language. What I'd taken for blacked-out windows had turned out to be monitor screens, and the only doors that looked as though they might lead somewhere were sealed tight. If I hadn't found a box full of food and medical supplies in one of the rooms and a few tools scattered among the others, I'd have thought I was the only person ever to set foot in this place.

I was slumped on a sofa in the abandoned lounge, wondering what would happen if I smashed one of the screens and whether I had enough willpower left to do it, when I heard a noise. Only a soft, distant click—but to me it was shocking as a gunshot. Not just because it was the first sound I'd heard in this place that I hadn't made myself, but because I knew instinctively what it meant. It was the sound of a door opening, and somebody coming out of it.

Coming for me.

My lungs constricted, and my heart burst into a gallop. I reached for the best weapon I had, blood-crusted fingers clenched around the grip. Then I sidled out the door and went hunting.

The corridor was curved, so I heard my visitor before I saw him. Even strides, firm footsteps—and luckily for me, he was heading in the opposite direction. I pressed back against the wall and edged sideways until he came in sight.

Crap, he was tall. Not too muscular, more on the lanky side. But his shoulders were broad beneath his grey uniform, and he moved with vigor and purpose. In a fair fight, I wouldn't have stood a chance.

But after what I'd been through, I had no intention of fighting fair.

I broke into a sprint, kicked off the corridor wall as he started to turn, and jammed the injector into his neck. It hissed, he gasped and swung around—

Then his knees buckled, and he collapsed at my feet, unconscious.

I'd done it! Now to get out of here. I raced to the door he'd come through, panting with anticipation. But he'd shut it behind him, and its surface was just as blank as before.

I wanted to pound on the door and scream, but I had enough bruises already. *Calm down, Tori,* I told myself. *There's got to be a key on him somewhere.* And sure enough, when I searched the man's pockets, I found a key ring and a wallet. But the keys were for a Volkswagen, and I wasn't going to get far with the credit cards or the Canadian driver's license.

I threw the wallet down and stomped off to look for something to tie the man up with. If I threatened to smash his head in with my tool kit, maybe I'd get some answers out of him.

(2.2)

I was in the supply room snapping a fresh dose of sedative into the injector when I heard the door creak again. Somebody had noticed the man missing and come to look for him.

Well, I'd pulled off an ambush once; with luck I could do it again. But even if I succeeded, it wouldn't be long before the sedative wore off. And since I hadn't found any rope, there was no way I could manage two hostages at the same time.

Number Two would just have to sleep longer, then. I cranked the dial of the injector up three notches and slipped back into the corridor.

The newcomer's steps sounded lighter, more hesitant. This one was nervous, so they'd be looking around as they walked. It wouldn't be so easy to sneak up on my quarry this time, unless I could come up with a distraction—

"Faraday!"

The voice was a girl's, high with distress. And was I crazy, or did she sound familiar? Ten more steps and I saw her crouching over the fallen man, her face invisible behind a veil of hair. "Faraday, wake—"

She never finished the sentence, because I launched myself at her and body-slammed her to the floor. She didn't even have time to cry out before I sedated her.

I stayed there with my knee on her spine until she went limp. Then I got up, giddy with adrenaline and triumph. Now I knew who she'd reminded me of, with those long skinny limbs and that reddish—

Misgiving seized me. I bent and rolled her over. Then I stood back and stared, unable to believe what I was seeing.

She didn't just remind me of Alison Jeffries. She *was* Alison. My schoolmate, my rival, my nemesis, was working for the people who'd kidnapped me.

The discovery shouldn't have shocked me as much as it did. After all, I'd been fighting with Alison right before I was abducted, so it made sense she'd had something to do with it. And there was no doubt in my mind that she hated me, even if I'd never understood why.

And yet I still found it hard to believe that Alison would sell me out like this. It didn't seem to fit somehow.

Well, there was no use brooding about it. I got up and checked the exit door again. It was still locked, so I jogged back to the supply room for my tool kit. Then I exchanged the injector for the heftiest blunt instrument I could find and stood over the man until he groaned and began to stir.

"No fast moves," I warned, "or I'll smash your head in." Not that I needed to worry at the moment: I'd had a dose of that sedative myself, so I knew he'd be sluggish and weak for at least five minutes yet. But I wanted him to know who was in charge.

Painfully the man pushed himself up onto his elbows, shaggy head hung low. Then with another groan he crawled to one side of the corridor and flopped over against the wall, blinking up at me. With his blue eyes half-lidded and his mouth hanging open he looked comically stupid—and surprisingly young. Still, I wasn't about to lower my guard. I hefted my tool kit, preparing for the interrogation, but the man spoke first.

"Tori Beaugrand, I presume."

It didn't surprise me that he knew my name—I'd already guessed that my kidnapper, or kidnappers, hadn't chosen me at random. I was about to answer when the man caught sight of the girl lying on the floor, and his sleepy look vanished with terrifying speed. "Alison!"

"Don't move!" I snapped, but he ignored me. He pulled Alison's limp body toward him, feeling her neck for a pulse.

"How much sedative did you give her?" he demanded.

"It was on six—"

"Six! Do you have any idea how much that is? How it would interact with the drugs she's already taken?" He was shouting now, eyes red-rimmed and big hands clutching Alison so tightly the veins stood out. "You little fool! You could have killed her!"

"She broke my nose!" I snapped. "Ask me if I care!"

"You should care," he said coldly. He gathered Alison in his arms and began struggling to his feet. "She's been through two and a half months of absolute hell because of you."

"What?" I asked in baffled outrage. "What are you talking about?"

The young man was standing now, swaying with the effort of keeping his wobbly legs steady. Cradling Alison against his chest, he began walking very slowly back the way we'd come.

So much for being in control of the situation. Exasperated, I slung the tool bag over my shoulder and headed after him. "Look, whoever you are—"

"Call me Sebastian," he replied shortly. "And before you ask, I am not one of the people who abducted you. Neither is Alison, for that matter. In fact, you might say we're here to rescue you."

My lips framed a soundless *what*.

"Problem is, it's not going to be nearly as simple getting you out of this place as it was getting in," he continued. "So when Alison wakes up—if she wakes, and you'd better hope she does—you'll have to work together."

"Or what?" I asked.

"Or neither one of you is ever going to see your homes and families again."

I clutched the tool kit tighter. "Are you threatening me?"

Sebastian looked at me over Alison's slumped head. "No," he said quietly. "It's just a fact."

I wanted to demand an explanation, but the look in his eyes silenced me. Subdued, I followed him as he carried Alison down the corridor, his stride lengthening with every step.

I expected him to stop at the door they'd both come through, but he walked right past it. He carried Alison into the nearest room with a bed—the same room I'd woken up in myself—and gently laid her down, smoothing the tangled hair back from her face before checking her pulse again.

"How is she?" I asked and was surprised to realize that I cared.

"Her heartbeat's slow," he said, "but stable. All we can do is wait." His fingers brushed Alison's cheek, tracing the pale oval of her face, and it came to me with a shock that this man was in love with her. When had that happened?

Sebastian looked back at me. "Sit down," he said.

"I'll stand, thanks," I said. He hadn't tried anything yet, but that didn't prove I could trust him. Or Alison, for that matter. "What are we waiting for, anyway? Shouldn't we be trying to get out of here?"

"We can't," he said. "Not yet."

"Why not? There's got to be a way to open that door from the inside." But he only looked blank, so I added impatiently,

"The door you and Alison came through."

"That's not an exit," he said. "It's just a storage space. We came here the same way you did, through the relay." He laid Alison's arm across her chest, walked to the foot of the bed, and sat down. "This is getting us nowhere. Why don't you start by telling your story, and then I'll tell you ours?"

"You first."

Sebastian sighed, but he didn't argue. Instead, he launched into a long explanation. What the relay device was for and what it could do, and how he'd accidentally lost track of it after taking it out for a scientific test drive. How it had stayed hidden and dormant for years, defying all his efforts to find it. How he'd almost given up hope when a girl named Tori Beaugrand vanished under mysterious circumstances, and he finally had a lead to investigate . . .

The story was interesting in its way, but I was starting to get restless. So I'd been zapped by a top secret experimental device and beamed back to its home base, I got that. What I wanted to know was, who'd brought me here, what did they want with me, and how soon were they going to let me go?

Now Sebastian was explaining how he'd discovered I'd been seen fighting with a schoolmate named Alison Jeffries only minutes before I disappeared. Which was no news to me—she was the reason I had a new bend in my nose and blood all over my shirt, after all. I was about to interrupt and tell him to get to the point when he dropped the A-bomb: that after I vanished, Alison, shattered by the horror of seeing me disintegrate, had confessed to my murder and ended up committed to a psychiatric hospital.

And they'd kept her there for *eleven weeks*.

That was what Sebastian had meant when he talked about Alison's two and a half months of hell. She'd been labeled a schizophrenic, dosed with antipsychotics and antidepressants, and kept in a locked ward against her will. All because she'd told the truth, or at least what she thought was the truth, about what happened to me.

Finding out that Alison had suffered even more than I had made me feel about half a nanometer tall. Not only had she paid for breaking my nose ten times over, she'd carried the guilt of believing that I was dead and that she'd been the one to kill me.

But selfishly, that wasn't the worst thing about it—not for me, anyway. The worst was realizing how much time had passed for Alison and Sebastian since I'd disappeared. That I'd been missing for nearly three months back home, even though to me it felt like less than a day . . .

Which meant that by now everybody I knew and cared about had given me up for dead. I slid down the wall and sat down on the floor, feeling like I'd been punched in the stomach.

"I don't know how you lost so much time," said Sebastian, when I found the voice to ask him. "Maybe you were stored in the relay's databanks for a while before anyone realized, or maybe they kept you there deliberately until they'd decided where to put you. But, Tori . . ."

I raised my head. Sebastian was regarding me with a quizzical expression, as though something about me didn't make sense. Then he said, "Could I have a look at your arm?"

My throat went dry. "Why?"

Sebastian slid off the end of the bed and knelt on the floor beside me. Then, deliberately, he rolled back the sleeve of his grey shirt and pointed to the inside of his elbow. "Because," he said, "before I went through the relay the first time I had a chip implanted under my skin, right about here. And if you have a chip as well, then I think I know why they took you."

(2.3)

I never told Alison half of what Sebastian and I talked about while she was sleeping or how hard it was to find out that my worst fears about myself were true. But by the time she woke up two hours later, I'd come to terms with it. I was even able to pass it off lightly when she guessed my secret, telling myself it wasn't so different from what my parents and I had always believed anyway.

And as it turned out, Alison had a secret of her own—her synesthesia. Seeing noises as colored shapes and tasting words in thirty-nine flavors was distracting and sometimes overwhelming for her, which explained why so many times at school she'd seemed to be living in another world. And when I was nearby, it was a hundred times worse, because she could both see and hear the chip in my arm—and its constant high-pitched buzzing had made her feel like she was going insane. No wonder she'd acted so prickly around me.

But the chip was quiet now, so we could talk freely. And as we worked through our differences, I realized that I'd misjudged her. She wasn't snobbish and unfriendly as I'd always thought, only cautious and a little shy. But the weeks she'd spent in the psych ward had changed her. She'd always seemed nervous, but now she was positively twitchy. Her pupils were dilated, her freckles stark against her too-pale skin. And though she'd grown two centimeters since I'd last seen her and put on some unexpected curves, she held herself as though she might shatter at any moment.

I wondered how long it had been since she'd taken her meds. I also wondered whether she needed them more than she and Sebastian thought.

I didn't say that, though. I put on a matter-of-fact attitude because it seemed like the best way to reassure her, and I pretended to have a plan even though I had no idea what I was doing. I marched out into the corridor, stopped at the only remaining door that looked like it might lead somewhere, and started trying to take it apart.

"Do you know where Faraday went?" Alison asked after a minute. She was shivering, though it wasn't cold, and her pupils had grown so huge I could barely see the grey around them.

"Probably sleeping," I said. "But why do you keep calling him by his last name? I thought you two were, uh, close."

Alison looked sheepish. "It's a synesthesia thing. His last name has three *A*'s in it, and his first name is a little too . . ." She broke off, biting her lip, and when I made a *go-on* gesture, she mumbled two syllables and looked away.

"Sorry, what?" I couldn't have heard her right. Had she actually said *sexy?*

She blushed. Yes, she had.

And there it was again. The feeling that came over me every time this subject came up, as though I was standing on one side of some vast and uncrossable abyss and everybody else I knew was waving at me from the other. Until two hours ago I'd thought it had something to do with the chip in my arm, but since Sebastian had a chip as well, I guessed not.

Not that it mattered. If there was a bridge over that particular chasm, I wasn't looking for it at the moment. All I cared about was getting through this door and finding whoever was behind it.

(2.4)

Sebastian found us in the hallway a short time later, and with his help, it wasn't long before I got what I wanted. But once I met Mathis, I wished I hadn't.

Not that there was anything especially intimidating about him at first glance. In fact, it surprised me that he was so young. Still, I'd read in a magazine once that the German language had a word meaning "a face that cries out to be punched," and if so, it was the perfect description of Mathis. Every time he smiled, I wanted to hit him.

Not that he cared what I thought. He spoke warmly to Sebastian, welcoming him back like a long-lost brother, and he seemed intrigued by Alison. But when he glanced at me, I understood why he'd kept me locked up in isolation for so long. There was no sympathy in his eyes, no shame or guilt, not even an acknowledgment that we were the same species. My anger meant nothing to him: I might as well have been a mouse squeaking as the needle went in.

But that wasn't the worst of it, not yet. The worst was when Mathis told me, in his heavy Dutch-sounding accent, that he couldn't send me home now even if he wanted to. I didn't believe him at first, but Alison could taste the truth, and she said he wasn't lying. And as my eyes stung and blurred, I saw Mathis's mouth curl at one corner, and I realized he was enjoying himself. He liked the power he had over me.

I knew then, even before Alison or Sebastian did, that Mathis wasn't merely ignorant or misguided. Every move he'd made had been calculated and carried out in cold blood. He'd selected me for this experiment as a baby. He'd put the chip in my arm, and programmed the relay to stalk me wherever I went. And though he'd beamed me here the moment I was injured, it wasn't out of compassion. He simply didn't want to risk losing a valuable specimen he hadn't finished studying yet.

I knew then that I had to get away from this man, whatever the cost. Because if I didn't, one of us was going to end up dead.

PART TWO: Amplification

(The act of increasing the intensity or range of a communications signal by means of a device constructed for the purpose)

010110

When I came upstairs, the house was dark and the only sound was the tick-tick-tick of Crackers trotting across the kitchen floor to greet me. I scratched behind his ears until he collapsed in a ginger-colored puddle of bliss. Then I opened the fridge, looking for the dessert I hadn't eaten earlier. After moving some jars aside, I spotted a storage container that looked promising, but it was in the back, so I had to stretch . . .

"Hey, pumpkin."

I snapped upright, cracking my head on the roof of the fridge. The container flew out of my hand, hit the floor corner-first, and burst open. Cherry cheesecake splattered onto the tile.

"Crap! Dad, don't *do* that!" I snatched up the container, but it was empty. Crackers was nose-deep in graham cracker crumbs and creamy white filling, and the floor looked like an accident scene.

"Sorry," Dad said. "Didn't mean to scare you."

But he didn't sound that sorry, and he didn't offer to help clean up the mess. Wincing at my sore head, I grabbed a dishrag and went to work on my ex-dessert. "What are you doing up?" I asked. "It's after midnight."

Most people would have asked me the same question, but Dad knew better. I hadn't slept more than five hours a night since I hit puberty, and my parents had long ago learned not to get agitated about it. I could function perfectly well on minimal sleep—another of the many weird things about my biology. I wondered if Dr. Gervais and her GeneSystem flunkies had seen *that* in my DNA.

"Well," Dad said, scratching his beard, "I was kind of hungry myself, but since you're here and the cheesecake obviously isn't . . ." He pulled a bag of potato chips out of the cupboard. "Why don't we share this instead?"

"Why don't we get to the point instead?" I asked, wiping up the last of the cheesecake and throwing the dishrag into the sink. "You might as well say it, Dad. We both know what this is about."

"That obvious, eh?" He gave a little sigh. "Well in that case, why don't *you* start? Tell me what's been going on. You've never treated your mother like that before."

"I slammed my door," I said with an effort at patience,

"because she wouldn't leave me alone. I know I've always talked to you guys about everything, but I'm seventeen now. There's stuff going on in my life that has nothing to do with you." Or at least it didn't yet, and I hoped I could keep it that way. "Is it wrong to want a little time and space for myself?"

Dad reached out and rubbed a big, calloused thumb along my cheek. "Nope," he said. "But we care about you, sweetie, and it's pretty hard for us not to notice when you're feeling down. Hard not to worry about it too. You haven't been yourself lately."

Back in my old life, a lot of people—Lara and Brendan for a start, not to mention half the girls on my hockey team—had told me they'd give anything to have parents like mine. I knew what they meant, and I didn't disagree. They really were just as loving and generous as they seemed.

But what they didn't realize was that my mom and dad divided everyone they met into two categories: Our Kind of People and Those People. The ones who were enough like them to earn the jokes and the invitations and the we-must-do-this-again-sometimes, and the ones they kept at a polite distance because they were just too different. And even if you looked like them and spoke their language, one careless word could transform you from an Us to a Them forever. Maybe even if you were their daughter.

So I'd put a lot of effort into making it easy for my parents to love me. To be the kind of daughter they'd always wanted, so they wouldn't regret the sacrifices they'd made for my sake. And right now it was taking everything I had not to burst into tears of frustration, because when had I *ever* been truly myself, even with them?

"It's nothing, Dad," I said. "I'm just a bit moody. You know, it's around *that* time."

Which wasn't remotely true, because I'd never had PMS in my life. But I knew it would make him back off, and it did.

"Oh," he said, flustered. "Right. Well, remember that if you need to talk about anything, we're here for you. Okay?"

"Okay," I said, bracing myself for the inevitable bear hug—and sure enough, Dad wrapped his arms around me and lifted me right off the floor. Then he ruffled my hair affectionately and plodded off to bed.

When he was gone, I slumped into a chair, staring at the thin slice of moonlight bisecting the table. I felt tired, more tired than I ought to be at this hour of the night. And the knot in my chest, the hard little cyst of anger that had been growing there since last summer, had grown three sizes today: once when Sebastian disappeared, again when he texted Milo, and last when I saw that stupid website.

Milo still wanted to e-mail the writer. I told him to go ahead, but not to expect any miracles. If he got a reply at all, it'd probably be a rant about how Meridian was just a front for the activities of evil aliens from another galaxy . . .

There was a salt shaker in my hand, and I couldn't even remember how it got there. But if I thought about Meridian one second longer, I was going to fastball it through the kitchen window. And I doubted even Dad would be naive enough to chalk that up to Girl Hormones.

With deliberate care I put the salt shaker back down, then got up stiffly and went to bed.

The last thing I did before I went to sleep that night was open a new e-mail account and write to Alison. I'd thought about contacting her once or twice before but decided it was too risky. Besides, she needed to heal and move on just as much as I did, and I'd only remind her of things she'd be better off trying to forget.

But if Milo was right about my past coming back to haunt me, then Alison might be in danger too. I was pretty sure Sebastian was keeping tabs on her somehow—probably electronically, knowing his talent for hacking. But if he was hiding from her, for whatever reason, she'd need somebody she could talk to if things got bad.

> From: tasteslikecoughsyrup@gmail.com
> To: keyofviolet@gmail.com
> Subject: Hey Ali
> I know you don't check e-mail that often, so you probably won't see this for a while. But I wanted to let you know I've been thinking about you. I hope everything's OK.
> No need to write back. Just saying hi.

I didn't sign the note. Alison was the one who'd told me that my old name tasted like cough medicine, so as soon as she saw my e-mail address she'd understand.

I was pretty sure she'd also understand that *no need* meant *don't unless it's an emergency*. I hadn't told her about GeneSystem or my run-in with Deckard, but she knew I was trying to get away from my past and that I didn't want anybody finding me. Still, it made me feel better to have given her my address. Even though I hoped she'd never need to use it.

011000

For the next few days I went through the motions of my daily life—walk the dog, do some schoolwork, put in my shift at Value Foods, tinker in the basement, and fall into bed when I couldn't keep my eyes open anymore. I felt edgy and short-tempered, and it was getting harder all the time to keep it in. But I did my best to pretend that nothing was wrong, and though Mom still gave me the occasional troubled look, my parents seemed willing to buy it.

Meanwhile, the danger Sebastian had warned about showed no signs of materializing, even figuratively. And by the time a week had passed, I was starting to wonder if all those trips through the relay had activated some kind of latent paranoia. Maybe that was why he'd ditched us back at the café, and it didn't have anything to do with logic or evidence—or me, for that matter—at all.

But deep down I knew better. Sebastian might be cryptic and high-handed at times; he could even be manipulative. But he wasn't the type to fall apart in the face of danger. He and I were more alike than most people would ever guess, and I had a gut feeling that whatever he was up to, it was part of some greater plan.

On Monday night I was walking home from the bus stop, absently counting my steps as I went, when my phone clanked.

–Are you all right?

I almost typed, *Seriously?* Because I'd seen Milo twenty minutes ago, so he ought to know better. But then I checked the screen again, and my blood went hot as I realized that the text hadn't come from Milo after all. It was from an unknown number, which could mean only one thing.

   –Sebastian you enormous jerk. Yes, I'm fine, no thanks to you.

   –Charming as always. I apologize for disappearing so abruptly, but something came up and there was no time to explain. But now, if you're willing, I could use your help.

   –With what? And why should I?

   –I think you'll be able to figure that out once you know the details. May I e-mail you?

   –You don't know my address already? You're losing your touch.

But he didn't rise to the bait. He remained silent, waiting me out with that maddening patience of his, until I sighed and typed in my e-mail address.

   –Thank you. You won't regret it.

   –Don't make promises you can't keep. Oh, never mind—too late!

He didn't respond to that dig, either. So I added:

   –Have you talked to Alison yet?

Still no answer. I rolled my eyes and started walking again. Eighty-two steps, eighty-three, eighty-four—

   –No. Have you?

If he didn't know, I wasn't about to tell him. But he had a lot of nerve trying to make me feel guilty, when he should know I couldn't afford to get close to Alison anyway. Not without running the risk that someone like Deckard would notice and use her to get to me.

On the other hand, the police were looking for Sebastian too. And unlike me, he was a wanted suspect, so it wasn't only Deckard he had to worry about . . .

Oh.

My self-righteousness deflated like a punctured tire. I shoved the phone into my pocket and broke into a run, heading for home.

011001

When I opened my laptop, Sebastian's message was waiting. No explanations, no apologies, no time wasted on coaxing or flattery. It said, simply:

–Specifications attached.

Well, at least he wasn't underestimating my abilities. Fifteen pages of technical requirements, describing a piece of highly sophisticated equipment that would have emptied my savings account if I hadn't been capable of building most of it from scratch. Even so I was wondering how I was supposed to pay for all of this, let alone why I would want to, when I got to the second-last page. He'd given me the username and password for his PayPal account.

And the final page, carefully unfolded and scanned to crisp perfection, was the brochure for the local makerspace.

Great idea, Sebastian, I thought sourly as I paged back to the beginning and began skimming over the specs again. *Wish I'd thought of that myself.* Sure, the electronics project he'd given me looked like an interesting challenge, but I'd need a better reason than that to—

A thousand watts of realization lit up the back of my brain. I scanned the pages again, mentally assembling the list of components into a single device. A high-power, long-range multi-band transmitter and receiver unit, to be exact. All that was missing was the antenna, but presumably Sebastian had his own ideas about that . . .

And now I knew why he'd been so certain I'd help him, once I'd read his message. From the minute Sebastian beamed into my bedroom the threat had been staring me in the face, but I'd been too busy sniping at him and resenting his interference in my life to notice. After all, he'd seemed so casual about the outcome of his confrontation with Mathis, so confident that the relay could be destroyed. Even when he'd sent that warning to Milo, part of me had wondered if he was just being extra cautious.

But I saw my danger clearly now, and there was no doubt in my mind what I had to do. No matter what my parents thought about me joining the makerspace, no matter how hard it might be to tackle such an ambitious project without getting noticed, I needed to start building this transceiver right away.

I closed my eyes and counted silently, giving my racing heart time to calm. Then I picked up my phone and texted Milo.

011010

"I can't believe we're doing this," Milo muttered as we got off the bus. It was seven o'clock on Tuesday, and the downtown was a wasteland of closed shops, bored teenagers, and the occasional homeless wanderer. We'd left the worst behind by the time we got to our stop, but being surrounded by auto body shops and decaying factories wasn't much of an improvement.

"You didn't have to come if you didn't want to," I said.

"I didn't mean it like that. I mean Sebastian and that list he gave you. If he needs some fancy high-tech communication device, why get you to build it for him? Wouldn't it be faster to just order the stuff or rent it from somewhere?"

"Not with these specifications," I said. "Among other things, he needs the transceiver to hook up with the relay, and I'm the only one who knows enough about the relay to make that happen."

"I thought he was going to destroy the relay."

"That was Plan A," I said. "But apparently that didn't work out, or he wouldn't have gone to Plan B. Which is to send a signal to the computer that controls the relay and force it to shut down." Which was oversimplified at best, and at worst downright misleading. But it was the safest way I could think of to describe it.

"What good's that going to do?" Milo asked. "All the people at Meridian have to do is turn it on again."

"It's not that easy," I said. "There's a complicated process in getting the two devices to talk to each other, and once the uplink's broken, it'll be next to impossible to reestablish it. It has to do with the data encryption and decryption algorithm," I added, in case he thought I was patronizing him. "It uses quantum entanglement."

"Oh, of course it does," said Milo, poker-faced. "I don't know why I didn't think of that myself."

I punched him in the arm, hoping to catch him off-balance. But his bicep had about as much give as rubber-covered concrete, and he didn't budge a millimeter. "The point is," I told him, "we can't get rid of the relay until we've made sure it won't activate again. We can't risk some random person coming across it and beaming themselves who-knows-where."

Milo looked unconvinced, but he didn't argue. He matched my brisk pace as we turned onto a side street, the sounds of traffic receding as we walked along. We passed a long row of barn-shaped wartime houses and finally stopped in front of an old factory with rust-colored brick and metalwork, its closed doors offering no hint of what lies inside. Only the faded number painted over the entrance reassured me I'd found the right place.

"Wow," Milo said. "Check out the picturesque old-world charm. What's that sign on the door say? ABANDON . . . HOPE . . ."

"Very funny," I said, walking up the steps and hauling the door open. "Actually, it says there's a Tae Kwon Do studio upstairs. Are you coming or not?"

"Remind me to tell you about the year I spent taking Tae Kwon Do sometime," said Milo, following me in. "Between that and the violin disaster, I could write a book on How to Fail at Being Korean—wow, those stairs are *really steep.*"

"Good thing we don't have to go up them, then," I said. There was no visible sign for the makerspace on this level, but I'd read the directions on the brochure and knew where to go. "This way."

We headed through a fire door into a narrow hallway with grey-white walls and no windows to be seen. Most of the doors we passed were shut, but the open ones gave glimpses of sagging ceilings, exposed wiring, and debris-littered cement. From somewhere upstairs came a steady pounding, and the whole place smelled like wood shavings mingled with incense or possibly marijuana smoke.

"This is fantastically squalid," said Milo. "We may never get out of here alive."

"You have no sense of adventure," I told him sternly, but deep down I was glad he was with me. All these empty hallways and closed doors reminded me uncomfortably of what it was like to be Mathis's prisoner, and it would have been hard to get through this place on my own.

We turned the corner and there was the sign for the makerspace, with a large friendly arrow pointing to the right. My pulse quickened with anticipation—but at the same instant my feet came to a stumbling halt.

"Niki?" asked Milo. "What's the matter?"

I'd stopped three meters from the junction, staring into the middle distance. My throat had closed up, and my lips were dry. I couldn't move.

"Hey." He stepped in front of me, waving a hand through my line of sight. "Earth to Niki."

Weak as the joke was, it snapped me out of my paralysis. I focused with an effort and said, "Milo, I asked my parents if I could come here weeks ago, and they said no. If they find out . . ."

"They'll do what? Hello, you're a teenager. This can't be the first time you've gone against—" He broke off as he saw the look on my face. "You're not serious."

"I couldn't. I mean, I didn't want to. Not really." I'd argued Mom and Dad into changing their minds sometimes, and now and then I got around them on a technicality. But I'd never disobeyed a direct order from either of them, for reasons I couldn't explain even to myself. "And now . . . I don't know if I can."

Milo frowned and pushed his glasses up his nose. "Why did they tell you not to? Don't they want you to go into engineering?"

"That's not the problem," I said. "They just think it's too much, too soon. And maybe they're right, but—"

"The alternative's worse. Yeah. I get it."

"So do I. I just can't get my body to cooperate." I leaned forward, trying to force myself to take the next step. But my feet stayed rooted to the floor.

Milo frowned at me, his head tilted to one side. Then he broke into a slow, wicked grin. I didn't even have time to brace myself before he ducked down and swept me, literally, off my feet.

I spluttered a curse and tried to wriggle free, but Milo didn't falter. He marched down the hallway, executed a military turn, and carried me over the threshold of the makerspace.

"Oh no," he said in mock dismay. "Look where you are. How did that happen? Clearly, it was all my fault."

I wanted to be irritated with him, and part of me was. I didn't like being touched without permission. But he hadn't put his hands anywhere he shouldn't—in fact, he'd been a positive gentleman about it. It was hard not to be impressed by how easily he'd picked me up too. So I collected what was left of my dignity, and said, "You can put me down now."

"Uh, hi," said the young man at the desk as Milo lowered me to my feet. "Can I help you with anything?"

Milo made an *over-to-you* gesture, and I realized to my relief that his ridiculous strategy had worked. The panic that had gripped me in the hallway was gone, and I could move again.

"We're here for the Open House," I said, giving the man my most winning smile. "Is it okay if we come in and look around?"

011011

Not only was Front Desk Guy happy to see us, he even gave us a tour. The makerspace wasn't that big, just two modest rooms with a small lounge area between them. But it had plenty of equipment. First, we wriggled through a curtain of clear vinyl strips to visit the woodshop and heavy tool room. They had lathes, sanders, a miter saw, and a couple of drill presses—most of them old and battered but still in good working condition. A scarred wooden worktop ran along the far wall, and in the middle of the room two men were arranging bits of scrap metal on a table, chortling and elbowing each other like old friends as they worked.

After that we came back out into the lounge, a rough square of old sofas and armchairs with a coffee table between them and a wall of bookshelves behind. Among the books on programming and electronics I glimpsed a complete set of *Monty Python* DVDs, a Yoda-shaped coffee mug, and a stuffed bison with six legs that caused Milo to break into a grin. Up a slight ramp we found the clean room, which had a soldering station even better than the one I had at home, four computers in various stages of disassembly, a plotter, a laser cutter, three different kinds of printers . . . and, to my immediate interest, an oscilloscope.

There were a few other people scattered around—a grey-haired woman frowning over her laptop, a pair of gangly college students poking at an old PC tower, and a little boy playing with a flight simulator. In the back corner a young man with a ponytail and a skull earring was building a sculpture from laser-cut plastic, while an older man tinkered with a 3-D printer. None of them spoke: most barely glanced up as we walked through. But I wasn't offended—I knew the feeling of being so absorbed in a project that nothing else existed, and I was happy to leave them to it.

"So," said Front Desk Guy, when we returned to the lounge. "Any questions?"

I glanced at Milo, but he only shrugged. It was up to me, then—but I hadn't really expected anything else. "I'm working on a surprise for my dad," I said, with a hint of bashfulness. "He's into amateur radio, and he's always wanted to do a moon bounce. So I . . . I'm hoping to build him a transceiver for his birthday."

"Wow," said FDG—I had to call him that because he wasn't wearing a name tag, and despite his enthusiasm, he'd forgotten to introduce himself. "That's awesome, good for you. So were you looking for some help with that? You should talk to Barry. He's our radio expert."

"That'd be great," I said, keeping my expression humble and a little nervous. Just an ordinary teenaged girl with an interest in electronics and a few modest projects under her belt, nothing extraordinary here. "But I was wondering, could I maybe bring the kit here to work on it? Because our house is pretty small, and I don't want my dad to see it until it's ready."

FDG blinked. "Uh, well, we only have Open House twice a month. You have to be a member to get in any time you want, and that takes—"

"I know," I said. "I'm new, and you'd want to get to know me better before you could vote me in. But I only found out about this place a few days ago, and Dad's birthday is coming up fast. I'd be glad to pay a month's membership up front, if that would help. And I'll bring my own supplies, and only work when the regular members are here. I mean, it's not like I can get in the door otherwise, right?" I gave him a hopeful smile.

"Hmm," said Front Desk Guy, sizing me up. "How old are you?"

"Seventeen."

"Give me a sec, okay? I need to talk to somebody." He galloped up the ramp to the clean room.

Milo flopped onto the sectional sofa, and after a minute I sat down in the armchair on the other side. A set of interlocking wooden hexagons sat on the table next to a sign reading PLAY WITH ME, but I wasn't in the mood. I was trying to make out the conversation from the next room, as the Desk Guy's chirpy tenor alternated with a deeper rumble that sounded ominous.

What would I do if they decided not to let me in? I needed that oscilloscope, for one thing, and I could hardly build the whole transceiver in my basement. I'd be ordering all kinds of new parts and supplies, and there was no way I could expect my parents not to notice . . .

"Hey," said Milo, nudging my foot under the table. "It's going to be fine. They'll love you. This is what they're here for, and besides, you offered them money."

I leaned forward, breathing into my hands, then bolted to my feet. FDG had reappeared at the top of the ramp, with 3-D Printer Guy beside him.

"Hi there," said the older man, walking to meet me. "I'm Len." He gave me a brisk handshake and said, "I hear you're building a transceiver for your dad. And you're on a tight deadline."

"Yeah," I said, reminding myself to bring out the shy smile again. "His birthday's in a couple of weeks, so I'd really like to get it ready as soon as I can."

"Understandably. And we'd like to help you. But we have a strict Health and Safety policy for insurance reasons, and we can't allow anyone under eighteen to work here without direct supervision. If you had someone older with you, like a parent or guardian—"

"What about me?" interrupted Milo. "I'm eighteen."

It took all my concentration to keep smiling, and not whip around and stare. Keeping me company on my first visit was one thing, but to come back here day after day? I'd never expected Milo to make such an offer.

And yet if he was serious, how could I refuse?

The two makers exchanged glances. "Well," said Len. "We can't guarantee anything. But we'll discuss it with the board at our next meeting."

"When will that be?" I asked.

"Monday night."

Nearly a week away. I'd hoped it would be sooner. But I still had a lot of parts to order, and they'd take a few days to arrive in any case. In the meantime, I could get started on designing the circuit board and trying to track down a vector network analyzer, which was the one piece of equipment even Sebastian couldn't afford.

I only wished I knew how much time I had left to do it. But when I'd asked Sebastian, he didn't seem to know any more than I did. *Too many variables,* he'd written. *Just work as fast as you can.*

"Okay," I said, trying not to let my worry show. "Thanks."

FDG rummaged underneath his desk and popped up with a duct-tape covered clipboard and a pen that looked as though it had been chewed by a Rottweiler. "We'll need your names, addresses, and a phone number or e-mail." He thrust the clipboard at me. "After the meeting, we'll give you and your boyfriend a call."

I started to protest that Milo wasn't my boyfriend, but then I realized that would just complicate the issue. It wasn't like I could pass him off as my brother or cousin, not without fabricating an adoption story at any rate. And if there wasn't some obvious reason for him to want to hang around and watch me solder components for hours on end, the board might decide he wasn't dependable enough to take the responsibility.

So I slid closer to Milo as I scribbled down my contact information and touched his arm lightly when I passed the clipboard on. Not enough to startle him, just to show we were comfortable with each other.

We could work out the details later.

011100

When Milo and I left the makerspace, the sun had dipped below the rooftops. We walked the two blocks to the bus shelter without speaking and stood there watching the traffic for a while. Finally, I cleared my throat and said, "That was . . . what you said back there . . . thanks a lot. I wasn't expecting you to do that."

Milo squinted out the doorway, shifting his weight from one running shoe to the other. "Yeah, well," he said, "I wasn't expecting them to mistake me for your boyfriend either. And I definitely wasn't expecting you to go along with it. So I guess it's been a night of surprises all around."

There were forty-three centimeters between my elbow and Milo's, and every picometer of it was charged with Awkward. I steeled myself and plunged in. "Sorry if I embarrassed you. I didn't know what to say, and—"

"You think I was embarrassed?" He gave me an incredulous look. "Why would I be? I scored about a billion Dude Points just walking in the door with you. Believe me, you don't have to apologize."

I didn't blush often, let alone for long. But right now I felt like I'd stuck my face in an oven. "Milo . . ."

"I know. I'm just a friend, and you want to make sure I'm okay with that, because you're a nice person. I get it, Niki. It's fine."

Somewhere along the line I'd got out of the habit of reading Milo—stopped running my usual diagnostic on his expression, stance, and tone of voice. In other words, I'd started trusting him.

But now I saw the tremor in his jaw, and I knew he was lying. It wasn't fine at all.

"That's not what I mean," I said, fighting to keep the anger out of my voice. Because it wasn't Milo I was angry at, it was the whole stupid world. A world where relationships like the one I'd had with Brendan were normal, and the one I had with Milo was not. "There's no such thing as *just* a friend, Milo. Friendship is one of the most important things there is."

Milo stuffed his hands into his pockets and glanced up the road, as though hoping the bus would come and rescue him. "Yeah," he said. "I know."

"I'm serious," I insisted, stepping in front of him so he'd have to look me in the eye. "I hate it when people talk like friendship is less than other kinds of—as though it's some sort of runner-up prize for people who can't have sex. I had a boyfriend once, but I never liked being with him the way I like being with you." I held his gaze, refusing to falter or look away. "You're one of the best friends I've ever had, Milo. And that is *everything* to me."

Milo was quiet for a moment. Then he said, "You mean that, don't you. You're not just trying to make me feel better."

"I'm not," I said. "I'm really, really not."

His eyes lowered, and his expression turned pensive. Then he looked up again and said, "Okay."

"Okay?"

"I mean, that's good by me." He gave a slight, tentative smile. "I'm not going anywhere."

I let my breath out in relief. Finding out Milo legitimately cared about me and wanted to be around me, even if there was no chance of the two of us hooking up, was enormous. I wanted to show him how glad I was for his friendship, how warm and bubbly it made me feel to have him by my side. I wanted to take his hand, lean my head on his shoulder, maybe even hug him.

Only knowing he liked me as something other than a friend—not *more than*, I'd never say that—held me back. I didn't want to be unfair to Milo. But I didn't want him to think I was repulsed by him, either. I wanted to give him something personal and precious, so he'd know how much his friendship meant to me.

"Milo," I said, "I'm going to tell you something I've only ever told one other person. And when I do, I . . . I hope you'll understand." Passionately hoped, in fact. Because if he said any of the things Lara had said to me when I told her, it would be hard to forgive him for it.

"I know," he said. "You're gay, right?"

"No," I said. "I'm not sexually attracted to anyone. At all. Ever."

Silence. I could see Milo blinking behind his glasses, his brain struggling to process this new information, and I prepared myself for the inevitable barrage of questions. *Have you seen a doctor? A psychiatrist? Were you abused? Are you scared? What if you haven't just met the right person yet?*

But when Milo spoke it was cautiously, his brow furrowed in thought. "What do you mean by that, exactly? You said you had a boyfriend once . . ."

Brendan Stewart, long gone and unlamented. Great hair. Great body. Great kisser, according to other girls he'd dated. But if so, his talents had been wasted on me. "I went out with Brendan because it was what he wanted," I said. "I thought if I tried to act like a real girlfriend, maybe I'd start to feel like one. That I'd want him to kiss me and put his hands on me, instead of counting the seconds until it was over. But . . . I never did."

"Oh," said Milo.

"I mean, it didn't help that he was a selfish pig who wouldn't take no for an answer. I would have broken up with him anyway, even if I'd liked the physical stuff. But going out with him made me realize that I wasn't shy or uptight about sex. I simply wasn't interested."

What I didn't say was that by that time, I'd also found out I wasn't alone. I'd discovered a forum on the Internet that was full of people—many of them young, healthy, social, even attractive—who felt the same way. They weren't against sex or trying to keep other people from having it. They just didn't feel the need. And once I'd seen that, it had given me the courage to stop trying to change myself.

"So you're never going out with anyone again?" Milo asked.

"I don't know," I said. "Maybe, if I met somebody who accepted me the way I am and didn't feel cheated that I didn't want to make out all the time. But how likely is that? Most people our age are crazy about sex. And don't tell me you're different, because I won't believe you."

Milo made a face. "I'm not. I wish I was sometimes, because my mom doesn't want me seeing anybody until I'm done with university. But I'd be lying if I said I don't think about it. A lot."

"How do you get anything *done?*" I asked, and Milo laughed. Only a short laugh, but the smile that went with it was real, and it dissolved all the tension between us.

"Cold showers," he said. "And lots of running. My thighs are steel. My abs are bronze. My biceps—"

"They are excellent biceps," I said. "I've noticed."

That got me a double take. "You have?"

"I'm in your bus shelter, messing with your worldview," I said, elbowing him. "Yes, I've noticed. I'm asexual, not blind."

Milo scratched the back of his neck, clearly at a loss. "So . . . what exactly are you noticing, again?"

I wanted to laugh. "Stop fishing for compliments," I said. "Yes, I like the way you look. I'd even say you're attractive. Just because I don't have the urge to tackle you and rip your clothes off—"

"*Please* don't say things like that," Milo moaned, and now I did laugh.

"Sorry. What I mean is, there's nothing wrong with you as far as I'm concerned. I wish . . ." No, I wasn't going to finish that sentence. I'd been honest enough for one night. "Anyway, if you don't mind the people at the makerspace thinking you're my boyfriend, I'm not going to argue with them. In fact—" My gaze turned inward, a new thought sparking alight. "It might help if one or two other people made the same mistake."

"Oh, no," said Milo. "I know that look. That's your I-have-an-idea look, and it means bad things."

"Not necessarily," I told him. "But if my parents thought I had a boyfriend, a mature, responsible, *strong* boyfriend . . ."

"Then you'd have the perfect excuse to go out every night and work on the transceiver. I get it. But remember what I told you about *my* mother? If she thought I was seeing anybody, she would flay me alive. With her teeth."

"You're already lying to her about the phys ed thing," I pointed out. "This wouldn't even be a lie. We *aren't* going out. We're just going to let a few people think we are."

"What about everybody at work?" asked Milo. "What do we tell them?"

"Nothing," I said. "It's none of their business."

The bus squeaked to a stop outside the shelter, blue and white paint glowing in the fading light. I climbed on, flashed my pass at the driver, and swung myself into a seat.

"So let me get this straight," Milo said as he joined me. "To the people at the makerspace and to your parents, we're going out. To my mother and between ourselves we're not. Everybody else gets to make up their own minds, because we aren't saying one way or the other. We're like the Schrodinger's Cat of relationships."

"Exactly."

"And if somebody asks if we're together? Like Jon, for instance."

"It's complicated," I said. "We have to play it cool because our parents don't approve. Like Romeo and Juliet."

"Who ended up dead, if you remember," said Milo.

"Only because they were stupid. You and I are not stupid."

"Thank you," said Milo dryly. "But there's another problem. You never asked me to pretend-go out with you."

"Should I pretend to get down on one knee?" I asked.

"I'm not sure I'm ready," he said. "It's a big commitment."

For three seconds I couldn't tell whether or not he was serious. I was beginning to worry that I'd assumed too much when he went on in the same grave tone, "Maybe we should pretend-see other people for a while."

I punched him in the arm. "Stop messing with me. Are you okay with this or not? Because if you're not, we need to come up with a better idea fast. My mom's seen us together a couple of times, and I'm pretty sure she thinks we're going out already."

"This has been the second weirdest evening of my life," said Milo, resigned. "But why not? Let's pretend-do it."

I was tempted to make that into a joke—*On the first date? What kind of pretend girlfriend do you think I am?*—but it would only embarrass him, and I was getting tired of bantering anyway. "Thanks," I said softly.

We rode a while in silence. The bus paused to let off a young woman in a hijab, then stopped again to pick up an old man, who tottered down the aisle and collapsed into the seat across from us, wheezing and mopping his nose. Two more blocks, and it would be my turn.

"So," said Milo. "We get off the bus together. Right?"

"Right," I said, reaching up to signal for our stop.

"And then what?"

"You walk me home." I got up, stumbling a little before I caught my balance, and headed for the exit. "We say good night. I go inside and start working on the transceiver."

"Oh. Okay."

I wouldn't have thought it was possible for anyone to sound relieved and disappointed at the same time, especially in three syllables. "What's the matter?" I asked.

"Nothing."

Liar, I thought. But I didn't call him on it, not until we'd got off the bus and crossed the four lanes of traffic to my street. Then I turned to him, held out my hand, and said, "Showtime."

"Really?" he asked. "You're okay with that?"

"I am totally okay with that," I said firmly and laced my fingers into his.

011101

"How was the movie?" Dad asked when I came in. He was kneeling on the kitchen tile with a pile of newspapers under him and a paint can in one hand, touching up the baseboards.

"Pretty stupid, actually," I replied. "I'd skip that one if I were you. Where's Mom?"

"Having a bath, probably," he said. "She's been painting all evening, so I told her to go relax."

"Oh," I said. I'd hoped at least one of my parents had seen Milo and I standing close together on the sidewalk, still holding hands, as I gazed dreamily up at him and told him that I was going to ship all the bigger transceiver parts to his house. He'd told me okay, but not to overdo it and could I please get that dopey look off my face before he threw up? So it had been a very special moment, and I was sorry to think it had been wasted on just the two of us.

"So who'd you go with?" Dad asked, painting a slow line across the top of the trim and dipping his brush again.

"A friend," I said.

He sat back on his haunches and gave me a quizzical look. "Just a friend?"

The next time I heard somebody use that phrase, I was going to hit them. "A good friend," I said shortly and turned to leave.

"Because," Dad continued, "your mother thought it might be a date."

I stopped.

The newspapers rustled as my father got to his feet. "Look, pumpkin," he said, "All I want is for you to be safe and happy. So you don't have to hide anything from me."

He had no idea how much I wished I could believe that. "I know," I said. "It's just . . . we've only gone out a couple of times, and I didn't want Mom to get worked up over it."

"Don't worry about her," he said, putting a burly arm around my shoulder and giving me a squeeze. "She'll be fine. So who's the lucky boy?"

Hello, Dad Cliché 32. Nice to know this conversation was still on a predictable course. "Milo Hwang," I said.

There was a fractional silence. Then Dad said, a little too heartily, "Well, good for you. That's . . . um, great. Hope it works out."

And there it was. Liberal on the outside, redneck conservative deep down. He wouldn't forbid me to see Milo because that would be narrow-minded, but that didn't mean he was ready to invite him over for hockey and popcorn.

"Why shouldn't it work?" I asked. "He's a nice guy."

"I'm sure he is," said Dad. "But when people from different cultures get together, it can be an adjustment—"

"He's not from a different culture," I interrupted. "Milo was born and raised here. He's just as Canadian as I am." More so, in fact, but that was the last thing I wanted to tell my parents. Because if I did, they'd react like this. "Anyway, like I said, we only just got together. It's not like we're planning the wedding."

"I'll say you aren't," Dad said with mock gruffness and made his Big Bad Giant face until I gave a reluctant smile. Then he continued, "All right, point taken. We'll stay out of it and let the two of you sort things out."

"Thanks," I said. "And . . . Dad?"

He'd stooped and picked up the brush again, but he looked back over his shoulder.

"Could you and Mom keep this to yourselves? Because Milo's mom thinks having a girlfriend is going to interfere with his studies, and he needs some time to prove to her that it won't before he breaks the news."

"Sure thing," he replied and went back to painting.

Relieved, I made myself a plate of cheese and crackers and

headed for the basement. I had some schematics to draw up, and a whole lot of parts and components to order.

011110

Sebastian texted me two days later.

> —How's the transceiver coming?
>
> —Fine so far. Though I can't do much more until I hear from the makerspace. And I'll need to borrow a vector network analyzer from somebody, unless you have $10K sitting around. Also, you forgot the antenna.
>
> —I didn't forget. It'll be ready when you are. Just keep working.

I hesitated, fingers hovering above the keys. Then I wrote:

> —How much danger am I in right now? Could the relay find me and beam me back to Mathis even without the chip? Or is there something else I should be afraid of?

But the phone was silent.

The weekend was largely uneventful, although Jon frowned when he saw me talking to Milo on Friday night, and I had a sinking suspicion he was going to ask if we were together. Not that I would have minded saying yes if I thought it would get Jon off my case, but Milo's grandparents came through Jon's register nearly every time they shopped, and if he said anything to them, it would be a disaster. So I kept my distance from Milo for the rest of the weekend, and for good measure—though I hated myself for doing it—I flirted with Jon a little. He perked up at once, and when he told me he was helping out at his aunt's bakery the following Saturday and that if I came in he'd give me a free cupcake, I knew I was off the hook.

All in all, if I hadn't been worried about what might happen if I didn't get this transceiver built in time, I might have been tempted to believe my troubles were over. Apart from her discomfort with me seeing Milo, my mother was happier than I'd seen her in months: she'd been having so much fun redecorating the house that she'd started talking about taking some night courses and becoming an interior decorator. Meanwhile, Dad was selling farm insurance policies as fast as people could sign them, so his boss had given him and Mom a gift card for a hotel and theater getaway in Toronto. Everything seemed to be going our way—or my parents' way, at least—and I was glad of it.

But late Sunday night, I got another message from Faraday.

–Check your e-mail. Now.

He wasn't usually so curt, even in text form. I put down my soldering iron, pushed my safety glasses up onto my forehead, and flipped my laptop open.

There were four new messages in my inbox, including one from Milo. But it took me less than a second to find the one Sebastian wanted me to see.

From: keyofviolet@gmail.com
Subject: URGENT — PLEASE READ THIS

It looked like spam from the subject line, but the address told me everything I needed to know. It was from Alison.

I braced myself and opened the message.

I'm sorry if this letter doesn't make much sense. I'm pretty shaken up right now, and my synesthesia's more intense than it's been for a while. But I had to write to you and tell you what's been happening.

I'm not sure if you ever met Constable Deckard, but he was part of the police investigation when you disappeared. He drove the van that took me to Pine Hills, and he questioned me a couple of times while I was in the hospital, trying to find out if I'd killed you. Even once it was obvious that I hadn't, he still didn't seem satisfied. He kept giving me these ice-dagger looks, like he knew I was hiding something. So I tried to keep out of his way.

But about a month after you left, he came to the house and asked me if I'd talked to you lately. He wanted to know if I had your address or phone number or an e-mail where he could reach you. I said no, but I could tell he didn't believe me. He told me it was a very serious thing to give false information to the police and that it was vital that he get in touch with you immediately. His voice was so vinegar-sharp it scared me, but I kept repeating that I didn't know where you were or how to reach you, and finally he changed the subject. If I hadn't heard from you, then what about Faraday? Had he tried to contact me since he left Sudbury? Did I have any idea where he was now?

That was when I couldn't take any more. I told him to leave me alone and shut the door in his face.

Then I went to my room and cried until I felt grey all over. I knew Deckard would never find Faraday no matter what I told him, and I doubted he'd find you either. But he'd made me feel like a criminal for not helping him, and I was afraid he'd find an excuse to charge me for it.

I clenched my jaw and flexed my fingers against my knee, wishing I could strangle Deckard. Yet this was only the beginning of the story. There was more, and probably worse, to come.

For weeks after that, I felt sick and shaky every time I saw a police cruiser. But it was never Deckard behind the wheel. And once I'd got through the whole winter without seeing or hearing from him, I convinced myself he'd given up. So when a car pulled into our driveway yesterday and a man got out, I didn't think twice about answering the door. I figured it was one of my mom's real estate clients come to drop off some paperwork.

It wasn't, though. It was Deckard.

He was out of uniform this time, but the way he carried himself was as intimidating as ever. He told me he was working on a special investigation and had some questions to ask me. I started to tell him no, but he said I'd be welcome to ask one of my parents to join us if it made me feel more comfortable. So, stupidly, I let him in.

Deckard asked me if anything had changed since the last time we'd talked and whether I'd found any way to contact you. I thought about the e-mail you'd sent me, and I tried not to hesitate or grimace at the taste when I said no. He gave me one of his steely looks, and I was afraid he'd threaten me again, but then he got very quiet and sober. He said that what he was about to tell me was confidential, but it was important for me to know. Then he told me that your doctor was trying to contact you with the results of some medical tests you'd done before you left. He said you'd been diagnosed with a very serious condition, and if you didn't get it treated right away, you could die.

"Oh, crap," I whispered, staring at the screen. "Crap, crap, *crap.*"

I should have seen it coming, even before I left Sudbury. Deckard's single-minded obsession with my case had been suspicious enough, but his parting shot about summoning me back from Vancouver if I didn't return Dr. Gervais's call had practically clinched it. Then to show up at Alison's house wearing plain clothes and driving an unmarked car and using the same line on her that Dr. Gervais had tried to use on me . . . there was only one explanation that fit the facts.

Deckard had left the police force and become a private investigator. And GeneSystem was paying him to hunt me down.

He held my gaze steadily as he spoke those words, and his voice didn't waver. But his words tasted funny, so I knew he wasn't telling the whole truth. I stammered something about being sorry and wishing I could help, but I really didn't know where to find you. He nodded and turned to leave, and I thought the interrogation was over. But halfway down the steps he turned back, and said he had one more question.

I knew he was going to ask me about Faraday, and I thought I was prepared. But when he asked which one of us had broken off our relationship, I was so flabbergasted I didn't know what to say. I'd never told anyone how close I was to Faraday, not even Dr. Minta. How did Deckard know?

But then I remembered that Faraday had taken me back to Champlain Secondary one night, so I could show him the spot where you'd disappeared. We'd hugged, we'd nearly kissed—in full view of the school's security cameras. And of course Deckard would have seen the tape. So I resisted the temptation to tell him it was none of his business, and I said, "He ended it."

For the first time, I saw pity in Deckard's eyes. He thanked me for my time and turned to leave. And I should have let him go, but I couldn't stop myself. I called out to him and asked why he'd wanted to know. That was when he told me that Sebastian Faraday had been spotted in southern Ontario ten days ago, accessing one of his old bank accounts from an ATM.

He wasn't lying, either. What he was saying made no sense to me, but there was no flavor of deception to his words at all.

Deckard must have realized my shock was genuine, because he gave me that pitying look again, and then he took out his phone and showed me the security tape. He hadn't been mistaken. It was Faraday, looking exactly as I'd last seen him. The hair, the way he moved, even the clothes he was wearing—he hadn't changed at all.

Things got a little fuzzy at that point, but Deckard said something about Faraday still being wanted for questioning and for several outstanding charges, and how if he tried to contact me again I should call him— Deckard, I mean—immediately. Then he handed me his card and drove away.

Once I calmed down, I tried to tell myself I should be happy. After all, hadn't I been waiting for Faraday to come back? Hadn't part of me always believed that he would? Every time I closed my eyes I could see his face so clearly. I could feel the warmth of his eyes on me and taste the last words I'd heard him say, "I don't love you."

I'd laughed through my tears then, because I'd known he was lying. But now that I'd found out he'd been back for days—maybe even weeks—and hadn't tried to contact me, I wasn't sure what to believe anymore.

Then I realized I hadn't checked my e-mail in a couple of days. Maybe Faraday had written to me, and I just hadn't seen it yet. So I logged on and found a message waiting, but it wasn't from him. It was from Sanjay, a boy I'd met at Pine Hills. He'd sent me a link to an article about a top secret experimental laboratory called Meridian . . .

I broke off, sick at heart, and pushed the heels of my hands into my eyes. Oh, Alison, I thought. I'm sorry. So sorry.

I'm shaking as I type now, irrationally terrified that writing down the way I feel will make it true. But if I know the fear is irrational, that means I can't be too far gone yet, right? So I'm just going to say it. Okay. Here it is.

I think I'm losing my mind.

No, worse than that. I'm afraid I lost it a long time ago.

How else can I make sense of what I saw on that website? How could a made-up story, or some paranoid schizophrenic's delusion, be so close to what I experienced—or thought I experienced—when Faraday and I went through the relay and found you?

I thought we'd beamed ourselves through a wormhole to the other side of the universe and ended up on a space station. But now I feel embarrassed even typing that, because where's the proof? There were no windows anywhere in that place, only screens that could show whatever the controller wanted. I believed I was in space because I saw so many stars, but I could have been underground the whole time and never guessed it.

And the drugs, the hallucinations, the men in grey uniforms—all of it fits roughly with what I remember, because I'd been on psych meds for weeks at that point, and everything felt strange and unreal to me, and both Faraday and Mathis were wearing grey. The part about people having chips implanted in their arms was familiar too, because you had one.

But the worst part of that article for me was reading about the helmet. Because I remember what it felt like to put it on, and that eerie feeling of floating in space. I thought I was doing it because I had to, because Mathis had closed the wormhole that led to Earth and my synesthesia was our only chance of finding it again. But what if all that was a hallucination or a simulation? What if it was simply part of some elaborate neuropsychological test?

I know Mathis was a real person, as real as you and Faraday. But was he actually an alien from another planet? Were you and Faraday aliens too? Or was that all in my messed-up head?

And now I've asked myself those questions, I keep thinking of more reasons I should have doubted myself all along. Like the way you acted after we got home, for instance. Because when you came to Pine Hills to try and convince Dr. Minta to release me, the story you told him was completely different from what I remembered. And when I teased you afterward about how your evil scientists driving black vans and helicopters weren't much more believable than my aliens and wormholes, you looked uncomfortable and said I shouldn't talk about "that alien stuff" anymore, even to you. Why would you say that, unless you knew I was wrong?

I thought I had the truth and that no one could take it away from me. But now I don't know what to believe. I need someone sane to talk to, someone who can tell me what's real. And since Faraday won't talk to me, you're my only hope.

Please, if you're reading this, help me.

Once I could have sworn Sebastian would do anything for Alison, no matter what the cost to himself. But he'd resisted every attempt I'd made to push him in her direction, and now he'd done this. Had I misread his character so badly? Or had something happened since I'd last seen him that had turned him into a different person?

I couldn't bear it anymore. I snatched up my phone and texted him.

—You unspeakable bastard. You should be on your knees right now in front of Alison, begging her forgiveness. And if she has any self-respect left, she'll never speak to you again.

I waited, but he didn't reply. Of course. So I texted again:

—Why did you make me read this? Just to spread the guilt around?

He knew I didn't dare write back to Alison, not with Deckard watching her every move. I knew manipulation when I saw it, and it was obvious that everything Deckard had told her had been calculated to make her panic and go running straight to Faraday—or to me.

Which, I realized as my anger subsided, was exactly why Sebastian had wanted me to read her letter. Not because he expected me to do anything but so I'd know to keep an eye out for Deckard. The struggles Alison was going through, her desperate pleas for help and reassurance, were incidental. She wasn't in danger of being caught and imprisoned, like Sebastian and I were; her freedom wasn't at stake right now, just her sanity.

As though there was anything *just* about it. I gritted my teeth and jabbed out one more message.

—Did you ever love her at all?

Not that he'd respond to that either, the coward. But it gave me a grim satisfaction to imagine his face when he read it. I put away my soldering iron, grabbed my laptop, and headed upstairs. Twelve minutes later, I'd changed into pajama pants and was climbing into bed when the phone clanked.

Probably Milo. Or with my luck, Jon. I picked the phone up and looked at the message. It said, simply:

–Yes.

1 0 0 0 0 0

"Hey," said Milo when I came out of the house the next morning. He took my hand, and I let him; it felt almost natural now. "What's the matter?"

He was dressed for running, just a T-shirt and track pants, same as me. It was still too cool for shorts, even this late in the spring. "Nothing," I said, stretching out one leg and then the other. "Just thought it was time to get back in shape. I've been sitting around way too much lately."

"Right," said Milo. "So you decided to go running with me at six thirty A.M., even though you don't have to get up for school. Seriously, what is it?"

"I'm here to run, not talk," I said and jogged away. With an exasperated noise, Milo shoved his earbuds into the pocket of his running belt and followed.

We kept a steady pace to the end of the block, then crossed the road and angled into the cemetery, where the pavement was smoother. Budding trees lined the path on both sides, breaking the sunlight into dazzling fragments, and the tombstones were glossy with dew. It was quiet here, open and private at once, and the only other person in sight was a grey-haired woman walking a pair of dogs nearly as large as she was. I breathed out and quickened my pace.

How fit was Deckard? Not that I was expecting to have to outrun him, or at least I hoped not. But as I recalled, he'd been in pretty good shape for a guy in his mid to late forties. The kind of guy who was seriously invested in taking down criminals, on foot and with his bare hands if necessary. So why would he retire from the force and go into private investigation? It might have been the money, but I suspected Deckard's loyalties weren't so easily bought. And it was a pretty huge step to take for a single case.

So now I had a tough, determined, and well-connected ex-cop searching for me full-time, not only because GeneSystem had hired him but because he was personally invested. And judging by how he'd treated Alison, he'd do whatever it took to—

"Whoa," said Milo. "Slow down, will you? We're not doing the hundred meters."

"Can't keep up?" I panted. My mouth was parched, sweat trickling between my shoulder blades, but I couldn't stop. I needed to test my limits, find out how hard and how fast I could run. "I'll see you at the top of the hill."

"Quit it, Niki." He stepped in front of me, arms outstretched to block my path. "You're going to injure yourself."

He was probably right, but I didn't like being told what to do. I set my jaw, dodged under his arm, and kept going.

"Tori!"

My old name echoed through the air like a thunderclap, freezing me in place. I stumbled and almost did a header before

Milo caught me and set me back on my feet. "Sorry," he began, "I didn't mean—"

I wrenched away and rounded on him. "Don't you *ever* call me that again!"

"There are plenty of girls named Tori," he said. "I know a couple just in my high school. You really think Meridian's got a satellite listening in on every conversation in Ontario?"

"That's not the point! If I can't trust you to keep a secret—"

"Oh, come on. That's not what this is about."

"What is it about, then? Reminding me you've got something on me, so I'd better do whatever you say?"

Milo's dark eyes narrowed behind his glasses. "Yeah," he said flatly. "Because that's the kind of guy I am. Good thing you spotted it before I could screw you over and sell you out, eh?"

Then he turned his back on me and walked away.

I gazed after him, anger fading to confusion. That wasn't how I'd expected the conversation to go at all. Milo had always been so easygoing, so willing to do whatever I asked. Every other time I'd lost my temper, he'd backed down. What had gone wrong this time?

"Wait," I called. "Please."

He stopped.

"I know you're not like that," I said. "It's just . . . you scared me. I don't like being scared."

Milo turned slowly. "I've noticed," he said. "When you get scared, you start picking fights with people. Or you run."

I sighed. "Yeah. I'm sorry."

"Okay," he said, walking back to me. "So what are you scared of?"

A wrought-iron bench sat by the edge of the path, three

and a half meters away. I limped over and lowered myself onto it, grimacing at the burn in my calf muscles. "Somebody from my old life has been searching for me," I said. "And I think he's getting close."

"Who is it?" asked Milo.

"An ex-cop named Deckard. I think—" No, I couldn't explain about Dr. Gervais. That would be far too complicated. Especially since I hadn't told Milo about my weird biology yet. "He knows there's a connection between me and Sebastian, and he knows Sebastian used an ATM here in town a few days ago. So I think he'll be coming here soon."

"What for?" Milo sat down beside me, offering me his water bottle. I took it gratefully and drank. "You haven't done anything wrong."

I waited for the question mark at the end of the sentence, the implicit *have you?*. But it never came. I handed Milo back the bottle. "Thank you," I said. "No, I haven't, but Sebastian has. When he visited Alison in the psych hospital, he impersonated a graduate student doing a study, with a faked-up website and credentials. Then he skipped town without paying his rent. And the police still think he kidnapped Alison and probably me as well."

"Wow," said Milo wryly. "And he seemed like such a nice guy."

"Yeah," I said. "He's good at that."

Milo must have caught the bitterness in my tone, because he stretched out his arm in a slow, deliberate movement and laid it along the back of the bench. Not touching me, just leaving it there for my consideration. "You don't like him much, do you?" he asked. "So why are you building this transceiver for him?

Why not let him deal with the relay on his own?"

"It's not that simple," I said. None of it was, not even the way I felt about Sebastian. In some ways he was like the older brother I'd never had. On the other hand, I'd never actually wanted an older brother. And whatever was going on between him and Alison was like looking into this weird alternate universe of emotions and passions that I'd never understand. "I have to do this, no matter what. I'm just afraid I'm not going to get it finished before Deckard finds me. Or Mathis does."

"Mathis?" asked Milo.

"One of the scientists Sebastian used to work with," I said, mentally kicking myself for the slip. "The guy who abducted me. I didn't think he could find me anymore, but if the relay's still working and the computer that controls it is still online . . . maybe he can."

"Yeah, but in that case, shouldn't he have found you a long time ago?"

A mournful whistle sounded in the near distance—a freight train chugging along the tracks at the north side of the graveyard, pulling its chain of boxcars toward the downtown core. Like Mathis, it was moving so slowly that I could almost outrun it. But that didn't make it safe to be in its way.

"I don't know," I said. "Maybe he got distracted or interrupted. Or it could be a timing malfunction—the relay system's a bit temperamental that way. But I can't assume anything." I slumped back, into the crook of Milo's arm. "All I know is that I have to get this transceiver built, and soon. Because Sebastian wouldn't have asked me for help unless he was desperate."

Milo sat still a moment. Then he slid closer and let his hand drop onto my shoulder. "You'll get it done," he said. "How's it going so far?"

"I've done pretty much everything I can at home," I said and sat up again. His arm was warm and solid and comforting, and I liked having it around me. But I didn't want him to forget what I'd told him back in the bus shelter—or make him think I was in danger of forgetting it myself. "Any more and my parents are going to start wondering what I'm up to."

Milo made a show of adjusting his glasses, then stood up and stretched in all directions. It was like watching a cat wash itself after failing to land on its feet. "Well, we're supposed to hear back from the makerspace today, right?"

"Right." I got up. "And if we sit around anymore, you're going to be late for school. So let's run."

"Fine, but I'll set the pace," said Milo. "I'm the expert, remember?"

I had a traitorous impulse to blow a raspberry and take off at top speed. But my muscles were sore enough already, and besides, Milo was right. "Yes, Mr. Hwang," I said in a childish lisp and matched my stride to his.

100001

I spent the rest of that morning failing to concentrate on schoolwork, which was unfortunate because it was English literature and I needed all the marks I could get. But I still hadn't figured out how to get hold of a vector network analyzer for less than ten grand or whether the makerspace would let me tinker with their oscilloscope—if they let me work in their space at all. And when I wasn't obsessing over the transceiver, I was feeling guilty about not writing back to Alison and frustrated with Sebastian for ignoring my questions about e-mail security and worried that Deckard might show up at any moment. So it was even harder to care about Shakespeare's sonnets than usual.

The afternoon passed more quickly, because Mom put me to work stripping wallpaper in the spare bedroom. I could tell she was surprised by how eager I was to help, but at least she didn't quiz me about it—or ask if I was still going out with Milo either, though I knew she wanted to. Instead, she tried to come at the subject sideways, asking me how "everyone" at work was doing and if I had any "special plans" for this weekend. I was tempted to ask if she'd been taking subtlety lessons from Jon, but that would open up a whole new can of awkward. So I just shrugged and kept working.

The evening, on the other hand, was torture. Two hours into my shift at Value Foods, I somehow misplaced a twenty and ended up having to pay for it out of pocket. At break I rushed to check my phone in case there was any news from the makerspace, but the only text was from my mother, reminding me we were out of milk.

I spent the bus ride home glaring at the screen, trying to compel the makerspace to call me by sheer force of will. There were no new e-mails in my inbox either, and by the time eleven o'clock came around, it was obvious I wasn't going to hear from them tonight. Sure, I wasn't as high on their priority list as they were on mine, but I thought I'd made it clear that this was urgent. Now I was beginning to wonder if they'd forgotten all about me.

Maybe it was time to start looking for alternatives—but

the problem was, I didn't know any. Where else would I get the space and the tools I needed on such short notice? Sebastian had obviously come to the same conclusion, or he wouldn't have sent me the brochure. But maybe I should have asked him to fake some references for me as well.

Listlessly I packed up the few bits of the transceiver I'd assembled so far and shoved the box into a corner. I still needed to get it out of the house before Mom or Dad got curious, but there was no point until I knew where I was going.

And right now, it looked like I wasn't going anywhere.

I was in bed and three-quarters asleep when my phone buzzed. I fumbled for it, thinking sourly that if it was Sebastian he was about to get an eyeful.

—Just got e-mail from the makerspace. Went to
spam so I didn't see it right away, sorry.

Well, of course they'd sent the message to Milo. He was the one who looked like a budding engineer. I was just the Manic Pixie Dream Girl in his personal life story, sent to wave her soldering iron around in a semi-competent fashion and awaken Milo to his true calling. The unfairness of it made me grind my teeth, but I reminded myself for the twenty-sixth time that I didn't want anyone to notice me anyway.

—So what did they say?

—Good news. We're in.

I collapsed onto the pillows, limp with relief.

—But we can't use the space unless there's
a member present. And we'll need to fill out a
couple of forms.

—Least of my worries. Thanks.

—No prob. Sweet dreams. See you tomorrow.

I smuggled my box of parts out of the basement late that night and stashed it behind the garden shed, wrapped up in a garbage bag in case of rain. It stayed there until dinner on Tuesday, when Milo sneaked into the backyard and took it away. When I got off the bus by the makerspace an hour later, he was standing there with the box under his arm, waiting for me.

"We're still going to have to get all the other stuff from your neighbor's," I said as we walked. Milo's next-door neighbor was an elderly widow, and Milo had been mowing her lawn and shoveling her driveway for years. So when he'd told her that he'd ordered a bunch of parts for a school project and didn't want the couriers to wake up his mother during the day, she'd been happy to sign for everything.

"Not a problem," said Milo. "But let's get this stuff dealt with first."

So we went inside and knocked at the makerspace, and when the door opened, it was Front Desk Guy, beaming at us. "Hey!" he said. "Come on through. I told Barry about your project, and he's pretty amped about helping you out. So between him and Len and me, you should be able to get in any night of the week."

"Thanks so much," I said. "I really appreciate this."

"It's what we're here for," he said cheerfully and led us up the ramp to the clean room. "Hey Barry! They're here. Wanna help them set up?"

We turned the corner and there was Barry, aka Radio Guy, short and stocky and goatee-wearing, elbow-deep in a large cardboard box. His eyebrows went up as he saw us, as did mine, and for the same reason.

"Hi," I said. "How's the quadrotor?"

"Uh, hi," he replied. He glanced at Milo as though for reassurance, then stepped back from the carton. "You want to do this?"

He was looking at me, holding out the battered utility knife he'd used to cut the box open. For a moment I was puzzled—until I saw the label on the box's side. Not to mention the other boxes and packages stacked up at the other end of the table, all of them bearing the same address.

"Milo, you didn't!" I exclaimed, and he grinned.

"My neighbor let me borrow her car," he said. "I brought it all down here after school. Surprise?"

I could feel FDG and Barry watching us, waiting for my reaction. I knew what they expected, and I knew better than to hesitate. But even as I threw my arms around Milo, I wished I could have thanked him without having to put on a performance. And when I felt his fingers tighten against my back, the way his breath caught when my lips brushed his cheek, my delight vanished beneath a rumbling landslide of guilt. He deserved better than this charade. I wished I had something better to give him.

"You're the best!" I enthused, breaking off the embrace and bouncing over to take the knife from Barry. "Let's get started."

In spite of our rocky start, I had to give Barry credit. It only took him a few minutes of watching me lay out the various parts and components to realize he'd misjudged where the enthusiasm for this project was coming from, and after that he started addressing all his comments to me. Soon Milo drifted off to a nearby table with his laptop and left us to it.

"What kind of antenna are you using?" Barry asked, following me as I carried my circuit board to the soldering station. "Dish or Yagi?"

Playing slightly dumb was a lot harder than playing completely dumb. I wasn't used to working in front of people who understood what I was doing, and I had to remind myself to act uncertain. "I haven't decided yet," I said. "What do you think?"

"Well, I know a guy who used to work at the cable company, and now he sells surplus electronics," he said. "He's got a couple dishes sitting around, if you need one."

According to Sebastian, I didn't have to worry about finding an antenna. But I didn't have to fake my interest either, because Barry had just given me an idea. "Do you think he might have a vector network analyzer?" I asked.

"Dunno," said Barry, looking surprised. "Maybe. I'll give him a call."

He wandered off to the lounge, while I laid out the remaining packages of capacitors and chips I needed to complete the microcontroller circuit I'd started at home. Most of the components had been simple to solder, but these last twenty-two were all surface-mounted, and some were so tiny that a single careless breath could send them flying in all directions. I swung the lighted magnifying glass over the board, picked up my tweezers, and went to work.

I'd been soldering for what seemed like only a few minutes, absorbed in the pleasure of concentration, when I became aware of fragmented whispers coming from behind me.

". . . should see how fast . . . barely used the magnifier . . ."

". . . no way can anybody solder that many SMDs in ten minutes . . ."

". . . look closer—oh man, she just picked up that SOIC."

I had too. The tiny square was at the end of my tweezers. Which meant Barry wasn't telling the others about some instructional video he'd watched online, as I'd vaguely supposed.

He was talking about me.

My tweezers shook, and the chip dropped onto the board a full centimeter out of place. My greatest worry until now had been that Barry would notice the modifications I'd made to my transceiver or ask me why it needed so much power. I never imagined I'd get busted for something as simple and basic as my soldering technique.

But I couldn't let that stop me. I had to keep working as long as I still had the chance. So I willed my hand steady and nudged the wayward chip back into position. I'd applied a thin line of flux and was drag-soldering the pins into place when Barry leaned over my shoulder. "D'you mind . . . uh, I mean, when you're done with that chip, could we take a look at your PCB?"

My instincts told me to play innocent. "Oh, sure!" I said, with an internal wince at how perky I sounded. "Hang on, I'm almost finished . . . okay, there."

I put down my soldering iron and slid out of the chair. Barry and the other two members crowded forward to inspect the circuit board, sweeping the magnifier across its surface. The tallest one frowned, and I held my breath—but then he leaned back and let out a sigh.

"Beautiful," he murmured. "Not a bridge in sight, and look at the size of that tip she's using." He turned his quizzical brown eyes on me. "Where'd you learn to drag solder like that, at your age?"

"She's homeschooled," Milo spoke up before I could answer and strolled over to join us. "Hey, baby," he said, in an exaggerated drawl that even a stranger couldn't have mistaken for anything but a joke. "Are these guys bothering you?" He pretended to crack his knuckles.

Barry and the others flicked me wary glances, and I laughed, as much with nerves as relief. "Oh no," I said. "It's fine."

The three men relaxed, and the stocky one gave a sly smile. "Mohan here was just about to ask you to marry him and bear him many beautiful geeky children," he said, elbowing the tall one in the side. "But since you're taken—"

"Excuse me, Jake," said the other with dignity, "You're forgetting *I'm* taken."

"Oh, right. Guess it's just me then." Jake flashed me a grin. "Seriously, nice work. I'll have to get you to give me a lesson sometime." Then he strolled off back to his own project, and after a slight hesitation, Mohan followed him.

"So," Barry said, when the others had gone, "let me tell you what I found out about your VNA. Surplus Steve doesn't have one, but he knows a guy who does and is willing to do you a loaner if you give him fifty bucks deposit. Sound okay?"

"Sounds great," I said. "Where can I pick it up?"

"Oh, I can do that for you." Barry waved my surprise aside. "I'm off work right now—wrecked my back doing long-haul trucking for sixteen years and can't start retraining until June. So it's no big deal to run an errand or two." He paused, his gaze sliding back to the circuit board at my elbow. "I've never seen a layout quite like that before. Who did the design?"

My pulse quickened, but I didn't let myself falter. "Oh," I said, "just a guy I know."

"Huh." He blinked and scratched the side of his nose. "Well, I'd like to meet that guy." He gave me a last, unreadable look and wandered back to his table.

"Everything okay?" asked Milo, when he was gone. "They weren't criticizing you or anything, were they?"

"No," I said, feeling the tension in my stomach beginning to unwind. "They were just looking."

And it was true, because nobody interrupted me for the rest of the evening. By nine o'clock I'd finished the microcontroller, made a good start on the oscillator, and was feeling good about my progress. At this rate, I might have the transceiver ready by the end of the week.

"Thanks for your help," I said to Barry, with a nod to Front Desk Guy—whose name, I'd finally found out, was Shawn. "So it's okay for me to leave my stuff here?"

"Sure thing," said Shawn. "But we've got a bunch of home-schoolers building robots in the morning, so if there's anything you're worried about, you might want to stash it in one of the lockers. And tomorrow night we've got the crafters coming in, so it might be a little crowded . . ."

"I just got called into work for tomorrow," said Milo, making a face at his phone. "Can Niki get in with one of you guys?"

"Uh," said Shawn. "Well, I'm teaching a night course—"

"I'll keep an eye on her," said Barry. "Is seven o'clock okay?"

Under other circumstances I might have hesitated before accepting that offer. But even if Barry turned out to be a creeper, he'd have to be pretty stupid to harass me in a room full of women armed with sharp objects. And besides, he was clearly a lot more interested in my transceiver than he was in me.

"That would be great," I said.

100011

Barry brought in the VNA the following night as promised, and it didn't take us long to convert the makerspace's old oscilloscope into a spectrum analyzer, so I finally had all the equipment I needed. And by the time I went home that night, I was starting to feel hopeful that I'd be allowed to finish the transceiver without interference.

Thursday went even better. Mohan watched me at the drill press, and Len helped me laser-cut the enclosure. When he saw me working on the bandpass filters, Jake hailed me as "Goddess of Solder" and pretended to worship me, and later that night a girl named Mandy told me she was a third-year engineering student and joked that we geek girls should stick together. But none of them questioned what I was doing at all.

Unfortunately, the transceiver still wasn't finished, so I had to beg off my usual Friday night shift at Value Foods. But I'd asked Kayleigh to cover for me, so I wasn't worried about getting in trouble. At least not until halfway through the evening, when Barry pulled out a chair and sat down next to me.

"You know," he said seriously, "this transceiver you're building is pretty hard-core, if all your dad wants is to bounce a radio signal off the moon. Not that moon bounces aren't a challenge, but . . ."

"You don't think it's going to work?" I asked, making an effort to sound anxious. Not that I wasn't concerned about getting it wrong, but so far everything I'd built had performed exactly as it should. I was more worried about whether Sebastian had given me the right specifications in the first place.

"I, uh, wouldn't say that," Barry replied with a sideways glance at the 3-D printer, where Len was working. "You seem to have a really good handle on what you're doing. I'm just not sure I understand *what* you're doing."

"Well," I said slowly as my brain scrambled for a plausible

answer, "I kind of wanted something more versatile . . ."

My phone rang, sparing me the rest of the sentence. "Excuse me," I said to Barry and hurried off to the lounge. "Hello?"

"It's me." Milo sounded tense. I could hear rumbling in the background and the slow beep of a truck backing up for a late delivery. "You know that ex-cop you said was looking for you? Becker?"

Cold crept up my spine. "Deckard. What about him?"

"He's here in the store. Right now."

PART THREE: Hunting

(The undesirable oscillation that occurs when a feedback control system is unable to reduce the error rate to zero)

100100

My legs felt shaky, and I gripped the corner of the bookshelf for support. I'd known Deckard might come to town looking for Sebastian, but I'd never dreamed his search would lead him so quickly to me.

"Niki?" asked Milo, faint and tinny. "You there?"

"How—" I cleared my throat. "How do you know it's Deckard?"

"Because he showed me your picture and asked me if I recognized you," said Milo. "Said you were a missing girl who'd been seen in the area, and there'd be a reward if I helped him find you."

I leaned harder on the bookcase and closed my eyes. Milo went on, "I told him you worked at the Tim Horton's on the corner. I thought if I could get him to leave, I could run around and tell Jon and the others he was a stalker. But when I came up to the front, he was by the manager's office, looking at the staff board."

Which had my picture on it, of course. With my name underneath, in large friendly letters. I groped along the sofa and sat down.

"I tried to sneak back to the stockroom, but he saw me," Milo said. "Then he called me over and showed me another picture. A still from a security video, with the two of us together. From the night you stopped the bus."

My throat felt like someone had soldered it shut. "Go on."

"So I played the stalker card myself," he said. "I said you'd told me you were hiding from a creepy ex-boyfriend and that I shouldn't talk about you to anybody but the police. That seemed to work, because he backed off and let me go. But he's still in the store. He's talking to Jon right now."

And not only did Jon Van Beek know exactly where I lived, he had my cell number. Friendly, trusting, farm-raised Jon, who would probably never guess this clean-cut, soft-spoken man would do me any harm. Especially if Deckard pulled out that medical emergency story he'd used on Alison, because Jon would love a chance to be my hero.

In short, I was doomed.

"So what are we going to do?" Milo asked, and his voice seemed to be coming from a billion miles away. I stared at the word clock on the wall, which said IT IS FIVE AFTER EIGHT, and tried to think.

I couldn't go back to Value Foods, not now that Deckard knew I worked there. So there went my job. I couldn't be seen with Milo, because Deckard would be watching him. So there went my best friend, quasi boyfriend, and partner in crime. I couldn't even go home, because now that Deckard had my name, it wouldn't take him long to hunt down my address. Nothing in my life was secure anymore, and nowhere was safe. The only thing to do was run.

But I couldn't do that, either. Not before I'd finished this transceiver. Because what was the use of hiding from Deckard and Dr. Gervais, if Mathis got to me first?

"I don't know," I said to Milo. "I don't know what to do."

For five seconds Milo didn't answer. Then he said in a decisive voice, "Stay where you are. I'll call you back in a few minutes."

100101

By the time my phone rang again, I'd pulled myself together. I even had the beginnings of a plan. "Okay," I told Milo, "so once Deckard leaves—"

"Wait," said Milo. "Let me go first. I just got off the phone with your dad."

"You *what?* He's not even home tonight. How'd you get his cell number?"

"Emergency contact," Milo said. "It was in your file. Anyway, I told him a guy you used to know came into the store looking for you, and you were scared, so you hid out in the back with me. And now you're afraid to leave in case he follows you home."

"Okay," I said slowly. It wasn't a bad story—it had the advantage of being simple and mostly true. It would also throw my parents into a panic, but I couldn't see any alternative. It'd be worse if Deckard showed up at the door and caught them unprepared.

"But I told him not to worry," said Milo, "because I've asked my grandparents to pick you up and take you to their house instead. You can even stay overnight with them, if you need to."

"You mean your *mother's* parents? Your mother, who's not supposed to know anything about—"

"Never mind that," he said. "I'll explain later. How soon can you get to the 7-Eleven on Caledonia?"

This whole conversation was beginning to feel surreal. "Twenty minutes?"

"Good. I'll tell my grandparents to pick you up there. And your dad said not to call him. He'll call you in an hour or so. Gotta go."

Click.

I lowered the phone and found Barry peering down at me from the top of the ramp. "Problems?" he asked.

"No," I lied. "I just have to leave a bit earlier tonight."

100110

From the outside Milo's grandparents' place didn't look like much, just the right side of a two-story semi with dirty white siding and peeling shutters. The driveway was cracked in three places, and the front steps had an eight-degree tilt to the left. But inside the house was cozy and spotlessly clean, with tropical plants standing in pots and spilling over the tops of the bookcases and framed Bible verses hanging on the walls.

Most of the verses were in Korean, but the one directly across from me was in English: LET THE BEAUTY OF THE LORD OUR GOD BE UPON US. It was done in brush calligraphy and decorated with silk flowers that looked hand-made. Maybe that was Mrs. Park's hobby.

"I am sorry you've had such a frightening experience," said Milo's grandmother, pouring me a cup of herbal tea. Her voice was soft and lilting, every word precise. "This must be very hard for you."

"Thank you," I said, suppressing a shiver. It had been raining when I left the makerspace, but I'd only got slightly damp, so why did I feel so cold? As Mrs. Park poured more tea for her husband and herself, I clutched the mug to my chest, inhaling deep breaths of grassy-smelling steam. *Relax*, I told myself. *You're safe here.*

Still, it was hard not to wonder why two near-total strangers would go out of their way to help me. Sure, they'd come to my register a few times, and I'd always smiled and tried to make conversation. But what had I done to earn their hospitality? Nothing, as far as I could see. So either they adored Milo so much that they'd do anything he wanted or they had some motive of their own . . .

Like suspecting their grandson was going out with me, for instance. It was the most natural explanation. But if they'd guessed that we were together, did they approve or disapprove? They'd treated me graciously so far, but that didn't necessarily mean anything. My parents were polite to everybody too, even people they despised.

Milo's grandfather broke into my thoughts, asking whether I had talked to the police about the man who was threatening me. I was wondering how to explain that my "stalker" was an ex-cop who apparently had half the local force eating doughnuts out of his hand when the phone rang, and Mrs. Park answered it. She spoke a few words in Korean and handed the receiver to her husband, who rose and went into the study, shutting the door behind him.

"Someone from the church," she said. "A pastor's life is very busy."

I knew there was a Korean church in town. I hadn't realized Milo's grandfather was the pastor. It should have been a relief to know that the Parks had taken me in as an act of Christian charity, but somehow it didn't help much. Especially when I glanced toward the dining room and spotted a text reading THE TRUTH WILL MAKE YOU FREE.

My phone buzzed in my pocket. "Please excuse me," I said to Mrs. Park, setting my cup down and getting up quickly from the sofa. "It's my dad calling."

100111

The conversation went better than I'd feared, at least to begin with. Dad had already guessed that the guy who'd come into the store must be Deckard, so he wasn't surprised to hear it. He even agreed that I'd done the right thing by going to Milo's grandparents instead of coming home. But the best plan he could come up with was for him and Mom to pack some suitcases, pick me up, and jump on the first plane to Calgary—and there was no way I could go along with that.

"Even if Deckard knows where we live, it's not like he's going to crash through the front door and hold us at gunpoint,"

I argued as I paced across the Parks' back patio and onto the lawn. It was too quiet inside for private conversation, so I'd gone outside to take the call. "This isn't the USA, and he's not a policeman anymore. Besides, it's me he wants, not you or Mom, so if I'm obviously not at home—"

"Obviously? I can't see how it's going to be obvious unless we let him in to search the place. And then what are we supposed to tell him? That you ran away?"

I almost said *yes*, but that wouldn't work, because then Deckard would have the perfect excuse to call out his cop buddies to search for me. "Not exactly," I said. "Tell him I've left town, with your permission. And that you don't know where I've gone or when I'll be back."

Dad spluttered. "Are you crazy? There's no way we'd let you take off on your own without—"

"I said you should *tell* him that, not I'm actually planning to do it. I don't want to go anywhere. I just want Deckard to leave you and Mom alone."

"And you think he'll give up that easily?" Dad asked. "I'm not afraid of Deckard: he can't do anything to me. But your mother's a different story. If he turns up at the front door looking for you, she'll never feel safe in this town again."

He lowered his voice on the last sentence, as though he'd only just realized how loudly he'd been talking. But I could tell there was more going on than that. "You mean you haven't told Mom anything about what happened tonight?" I asked. "She doesn't know about Deckard or—any of it?"

"Not yet." He sighed. "She was in the washroom when Milo called me. He told me you were safe for now, and I . . . didn't want to spoil her evening out."

But that wouldn't stop him from telling her the truth eventually, unless I gave him a reason not to. Somehow I had to convince him to let me stay here until I'd finished the transceiver . . . but how?

Then, in a white-lightning flash of intuition, I knew.

"Okay," I said. "How about this? Don't tell Mom anything yet. Take her out of town for the weekend—use that getaway package you got from work or something. I'll stay with Milo's grandparents, where Deckard can't find me. If he comes to the house tonight or tomorrow, it'll be empty and he can draw his own conclusions."

"And what good's that going to do? All he has to do is stake out the place and wait until we get back."

"He won't if he thinks we're gone for good," I said. "There's a guy I know who's brilliant with computers, and he owes me a favor. He can fake up some flight and hotel reservations, and make Deckard think we've gone to Newfoundland or something." Assuming I could get hold of Sebastian on short notice, of course. But I suspected that if I really needed him, he'd be around.

"Then what?" Dad asked. "Seems to me we're just delaying the inevitable. He's going to figure out the truth eventually."

"Maybe," I said. "But isn't it worth trying? We can't keep moving and changing our names every six months. I've seen the bills, Dad. I know how hard you've been working. Next time we move we're going to end up in a trailer park if we're lucky, and after that we'll be living on the streets. Do you really want that? Because I don't."

Dad was silent, and I knew I'd hurt him. He'd worked hard to protect his family, and I'd as good as told him that he'd failed.

But he wasn't arguing, either, and that meant he was close to giving in.

"Dad," I said, "It's not that I don't appreciate everything you and Mom have done for me. You've given up so much . . ." My voice wobbled on the last word. I swallowed and tried again. "Look, if my plan to get rid of Deckard doesn't work, then fine, we can run. But can we at least try my idea first? Please?"

Six seconds ticked by in silence. Then my dad said heavily, "All right. I'll talk to your mother."

101000

As soon as I got off the phone with Dad I texted Sebastian, and this time he answered right away. Once I'd explained the situation to him, he even seemed to relish the challenge.

–Leave Deckard to me. I'll keep him busy.

–Good to know you haven't lost your knack for messing with people's heads. At least this time you can do it to somebody who deserves it.

Which was rude and possibly ill-advised, but I wasn't worried about offending Sebastian. He needed this transceiver too badly to risk losing me, and he was hardly going to sell me out to Deckard because he didn't like my attitude. In fact, he was probably smart enough to have guessed where my sniping remarks were coming from—because it was easier to blame him for Alison's unhappiness than to admit that I was just as guilty.

And I was. Because I knew the truth about Meridian, about what had really happened last summer. I'd just been too much of a coward to talk about it, even to the one person who needed my honesty most.

"Niki?" Mrs. Park was leaning out the sliding door, looking around for me. I stepped back into the light.

"I'm here," I said.

"It's too dark outside," she chided. "Come in now. I have your room ready."

I took off my shoes and followed her up the stairs to where the spare bedroom waited for me, its double bed draped in white linens. There was a flowery nightgown laid out on the bed, faded but clean, with a set of towels and a new toothbrush—still in the package—beside it.

"You should sleep," Milo's grandmother said. "You have had a shock and you must be tired. You will feel better tomorrow."

In fact it was barely ten o'clock, and I wasn't tired at all. But though her voice was sweet there was steel in it, and I knew better than to protest. "You've been very kind," I said. "Thank you for everything."

Mrs. Park gave a satisfied nod and closed the door. I waited until her footsteps receded, then pulled out my laptop and phone. If I was stuck here, then at least I could get some work done.

I was halfway through a resignation letter to my manager when Milo texted me.

> –Settled in all right? GPs taking good care of you?
>
> –Very. What did you tell them???
>
> –Same thing I told your dad. Only with bonus stuff about how you were a nice girl and this was totally not your fault. And how we were just friends (sorry about the "just"), but I couldn't

put you up at my place because my mom's still
on night shift, and What Would The Neighbors
Think?

    –Nice.

And I meant it. I'd been feeling guilty about making Milo
lie to his grandparents, but that was essentially the truth, or at
least as much of it as they needed to know.

    –I'd come over, but my grandmother would give
    me the stank eye if I showed up at this hour. Still
    OK to get into the m-space tomorrow?

    –Yeah, no problem. Shawn's letting me in at 10.
    You coming?

    –For a while. See you then.

I finished my letter of resignation and sent it off to my
manager via phone, since the Parks didn't have Wi-Fi. Then
I undressed and climbed into bed. But no matter how many
binary numbers I counted, sleep refused to come. I couldn't
stop thinking about Deckard and my parents and Sebastian . . .
and now more than ever, Alison.

For the past week I'd allowed the urgency of building
the transceiver to push her to the back of my mind, telling
myself it wasn't safe to reach out to her anyway. But Deckard
wasn't in Sudbury spying on Alison anymore. He was here in
southern Ontario, looking for me. And what had happened
tonight had made me realize just how selfish I'd been to ignore
Alison's letter.

The fear that had jolted through me when Milo told me
Deckard was in the store, that sense of being vulnerable and
horribly alone . . . that was nothing compared to what Alison
must be going through. Because I wasn't alone, not really: I

had Milo, and I had my parents, and in a weird way I even had Sebastian. But Alison had nobody who understood what she'd been through or how she was feeling. Nobody who was willing to admit it, anyway.

I'd had enough of waiting for Sebastian to do the right thing. It was time to throw away my pride, my guilt, and all the fears that had been holding me back and tell Alison the truth.

I sat up quickly and switched on the bedside light. Then I picked up my phone and started typing.

101001

The next morning I ate an early, quiet breakfast with Milo's grandparents, helped Mrs. Park wash the dishes, and thanked them profusely for their kindness. I told them I had plans for the day and wouldn't impose on them any longer, but I'd always be grateful for their hospitality.

"Your parents," said Pastor Park. "Are they coming to get you? Or would you like us to take you home?"

He spoke mildly, and the lines of his face were gentle. But there was something unnervingly shrewd in the way he looked at me, and I found myself stammering out the truth before I could even think to lie.

"My parents aren't home right now. They've gone to Toronto for the weekend."

Mrs. Park gave me a sharp look, and I could tell she didn't think much of my parents. So I added quickly, "It's not their fault. They wanted to take me away with them, but I told them I'd rather stay here. I have a lot of work to do on a—a school project, and I can't afford to leave it."

That struck the right note. Milo's grandparents exchanged looks, and I could see they were impressed by my commitment to academics. "So, then," Milo's grandmother said, "you will stay here until your parents come back."

"Oh, I couldn't—"

"Don't argue with my wife," Pastor Park told me with a half-smile. "She's a very determined woman. Now, tell us where you need to go, and we'll drive you there. Would you like to stop at your house first?"

So that was how I ended up in front of the makerspace at precisely ten o'clock, with clean clothes and a packed lunch in my bag, waving to Milo's grandparents as they drove away. I was heading inside, still a little dazed by all this efficient care, when Dad texted me with an update.

He and Mom had packed up and left the house last night without any sign of Deckard. They'd left Crackers with our next-door neighbor, who adored him and would spoil him rotten. They were staying at a nice hotel in downtown Toronto, and Mom was going to call me in a few minutes to see how I was getting along.

Which meant that somehow, Dad had convinced Mom that he'd been planning this trip for ages. He'd told her I'd arranged to stay with Milo's family for the weekend, so she wouldn't worry about leaving me alone. Then he'd whisked her straight from their Friday night date to a romantic getaway weekend without a hint that there was anything unusual, let alone dangerous, going on.

So when she called, I kept my voice bright and confident. I asked her what shows she and Dad would be seeing and told her to have a great time and promised that Milo and I wouldn't throw any parties while the two of them were away, ha-ha. By the time I hung up, I felt thoroughly sick of myself.

When I walked into the makerspace, Barry was there, peering under the dust cover at my nearly completed transceiver. I braced myself for another barrage of questions, but when he saw me, he only mumbled a greeting and went back to work on his own project, a vintage radio he was converting to an MP3 player. So I wasn't busted yet.

Still, the faster I got the transceiver finished and out of here, the better. And I was so close now—two or three hours of work at most. Test the power amplifier, finish up the relay circuit and cabling, and assemble it all in the enclosure. Then all I had to do was install the firmware Sebastian had sent me, and I'd be done. I switched on the soldering iron, dumped out the last of my components, and went to work with a vengeance.

My hands moved smoothly from one task to another, obeying my slightest thought without hesitation. My eyes stayed focused on the board, immune to all distractions, while my mind slipped into a heightened, almost dreamlike state. It had been a long time since I'd allowed myself to sink this deep into a project, and the cautious part of me warned that I might regret it. But I didn't care anymore. I loved this feeling too much.

Closer and closer. The enclosure took shape beneath my hands, back and sides slotting smoothly into the base. I mounted the transceiver board, slotted in the relay module, and hooked up the cables. Almost complete now—just a few more steps and I'd be ready to power on. I could feel my confidence soaring, the old thrill tingling inside me . . .

Behind me, Milo cleared his throat.

"Oh, sorry," I said, blinking up at him. "How long have you been there?"

"Half an hour," he said. "But don't let me stop you. You look like you're on a roll."

"I'm almost finished," I said. "Just give me a few more minutes." I dived back into the enclosure, and the world vanished again.

A few in this case ended up being *twenty-three*, thanks to my perfectionist streak. Even once the transceiver was fully assembled, I couldn't declare victory until I'd hooked it up to my laptop and installed Sebastian's firmware. But when the green light glowed on the transceiver's front panel, and I saw that the test sequence had run perfectly, I let out a whoop and punched the air. "Done it!"

Milo came over to inspect my handiwork, running his hands over the smooth top of the case. "Looks fantastic," he said. "Like you bought it from some high-tech dealer. I can't believe you put all those components together so fast."

"Neither can I," said Barry, swiveling to face us. "This is top-notch work, Niki. How do you know all this stuff at your age?"

"I'm highly motivated," I said blithely. I knew I ought to be more cautious, but right then I was too busy savoring my triumph to care. Besides, the transceiver was finished, so what did it matter what Barry thought of it anymore?

Barry lumbered to his feet and came over. "So when are you planning to take it for a test drive?"

He was obviously eager to see the transceiver working, and I felt bad for not giving him the chance. But I suspected that when the time came to use it, Sebastian wasn't going to want a lot of spectators.

"Not today," I said. "I'm not exactly sure when it's going to work out."

"Oh, sure," said Barry, sounding disappointed but not angry, and I thought I was off the hook. But when I pushed the transceiver back against the wall and started draping the dust cover over it, he spoke again. "But, uh, let's be honest here. This isn't really for your dad's birthday, is it?"

Immediately my brain started shuffling through a pack of semi-plausible lies. But when I looked into Barry's earnest brown eyes, I couldn't do it. He loved electronics, and he knew radio, and even if I hadn't really needed his technical advice, he'd been a big help in other ways.

So I looked straight at him and said, "No. It's meant to beam a quantum-encoded data signal over a distance of 68.4 million kilometers, ordering a certain piece of scientific equipment to turn itself off. And if it doesn't work, I'm in big trouble."

Barry regarded me for a few seconds without expression. Then he said, "Thought it was something like that," and went back to his work.

I was staring at the back of his head, unable to believe it could be that easy, when Milo nudged me.

"Hey, Girl Genius," he said. "You've done an awesome job. Let's go celebrate."

101010

I'd thought Milo was joking about the celebration. But when we got outside and he started marching toward downtown, I realized that he meant it. "Wait," I said. "I can't. I need to text Sebastian—"

"You can do that when we get there," he said. "The Cakery's only a couple blocks away, and there's a slice of chocolate banana pecan calling my name."

So I gave in. Because, well, it was cake. While we waited for the waitress to bring our order, I wrote Sebastian to tell him the transceiver was finished. I expected he'd get back to me as promptly as he had last night, but by the time I cleaned my plate and drank two cups of coffee, he still hadn't answered.

"He's probably just busy," said Milo. "Didn't you say you'd asked him to lead Deckard on some kind of virtual wild-goose chase?"

"Yeah, but that shouldn't stop him from answering a text. Especially from me."

"So you think something happened to him?"

I considered the infinite set of possibilities, most of them unpleasant. He'd lost his phone or had it stolen. He'd been arrested; he'd been in an accident; he'd blown himself to atoms tinkering with the relay...

Or, more likely, he'd just pulled an all-nighter and fallen asleep on the keyboard. I forced a smile. "It's probably nothing. I'm just impatient, I guess."

Milo gave me a level look that reminded me of his grand-father. "No, you're not. You're worried about him, and you're stressed out about Deckard, and you look like you're about to fall over. I'm taking you home."

Normally I would have resented being told how I felt and what I should do. But the exultation of finishing the transceiver had faded, and I didn't have the energy to fight. "Fine, but which 'home' are we talking about? Because your grandparents seem to think I'm staying at their place until my parents get back. No arguments allowed."

"Arguments are never allowed," said Milo. "Not if you're under the age of seventy, anyway. The last time I talked back to my *halmunee*, she made me stand in the corner and hold my arms above my head for twenty minutes."

"Wow."

"Yeah. I didn't get supper, either." He pulled a doleful face, then grinned at my expression. "Don't worry, non-Koreans get a free pass. But if you really want to get on her good side, keep your eyes down, speak softly, and eat lots of kimchi."

"I'll keep that in mind," I said.

101011

Milo was on evening shift that night, so he rode the bus with me as far as his grandparents' neighborhood and jogged off to Value Foods from there. Once he was out of sight I checked my phone again, but there was still no word from Sebastian.

When I reached the Parks' house, a car I didn't recognize was sitting in the driveway. My heart skipped a beat—but then I noticed the Korean flag pasted into its back window. Not Deckard, then. I rang the doorbell and Mrs. Park answered, looking harried but relieved to see me. She scolded me for not calling for a ride, shepherded me into the living room, and hurried back to her kitchen, where something red and sweet-smelling was cooking.

Pastor Park was nowhere in sight. But muffled voices came from the study, a woman's voice rising in impassioned Korean and a male voice barking out denials. Milo's grandmother made a disapproving noise and went on stirring her pot.

"Is everything all right?" I asked.

"These young people," she said. "So many of them come to us for advice, saying they want to save their marriage. But the women only want to hear that they are right and their husband is wrong, and the man is just the same. They don't want to work or make sacrifices. They fight all the time, and soon they want a divorce."

"Oh," I said blankly. That was more information than I'd really wanted to know. "So . . . can I help you with anything?"

I ended up setting the table, while Mrs. Park prepared fried chicken with sauce, rice, and about five other side dishes without consulting a recipe book even once. After quizzing me about my parents' marriage, my religious background, and my academic goals, she inquired with disarming sweetness whether I thought it was a good idea for young people to date before they finished university. But thanks to Milo I knew the right answer and could even tell her honestly that I wasn't looking for a boyfriend, which appeared to settle any doubts she'd had about me. By the time Pastor Park came out to show the sulky-looking couple to the door, she'd relaxed enough to tell me about her daughter's early, failed marriage and how hard Milo's mother had worked to finish her education and raise two fine, handsome, brilliant sons.

"Jeremy is in his second year of business school," Mrs. Park announced with pride. "And Milo is going to be a doctor."

"Oh?" I said faintly. If Milo still hadn't worked up the courage to tell his family what he really wanted, I wasn't going to do it for him. But the reverent way his grandmother said the word *doctor*, as though it were the embodiment of everything that made Milo great, made me feel sorry for both of them.

Meanwhile, Pastor Park came back and sat down in the living room with the Korean newspaper, but his eyes were weary and the lines around his mouth deeper than before. Being a minister seemed to take up a lot more time and energy than I'd realized. And judging by the Parks' modest home, it didn't pay all that well, either.

So maybe Milo's family wasn't quite as unanimous about wanting him to be wealthy and successful as he'd thought. Maybe his grandfather, at least, would understand. "What did your husband's family think about him becoming a pastor?" I asked.

"They were not happy," Mrs. Park said. "They told him he was throwing his life away. But he knew that what he was doing was right in God's eyes."

Which wasn't going to help Milo much, as far as I could see. Not unless he could convince his family that God had enough pastors now and was looking for a few good gym teachers.

"So you think it's important to do something you really believe in," I said, "not just what your family expects?"

Mrs. Park gave me a narrow look, and I could see she suspected I was up to something. "I am saying," she replied with dignity, "that if a person has to choose between God and family, then God must come first. But family is very important. Children should respect their parents and their elders, and listen to their advice. Because that is how God gives young people wisdom." She picked up the platter of chicken, glistening in its red sauce. "We will eat now."

I knew when I was beaten. I lowered my eyes meekly, took the bowl of rice off the countertop, and followed her.

After dinner I checked my e-mail, but it was empty. I sent off another text to Sebastian, and a couple to my parents to reassure them that I was okay. Then I watched TV with Pastor Park, while Mrs. Park sewed more of her silk flowers. After all the frenzied effort I'd put into finishing the transceiver that morning, plus the suspense of wondering what Deckard was up to, whether Alison had got my letter, and why Sebastian hadn't got back to me yet, the quietness felt so anticlimactic I wanted to scream.

Milo texted me that night after the Parks had gone to bed, but he hadn't heard from Sebastian any more than I had. Though on a positive note, he'd seen no sign of Deckard either.

–I biked past your house on my way home,
and there was nobody parked on the street. If
Deckard's staking out the place, I'd like to know
how he's doing it.

I could think of a few ways, but I doubted Deckard was that talented with electronics. I was about to reply when Milo continued:

–So how are you doing? Everything OK?

There was no easy answer to that question. What could I tell Milo that he didn't already know, without getting into all the things I wasn't ready to tell him? I shifted into a cross-legged position on the bed and picked the safest answer I could think of.

–I'm worried about Alison. She's been going
through a hard time lately. Especially since she
found out Sebastian was back.

–Why? What's the deal with her and Sebastian?
I'd forgotten. He didn't know.
  –She was in love with him.
    –Ouch. So did he brush her off or let her down
    easy?
I couldn't blame Milo for assuming it had been one-sided. Whatever Sebastian's faults, he didn't come across as the type who would take advantage of a seventeen-year-old girl, especially one who was going through a massive emotional and psychological crisis. He didn't even seem like the kind of guy who'd be tempted. But somehow it had happened anyway, and it had taken him a surprisingly long time to clue in and do the right thing.
      –Neither at first. But when he helped her and
      me escape from—
My stomach clenched. Not only could I not say the word *Meridian*, I couldn't even bring myself to type it. Instead, I wrote:
      –From the lab. He said he'd made a mistake.
      That she was too young, and it should never have
      happened. But he did it in this noble, sacrificial
      kind of way, so it wasn't a breakup so much as a
      big romantic Hollywood moment.
      –Seriously? Sebastian did that?
Yeah. I don't know why. Maybe he thought it would make it easier on her, or— I stopped mid-sentence, a tiny spark of suspicion flaring to life. I cast my thoughts back over the past three weeks, finding nodes of memory and drawing connections between them. The dismay in Sebastian's voice as he asked, *Six months? Is that all?* His reluctance to answer my questions, using Milo to keep me at arm's length and then running off

before I could pin him down. How he'd admitted to loving Alison once, but acted as though he had no intention of seeing her ever again . . .

And the one piece of information that made sense of everything.

Alison could taste when people were lying.

Sebastian had told her she needed time to decide who she was and what she wanted, and that if he came back to Sudbury with her, he'd only get in the way. Apparently he'd meant it. But how could he expect Alison to let go and move on unless she believed she'd never see him again? Or since that plan had gone down in Deckard-shaped flames, unless he could make her believe that he was no longer interested?

No wonder he'd been avoiding her. Not because he'd stopped caring, but because he hadn't. And the moment he spoke to her—maybe even the moment he *wrote* to her—she'd know it.

I knew, then, that I'd misjudged Sebastian. Worse, I'd handled the situation so clumsily and made myself so obnoxious that I'd practically forced him into avoiding me. I might be able to fix things if I could get in touch with him again—but I had an unhappy feeling that I'd already blown my chance.

—Niki? You still there?

I'd just started to apologize and explain when the phone chimed. Sebastian! Maybe it wasn't too late after all. Abandoning Milo mid-sentence, I picked it up and blurted "Hello?"

There was a two-second pause. Then a soft tenor voice said, "Hello, Tori."

It wasn't Sebastian. It was Deckard.

"Why did you run away? No one wants to hurt you, Tori. I only want to talk to you."

He spoke gently, with a faint undertone of reproach. As though I should be ashamed of myself for making him go to the trouble of stalking me.

And that was his mistake. Because unlike Alison, I knew when I was being played. "Excuse me?" I said, blandly and a little more quietly than usual—I didn't want to wake the Parks. "I think you have the wrong number."

"I don't think so," said Deckard, unfazed. "I'm very thorough about these things. But a lot of good people are worried about you, Tori. You're a sick girl, or you soon will be. Why don't we meet for coffee somewhere—wherever you feel most comfortable—and talk about it?"

Tori. Tori. Tori. The sound of my old name was like a slow drip on the top of my skull. "I'm not sick," I said tightly. "And I have nothing to say to you, or the people you work for."

"There's no need to be hostile," Deckard replied. "I'm only trying to help. I'd hate to see you throw your life away over a misunderstanding."

If this had been an old-fashioned landline, I'd have hung up before he could trace the call. But cell phones worked differently, and I'd taken every precaution to make mine secure. Now that he had my number, he might be able to check my recent phone records to see who I'd been talking to and what towers the calls were coming from, but not without a warrant and definitely not on a weekend. Besides, if he knew where to find me, he wouldn't have bothered calling.

"You don't care about me," I told him. "All you want is to know what really happened to me last summer. And all

GeneSystem wants is to put me under a microscope and figure out what's wrong with my DNA. Well, I guess you're both going to be disappointed. Because I've left town, and I'm not coming back until you're gone. Maybe not even then."

For two seconds Deckard was silent, and I thought I'd beaten him. But then he said, "So how are your parents doing, Tori? Are they having a good weekend in Toronto?"

He knew. He knew where they were. Fear knifed into me, and my blood went cold.

"You know," Deckard went on, "I have to wonder what the police would think of some of the people your father dealt with when he set up your new identities. I also wonder what would happen if your dad's employers knew he was living under an assumed name."

If I'd ever been tempted to doubt that Deckard was dangerous, that ended it. My first impulse was to shout at him and tell him to leave my dad alone—but then the analytical part of me kicked in. *Some of the people*, he'd said. *His employers.* No names, no specifics. And even if he'd tricked the neighbor into telling him where my parents had gone, Toronto was a big city. Big enough to disappear in, if it came to that.

"Good questions," I told him, forcing myself to sound calm and even slightly amused. As though he hadn't shaken me at all. "But if you're so sure you know where my parents are, why don't you go and ask them? Maybe if you buy them a few drinks, they'll tell you where to find me."

"I doubt that," said Deckard. "But I suppose I could always try Alison again. I'll probably get more out of her this time, now that it's obvious that the two of you are back in touch."

Which made me wonder how it was obvious, but I doubted

he'd been reading her e-mail. Because if he had, he'd already know everything she could tell him about last summer—and everything I had to say about it too.

Still, I couldn't bear the thought of him harassing her again. Especially now.

"Alison Jeffries is mentally ill," I snapped, though it sickened me to say it. "She's got a head full of psych meds and sci-fi novels, and she can barely keep her feet on the ground. You know what she'll say, if you push her hard enough? She'll tell you we were abducted by aliens. Is that the kind of answer you want?"

Deckard let out a short laugh. "I really don't think—"

"Fine. Try it, then. But when she ends up back in the hospital and her family sues you for mental cruelty, how about you give me another call? Just so I can say I told you so."

"There's always Sebastian Faraday," said Deckard, recovering quickly. "Now that he's back in the country."

I couldn't see any point in pretending I didn't know. Especially since the ATM where he'd been spotted was only a few blocks from my place. "Sure," I said. "If you can find him. But I don't think you will, because right now I can't even find him myself."

The pause that followed told me that I'd surprised Deckard, but it didn't keep him from trying again. "Look," he said. "There's no reason this has to be so complicated. What do you want? I'm sure we can come to some kind of agreement."

Until now I'd been holding myself together by acting like my mother—not imitating her voice this time but imagining how she'd behave if she were in my place. Pretending to be someone older, someone who was Deckard's equal, so I wouldn't have to think about how much he scared me. But I couldn't do it anymore.

"I want you to stop chasing me," I said thickly. "I want you to stop threatening the people I love. I want to live my life in peace, without always having to fight and hide and run away. I'm not hurting anybody. Why can't you leave me alone?"

Then I hung up, blocked Deckard's number, and burst into hot, humiliating tears.

Sebastian was missing, and without him, the transceiver I'd built was useless. I had no way to protect myself from Mathis if he came after me and no guarantee that I'd be safe even if he didn't. If Deckard was willing to threaten innocent people like my parents and Alison just to try and get me talking, what would he do when he got his hands on me? And how long would it be before he did?

I rubbed the wetness from my eyes, hating myself for letting Deckard get under my skin and Jon for being stupid enough to give him my number. Though in a way that was my fault too, because I'd let Jon go on thinking he still had a chance with me, instead of telling him honestly to forget it . . .

–Niki? You still there?

Milo's last text still glowed on my screen. I gulped a breath and typed my reply:

–Deckard just called. I'm a mess. Sorry.

I half expected Milo had given up on me by now, but it took him less than ten seconds to answer.

–Want me to come over?

I could think of at least three good reasons to tell him no. It was late, it was dangerous, and there was nothing he could do to fix the problem anyway. And what if his grandparents woke up and caught us? But I was past reasoning now. All I wanted was comfort.

–Yes. Please.

Then I sneaked downstairs and sat on the front steps, shivering and hugging my knees until the light of Milo's bicycle came flashing around the corner. He leaped the curb, dropped the bike onto the lawn, and started toward me, and I leaped up and ran to him, and if he'd been Brendan, he would have tried to kiss me and ruined everything, but he wasn't, and he didn't. He just stood there and held me until I stopped shaking and could breathe again.

101101

When Mrs. Park knocked on my door the next morning and told me it was time for breakfast, I was so tired I could barely open my eyes. Milo had been a comfort while he stayed, but he hadn't stayed long, and after he left, my mental gears had been too busy whirring and grinding with anxiety to let me sleep.

But as soon as I checked my phone, I was instantly awake. Sebastian had texted back at last.

–Sent Deckard to Montreal. Sorry to keep you waiting, I wanted to make sure he took the bait. Excellent news about the transceiver. How soon can I pick it up?

Montreal was 635 kilometers away. Not nearly as much distance as I'd like to put between myself and Deckard, but if he thought that was where I was hiding, it would keep him out of my way for the next few days at least. The relief was so enormous I felt like I could sleep for a week.

"Breakfast!" called Mrs. Park again, impatient now. I'd better get moving, though why she felt the need to get me up this early on a Sunday was beyond me . . .

Oh. Oh no.

I threw on a T-shirt and jeans, ran my fingers through my hair, and galloped down the stairs. Maybe when they saw me with dirty, wrinkled clothes and no makeup, they'd realize I couldn't possibly go to church with them.

As soon as I reached the dining room, though, I knew I was in trouble. The Parks were seated at either end of the table, dressed in their Sunday best, while between them sat a platter full of plump golden pancakes . . . and Milo.

"Hey," he said, waving me to a chair. "Sit down, quick. *Harabuji* needs to pray before the *hoddeok* gets cold."

His tone was so casual, you'd think we barely knew each other. There was no sign of the boy who'd raced ten kilometers to hold me last night. I sat and bowed my head while Pastor Park said a blessing in Korean, and then we all dug in to the pancakes, which were frankly the most amazing thing I had ever tasted in my life. There was no need for butter or syrup, because they had this incredibly sweet, nutty filling inside. By the time I'd eaten two of them I felt ready to slide into a sugar coma, and Milo was grinning at me across the table.

"I should send friends to stay with my grandparents more often," he said. "I haven't had *hoddeok* in forever."

"You should come to see us more often!" said Mrs. Park reproachfully, but she was smiling. She offered Milo the platter, and he helped himself to another pancake.

Once we'd finished and Mrs. Park was washing the plates, I leaned over to Milo and whispered, "Am I supposed to go to church with them?"

"Well, I am," he said. "I've been bribed with pancakes. But if you really don't want to go, they won't force you."

"Good," I said. "Because I just got a text from Sebastian, and he's on his way." I glanced at Pastor Park, seated quietly on the sofa with his Bible open in front of him. "We're going to meet at the makerspace in three hours."

"And then what?" Milo asked. "You hand over the transceiver and he takes off again?"

"No," I said. "This time, I'm going with him."

101110

As expected, Milo didn't like my plan at all, but it didn't take him long to soften up and come around. Ever since the moment he'd seen Sebastian come through the relay he'd been irresistibly hooked on this adventure, and he'd never be able to rest until he'd seen how it all turned out.

Besides, if last night hadn't been proof enough, he really liked me. Even after seeing me first thing in the morning with messy hair and no makeup, apparently—or at least that was how I interpreted the way his gaze lingered on me before he followed his grandfather outside. It was a good thing Mrs. Park's back was turned, because if she'd seen that look, there would have been some serious Korean drama.

"Thanks again," I said to Milo's grandmother, shouldering my overnight bag. "The food was amazing. I'm sorry I couldn't come to church with you, but maybe another time."

"You are welcome," she said. "And we were glad to help. To show you the love of Jesus." She reached into the living room cabinet and took out a wrapped present, presenting it to me formally in both hands. "This is for you."

Even covered in stripes of red and gold, that flat rectangle looked uncomfortably familiar. I had a feeling I was about to inherit a pointed Bible message about honoring my parents or honesty being the best policy or some other platitude I really couldn't stomach right now. "Oh, I couldn't—you've already been so kind—"

"I insist," she said firmly. So I gave in, and the two of us went out to the car.

I'd assured the Parks that it was safe for me to go home now, because my stalker had left town and my parents would be back in a few hours. And it was the truth—for certain values of "safe" and "few", anyway. As they let me off in front of my house, Milo signed at me through the rear window: *I'll text you later.* I nodded and waved as they drove away.

It felt strange being home after two days' absence and even stranger not to see Crackers toddling down the hallway to welcome me. I shut the front door and locked it, then headed off to dump my overnight bag and throw my dirty clothes in the laundry.

I'd unearthed my old duffel bag from the closet and was stuffing clothes into it when I realized I hadn't opened Mrs. Park's gift. Feeling guilty for my lack of enthusiasm, I picked it up and tore off the wrapping.

As expected, it was one of her handmade texts. It wasn't in English, though. It was in Korean, and I couldn't read a single character except for the reference at the bottom: ISAIAH 41:10.

She must have given me the wrong package, but I wasn't sorry. The calligraphy was beautiful, as were the flowers and leaves that surrounded it, and now I wouldn't have to wonder what not-so-subtle message she'd been sending me.

Still, I could at least look up the translation. I opened the browser on my phone and tapped the reference in.

> "Fear not, for I am with you;
> Be not dismayed, for I am your God.
> I will strengthen you,
> Yes, I will help you,
> I will uphold you with my righteous right hand."

That wasn't anything like I'd expected. It was kind of a nice thought, actually.

I only wished I could make myself believe it.

101111

When I got to the makerspace, Sebastian was leaning against the door with his hands in his pockets, waiting for me. He looked thinner than the last time I'd seen him, with shadows circling his eyes and dragging at the corners of his mouth, and I could tell I wasn't the only one who hadn't been getting much sleep. But when he saw me, he broke into a smile that made him look ten years younger, and he came bounding down the steps to meet me.

"Let me get that for you," he said, tugging the backpack off my shoulder. "I'll put it in the truck."

So it didn't surprise him that I'd figured out his next move and come prepared. I followed him around the corner to the old black Silverado he'd parked in the factory's loading zone and studied its rust-eaten wheel wells and sagging exhaust with misgiving. "If you paid more than two grand for that thing," I said, "you got robbed."

"Ah. Well, never mind." He opened the door and tossed my pack into the back seat. "I didn't. Much."

So much for the small talk. I took a deep breath. "Sebastian? I owe you an apology."

For a moment Sebastian didn't move. Then, quietly, he shut the door and turned to me. "What for?"

"Well, I've been pretty hard on you about the Alison thing," I said. "Especially since I should have talked to her myself, before things got so bad. But I kept telling myself it was too risky, and once you came back, it was easier to put the blame on you. Even though you didn't deserve it."

"You don't think I'm to blame for the way I've treated her?" His voice sounded rough. "I find that hard to believe."

"Well, it took me a while to figure out what you were doing," I said. "But now I get it, and I understand."

"Do you? "

"Sure," I said. "I know you want what's best for her. Even if it's hard for her to see it that way."

Was he buying it? I couldn't be sure. Sebastian's poker face was even better than mine. But when he cleared his throat and said, "Well, then. Apology accepted," I knew I was still in the game. I was breathing a mental sigh when Sebastian looked around and said, "Where's Milo?"

"At church with his grandparents," I said. "Why?"

Sebastian's eyes narrowed, and I could practically hear him thinking. Then he took out his phone, tapped a quick message, and put it back in his pocket. "All right," he said. "Let's go and take a look at your transceiver."

So we went inside and knocked at the makerspace's door. Shawn opened it, looking startled to see Sebastian behind me instead of Milo. But when I told him we'd come to pick up the transceiver, his face cleared. "Oh, you're done already? Awesome. Your dad's gonna love it. Hey, need a hand trolley? I can get you one."

"Thank you," said Sebastian warmly. "That would be very helpful."

Shawn darted through the vinyl-strip curtain into the woodshop and started banging around in one of the cupboards. I led Sebastian up the ramp to the clean room and unveiled the transceiver.

"It's been tested and calibrated," I said. "It should be good to go."

Sebastian stooped to inspect it, examining the enclosure from all sides. "Niki, it looks superb. You've outdone yourself."

Once the compliment would have made me glow. Now it just made me feel queasy. Not because I doubted Sebastian's sincerity but because I knew how much faith he was putting in my abilities. If the transceiver didn't work, after all this . . .

"Wait," Sebastian said. "Where does the relay fit?"

That, at least, I deserved credit for. I tapped the barely visible square panel on the cabinet's side, then popped it open to show him the slot I'd custom-built for the purpose. "Here are the connectors," I said, pointing out the plug at the bottom and the thin metal probe dangling above. "All we have to do is hook it up and close the panel, and nobody will even know it's there."

"Excellent!" Sebastian straightened up. "You've thought of everything." He glanced around the room, taking in the darkened computer terminals along the back wall, the shelves crowded with small tools and parts, and the assortment of half-finished projects waiting for their makers' return. "This is quite a place," he said, as Shawn came up with the trolley. "You've obviously put a lot of work into it."

"Yeah, and we've got some great plans for expansion too," said Shawn. "You should—whoa, you okay with that?"

"I'm fine," I said, lowering the transceiver onto the foot of the trolley. I stepped back and Sebastian took over, wheeling it down the ramp toward the door.

"You guys have been great," I told Shawn. "Thanks for helping me out."

"Hey, no problem," said Shawn. "Come back any time. When you hit eighteen, maybe we'll even give you a key." He flashed me a grin and went back to his laptop.

I smiled too but wistfully. Between running from Deckard and hiding from Mathis, I'd probably never see this place again. I gazed around the clean room one last time, letting myself imagine all the things I might have built here, the friends I could have made, if my life had been different. Then quietly I collected my tool kit and my box of spare parts from the locker and slipped out.

1 1 0 0 0 0

The inside of Sebastian's truck smelled like diesel, grease, and old leather, with an afternote of cheap pine freshener. I couldn't help wondering what colors and shapes those smells would have for Alison—but I knew better than to say that out loud.

"So," I said briskly as I buckled myself in, "where are we going?"

Sebastian turned the key in the ignition, which caused the truck to cough and give a full-body shudder. He slung his arm across the top of the seat, watching out the back window as he reversed. "To get Milo," he said.

Somehow, I wasn't surprised. Sebastian seemed to like having Milo around—probably because it kept me from asking too many questions. "And then where? Because my parents are coming home tonight, and I need to know what to tell them."

"You mean you haven't guessed?" asked Sebastian. "We need a large antenna to transmit that signal. We're not going to find anything of that size here."

I drew a sharp breath. The biggest radio antennas I knew of were down in the States—a *long* way down. "Tell me you're not serious."

"Is it that bad? I thought it would be an adventure, myself." He patted the dashboard. "And this seemed like just the vehicle for the purpose."

"You want to drive all the way to *New Mexico?*"

Sebastian made a spluttering noise, and then he started to laugh. The truck swerved, and I grabbed the steering wheel and straightened us out just in time—hello, déjà vu.

"All right, fine!" I snapped. "I don't have any idea where you're talking about. Does that make you feel superior enough? Because you seem to enjoy that."

That sobered him. He sat back, curling his long fingers about the wheel. "I apologize," he said. "No, we're not going to Arecibo. We're not even leaving the province. Have you ever visited Algonquin Park?"

It was the largest wilderness preserve in Ontario, a massive seven thousand square kilometers filled with pine trees, rocky lakes, and bears. Camps and cottages dotted the outskirts, but the interior was infamously remote. Lara had gone on a Girl Guide canoe trip to Algonquin two years ago, and when she got back, she couldn't stop talking about it. She'd described the haunting calls of the loons that glided by their campsite in the morning, the bull moose they'd nearly bumped into while navigating a swamp, and I'd envied her every moment of it, even the mosquito bites. Because back then I'd still had that stupid chip in my arm and I couldn't go anywhere.

"No," I said shortly. "I haven't."

"Well, about sixty years ago the National Research Council set up a radio observatory in the middle of the park, including a forty-six-meter antenna on an equatorial mount. The antenna broke down in the mid-eighties, and the government abandoned the site rather than spend the money to repair it. But a few years ago a small space communications company leased the property and fixed the antenna, and now it's a private venture. So I've made arrangements for us to stay at the observatory for a couple of days and use their antenna for our little experiment."

If calling the experiment *little* was an understatement, *made arrangements* was an even bigger one. It wasn't hard to guess why Sebastian looked so tired—he must have spent days faking some academic credentials and writing a bunch of articles about his so-called research before he called the observatory and introduced himself. Then he'd had to work out all the equations to figure out the technical requirements for the transceiver, write the specs so I could get started building it, and design a complicated piece of software to get the antenna, the transceiver, and the relay to talk to each other. And just when he was as busy as he'd ever been in his life, I'd texted and asked him to get Deckard off my tail.

No wonder he hadn't replied right away when I told him the transceiver was ready. By then he must have been practically in a coma.

"I had no idea," I said, and I wasn't just talking about the antenna. "So how are you paying for all this? You must be scraping the bottom of your bank account by now, and if Deckard and his police buddies used it to find you once—"

"That was carelessness on my part," said Sebastian. "I should have known my main account was being watched. But I had a couple of other, better guarded accounts as backup. And I always made sure to keep a decent amount in each one of them, since I knew I might have to change my identity at any moment."

Even so, I suspected that a *decent amount* wasn't more than a few thousand dollars all together, or Sebastian wouldn't have needed me to build him a transceiver from scratch. Not to mention that when Alison met him, he'd been working as a janitor and living in a tiny little basement apartment—hardly the lifestyle of a secret millionaire.

"You didn't answer my question," I said.

"No," said Sebastian mildly, "I didn't. It's being looked after, Tori. That's all you need to know."

And there he went playing big brother again. "It's Niki," I said. "Like Nikola Tesla, Mr. *Faraday*, and you really need to get out of that habit. Or I'm going to start calling you by your real name, and we'll see how much you like it."

Sebastian was silent, his eyes on the road. Then he said, "You know, at times it's difficult to imagine how you became the most popular girl in your high school."

"You know exactly how I did it," I said. "I watched people and did whatever it took to make them like me, or trust me, or feel like they owed me a favor. So they had to stop seeing me as an outsider, and accept me as one of their own. And don't tell me that you don't do the same thing, for exactly the same reasons." I folded my arms. "The only difference between us is that you think you can manipulate me the same way."

"So there's no such thing as kindness, only manipulation?" Sebastian shook his head. "That's quite a cynical outlook, Niki."

"Oh, please. You know that's not what I meant."

"Do I? I don't think you know me half as well as you seem to believe."

I rolled my eyes. "Fine," I said. "Far be it from me to violate your impenetrable air of mystery."

Sebastian gave me a sideways glance, and I could see I'd surprised him. "That's interesting."

"What?"

"Your vocabulary and diction just jumped several grade levels. That's deliberate too, isn't it? You keep your language simple so people won't be threatened by your intelligence."

"Well, you see," I said, "my mother taught me that it's rude to make other people feel inferior."

Which was catty, and I knew I'd probably regret it. But Sebastian only looked thoughtful. "Yes, of course," he said. "Your parents have obviously had a powerful influence on your life. Do you ever resent that? Have you ever tried to rebel?"

"Are we playing Twenty Really Personal Questions now?" I asked. "Because I'd rather stick to Animal, Vegetable, or Mineral, if it's all the same to you."

"Sorry," said Sebastian. "I was only curious. I hardly remember my own parents at all."

Well, that was awkward. I looked away quickly, counting the telephone poles flashing by the window, and we drove in silence all the rest of the way to Milo's house.

110001

Milo was waiting at the end of his driveway, casually dressed and with a sports bag slung over his shoulder. "This trip had better be educational," he said as he climbed in behind me. "Because not only do I have to write an essay about it, but there is *zero* legroom back here."

"What did you tell your mom?" I asked.

Milo slid to the middle of the seat and leaned between us. "The truth, more or less," he said. "Left her a note saying I knew this guy who was a scientist, and he'd invited me and another student to help him out with an experiment for a couple of days. Told her I'd cleared it with my physics teacher, which I actually did because Mr. Vanacek is on Facebook all the freakin' time. So I'm sure Mom'll be fine with it. Whenever she wakes up."

"Your mother's still working nights, then?" asked Sebastian. "Where?"

"Hospital," said Milo. "She's a trauma nurse. She wanted to be a surgeon, but, uh . . . that didn't really work out."

We made a fuel stop before we hit the highway, and Milo followed Sebastian into the store to get some snacks. While they were gone, I threw our luggage into the truck bed next to the transceiver, then climbed into the back seat so Milo could have the front. He tried to argue with me about it, but I told him to shut up because I wasn't being noble, I just wanted to go to sleep. Then I lay down and pulled Sebastian's car blanket over my shoulders, in case anyone was tempted to doubt it.

As I was drifting off, it occurred to me that Sebastian was even more tired than I was and probably shouldn't be tackling an eight-hour drive at the moment, Sunday traffic or not. I was wondering fuzzily if I should say something to Milo about it when I fell asleep.

110010

When I woke up, my mouth tasted thick and furry and my face was stuck to the seat. I rolled over, wincing, and rubbed my eyes. How long had I been sleeping? Longer than I'd planned, for sure. The sun was halfway to the horizon, and my left contact lens felt like it had been put in with superglue. Worse, the right one didn't feel like it was there at all. I was lifting a tentative finger to check when I spotted the thin circle of grey stuck to the edge of my hand.

Great. How was I going to put it back in now? My lens kit was in the bed of the truck.

". . . Literally, it means *'joined sensation.'*" Sebastian's voice rose over the sound of the engine. "When two or more of the five senses are interconnected, so that when one is stimulated, the other responds at the same time. When I met Alison, I discovered that she not only had multiple forms of synesthesia—seeing sounds, tasting words, and so on—but that her perceptions were extraordinarily acute."

I'd propped myself up on both elbows, ready to ask Sebastian to pull over. But if Milo had got him talking about Alison, there was no way I was going to interrupt now. Carefully I lay back down and listened.

"So there was no real reason for her to be in the psych hospital?" asked Milo. "They just put her there because they didn't know what was wrong with her?"

"Well, they had legitimate reason for concern," Sebastian said. "There was a family history of schizophrenia, for one thing. Alison's insistence that she'd seen Tori—sorry, Niki—disintegrate didn't help either. And at times her reactions could be . . . violent."

"Whoa," said Milo. "How violent?"

"No weapons were involved, if that's what you're thinking," said Sebastian dryly. "Even in her worst moments, Alison never hurt anyone on purpose. But being exposed to the relay had a powerful effect on her synesthesia. After Niki disappeared, Allison's senses were so raw that even the slightest touch felt like an assault, and when it became too much for her, she panicked and lashed out. So you can see why the police, and even her own family, made the mistake they did."

"And you're sure it was the relay that did it?" asked Milo. "Because Niki and I were standing right there when you came through, and it didn't do anything to us."

"No, but neither of you are synesthetes, let alone as sensitive as Alison. I admit I was skeptical myself at first, but once I'd seen the relay's effect on her firsthand, there was no doubt."

And that was another good reason for Sebastian to keep his distance from Alison, now that I thought about it. Especially since he was still carrying the relay around with him, and there was no way—yet—to be sure it wouldn't go off again.

I played possum for another five minutes, hoping Sebastian would let something slip that I didn't already know. But soon the conversation shifted to more casual topics, and by the time they'd started talking about the best places to eat in Sudbury, I'd had enough. I sat up, yawning, and asked, "What time is it?"

"Four twenty," said Milo. "That was a pretty impressive nap you took there. Want some Doritos?"

With the taste of sleep lingering in my mouth, I couldn't think of anything I wanted less. "Ugh, no," I said. "Can we stop at a Timmy's somewhere? I need coffee."

"We left civilization behind an hour ago," Milo said, tipping his head at the windscreen. Rocky outcroppings and stands of evergreen trees lined both sides of the highway, with a glimpse of blue lake around the next curve. "I don't think there's anything for . . ." He trailed off as our eyes met.

"What?" I asked, and then I remembered my missing contact. Which was really missing now, because while I was pretending to be asleep, it had dried up and fallen onto the floor. So now I had one grey-blue eye and one turquoise. "Oh. Yeah, I know. I lost a lens somewhere."

"And that doesn't bother you?" asked Milo. "When I had contacts, I couldn't stand to—" He frowned. "Wait. Who gets tinted contacts to make their eyes look *less* blue?"

"People who are trying not to get recognized, that's who," I said. "You had contacts?"

"For a couple years. But they bugged me and I kept getting eye infections, so finally I gave up and went back to glasses." He studied me, still looking troubled. "But yours . . . they're just for show, aren't they? You don't have any prescription at all."

I sighed and swiped the remaining lens out of my eye, rolling it between my fingers and let it fall. It wasn't like my disguise had protected me from Deckard, and I was tired of wearing contacts anyway. "Yeah," I said. "And for the record, I also dye my hair."

"Sure," said Milo. "Makes sense." But his voice was subdued, and I could guess why. He'd thought we were close, but he was starting to realize how little he knew about me. How many other secrets had I been keeping from him all this time?

Too many. But even now, I was afraid of telling him the truth. I still wasn't sure how he'd react.

"I dye my hair too," announced Sebastian. "Premature grey is so unflattering. Oh, look—is that a porcupine?"

As distractions went, it was a brave attempt, or at least the parody of one. But since the porcupine in question was lying half-smashed at the side of the highway with one paw stuck pathetically in the air, it didn't help much.

"No," I said wearily, "it's a metaphor for this conversation. Can we switch seats now?"

110011

We stopped for coffee and supper at a roadside diner north of the park. I'd eaten as much of my burger as I could stomach, and Sebastian and Milo were polishing off their slices of pie, when I remembered I still hadn't texted my parents.

Well, no point in putting it off any longer. I pulled out my phone.

> —On road trip with Milo and friend (responsible adult—no worries). Back in a couple of days.

I sent that one to my mother, then added a line about Deckard being safely out of the picture for the time being, and sent it again to my dad. Of course my phone clanked and lit up in seconds with Mom demanding to know where I was going and why I hadn't asked permission first. But when I explained that the trip to the observatory had come up at the last minute and that Milo had cleared it with his mom and teachers before we went, she calmed down.

Dad's response was shorter.

-Stay safe and keep in touch. We'll talk when
you get home.

Which would have sounded positive, except that I knew "we'll talk" was Dad Code for "You're in big trouble, young lady." But the important thing was, my parents knew I was alive and well—which was a lot more reassurance than I'd given them the last time I disappeared.

I just hoped this plan of Sebastian's would work. Or else the next time I went missing, it really would be the last.

Sebastian paid the waitress—in cash—and we headed back out to the truck. The sun was low in the sky now, casting long shadows through the trees and streaking the rocks with gold. The air smelled crisp and earthy. I breathed in slowly, savoring the wildness of it, and was surprised by a stab of homesickness—not for the south where I lived now, but for the north I'd left behind. I hadn't thought I'd feel that way, after being trapped in one place so long. Maybe it hadn't been quite so easy to pull up my roots as I'd thought.

Or maybe it was just the untamed beauty of the landscape that made me hurt inside, because it reminded me of what I'd always wanted and was afraid I'd never have—a life that was simple and honest and free.

Milo offered me the front seat again, and I took it without argument. According to the directions, we only had an hour and a half left to drive anyway. But when Sebastian returned from the back of the truck with a handheld CB radio, gave it to me, and said, "Channel 23. Once we get into the park, you'll need to call out our direction and location every kilometer so the logging trucks don't run over us," I realized that we were heading into some seriously remote territory. Places where only loggers and hard-core wilderness trippers ever went, and if we broke down, there'd be no handy tow truck or passing Good Samaritan to help us out.

In fact, once we turned off the highway, it quickly became clear that there would be no passing anything, period. The road was gravel and dirt, deeply rutted, and not much wider than the truck. We bumped along in silence for several kilometers, until we reached a closed gate with a warning sign beside it reading NO ENTRY. ROAD CLOSED TO UNAUTHORIZED VEHICLES.

"Now what?" asked Milo, but Sebastian merely shifted into park and jumped out to open the gate. He climbed up into the truck bed to check on the transceiver, making sure the straps that anchored it were holding and that the padding was still in place. Then he got back in and we started off again.

"Now would be a good time to start calling out our location," Sebastian told me, so I picked up the CB and spoke. "Black Chevy Silverado heading east at the two-kilometer mark. Over."

"This is amazing," breathed Milo, draping his elbows over the back of the seat and resting his chin on his wrist. "I bet we see moose. Maybe even a bear."

"Moose are good eating," I said. "Bears are just a nuisance. Move to Sudbury, and in a few weeks, you'll be sick of them."

"You have no soul," said Milo reproachfully, but I could see he'd recovered his good humor. Either the meal had lifted his spirits, or he'd finally got over the shock of finding that his pretend girlfriend was even more pretend than he'd thought. "So what's the deal with building a giant antenna in the middle of nowhere? Was it some kind of secret military project or what?"

"Nothing so exciting," said Sebastian. "They just wanted to avoid radio interference. Niki, you've missed another mark."

This was getting tedious. I raised the CB to my mouth and called out our location again, this time in my chirpiest shopping-channel voice, which made Milo snicker. At the next mark I did it in broad Cockney and the one after that in a southern drawl—I figured if the loggers had to listen to me babble the same message thirty-eight times, the least I could do was give them some variety. By the time I'd worked my way through Bored Hipster Girl, Scottish Lassie, and Indian Telemarketer, Milo was wheezing with laughter. But Sebastian didn't even crack a smile. His shoulders were hunched, hands tight on the wheel.

Nervous driver? He hadn't seemed that way before, but I suppose this part of the trip would be a challenge for anyone. With each passing kilometer the trees grew thicker and the swamps and lakes rose higher, so close to the road in places that a single rainstorm could have washed it out. And when I glimpsed a clear-cut patch in the bush and saw an enormous logging truck rumbling toward us, I realized just how vital that radio really was. If the driver had started off any earlier or been moving any faster, he'd have smashed us to bits.

Suddenly playing with the CB didn't seem like a game anymore. I called out our location one last time and handed it off to Milo.

The shadows deepened as we drove on, clouds flocking in from the east to darken the sky ahead. Sebastian switched on the headlights, but with so many sharp corners in the road, even high beams made little difference. Then a pair of luminous eyes shone out from the underbrush—and something galloped right in front of us. Milo yelled and Sebastian slammed on the brakes, but too late. The wheels went over it with a soft, sickening thump, and we nearly skidded off the road before Sebastian wrenched the truck back on course.

"What was that?" I gasped, twisting to look behind us. But the darkness in our wake was too thick.

"Raccoon, I think," said Milo, sounding equally shaken. "What is it with those guys, anyway? I thought they were supposed to be clever."

Sebastian didn't reply. His expression was bleak, his eyes narrow, and his mouth a thin line. "You okay?" I asked him.

"Fine," he said shortly, but I didn't have to be Alison to know that was a lie. I watched him, my uneasiness growing. Sebastian had been driving for seven and a half hours, and I was willing to bet he hadn't had a decent night's sleep in the last seventy-two. How much longer could he go on before he collapsed?

Fortunately, it was only three more marks before we spotted the yellow light pulsing out from the trees ahead, and our beams flashed over a sign reading MAGNUS LAKE RADIO OBSERVATORY. The crossroads offered us a choice of two gates, one chained shut and one angled half-open.

"It's too late to go to the antenna tonight," said Sebastian, before I could ask. "It'll take at least a couple of hours to set up our transceiver and connect it to the existing hardware, and we can't send the signal until tomorrow in any case." He steered the truck through the open gate, onto the paved laneway beyond. "We'd better check in at the bunkhouse. Dr. Newman's waiting for us."

110100

Dr. Hal Newman, the director of the observatory, was a stout, grey-haired man with rosy cheeks and sparkling eyes—in fact, if he hadn't been clean-shaven, he would have made a fantastic Santa Claus. He seemed delighted to see us, especially Sebastian, and lost no time introducing us to his staff (Liz the site manager, Brian the engineer, and graduate student Jacques) and showing us around. The wood-panel walls and burnt orange carpeting hadn't been updated since the disco era, but otherwise, the place was as clean and well equipped as any reasonable person could expect. I'd even scored a queen-size bed and a room all to myself, so I wouldn't have to listen to Sebastian and Milo snore.

"We're all very interested in your research," Dr. Newman enthused as we sat together in the lounge and dining area, where a row of windows looked out across the darkened lake. "If you're right about the nature of this anomaly, Dr. Ashton, it would be a tremendous discovery. My staff and I will be glad to help you in any way we can."

"Thank you," said Sebastian. "And please, call me Stephen."

Milo gave me a look that said, *"Seriously?"* I leaned against his shoulder and whispered, "You can have an alias too if it makes you feel better. How about 'Fred'?"

"It's too late to set up tonight," Dr. Newman continued, oblivious to Milo's snort, "and there's a storm moving in. Why don't we start first thing tomorrow?"

"That would be fine," said Sebastian. "But we should get the transceiver safely under cover, especially if it's going to rain."

"Oh, yes, of course." He gestured to his assistant. "If you want to drive over to the antenna now, Jacques here can open up the control building and help you unload."

"Thank you," said Sebastian. He pulled out his truck keys and tossed them to Milo, then looked meaningfully at me: *Go with them. Make sure nothing gets damaged.*

He didn't need to tell me. I nodded and followed Milo out.

110101

Night had settled over the observatory site, and it was too black to see more than the dim silhouette of the antenna, with its inverted-flowerpot base and its great dish angled up toward the sky. Still, even in the darkness it was impressive.

"Wow," murmured Milo, leaning over the steering wheel. "That's . . . big."

The control building was an A-shaped building of brick and glass, built in classic mid-sixties style, and the banks of old equipment inside looked more like an exhibit from a space history museum than anything useful. But there were newer devices and computer terminals scattered around the room as well—enough to reassure me that I'd have something to work with when the time came.

I held the door open for Milo and Jacques as they carried

the transceiver inside and set it down. A quick once-over reassured me that the wrappings were secure and that it had survived the bumpy ride intact. I'd give it a more thorough inspection tomorrow.

Raindrops pattered on the windshield as we drove away, turning quickly to a hammering downpour. We sprinted to the bunkhouse with our coats over our heads and reached the porch as the first fork of lightning split the sky.

"All settled?" asked Dr. Newman, as the two of us came in. He'd tucked his laptop under his arm and was heading for the east wing of the house.

"Looks to be," I said, shaking rain from my hair. "Where's, uh, Dr. Ashton?"

"In the library," he said. "We're going over the link budget calculations for tomorrow. Care to join us?"

I glanced at Milo, who was giving me a *please-don't* look that I understood completely. I liked math, but not at the end of a day like this. "That's okay," I said. "I think we'll take it easy."

"Of course. Make yourself at home—and stay up as late as you want. We're all grown-ups here!" He winked at me as though sharing a private joke and went off down the corridor whistling.

I turned accusingly to Milo. "I thought you said I looked older than my age."

"Well, with makeup and those grey lenses, you did. But right now, you look about fifteen."

I sighed. "Great. Now nobody's going to take me seriously."

"Did you want them to? I thought you were trying not to get noticed."

"Only to hide from Deckard and the people he's working for," I said. "And you know how well that went."

Milo gave me a sharp look. "He's working for somebody? Who?"

Crap. I'd grown so comfortable with Milo, I'd forgotten how little of my history he actually knew. "It's just a guess," I said. "It doesn't really matter."

"It matters to me," said Milo. "I like to know what's going on."

The reproach in his voice warned me that this was about a lot more than Deckard. "Milo, I wish I knew what to tell you. It's just so complicated—"

"Yeah." He spoke flatly. "You said that before. Look, I'm pretty tired, so . . ." He jerked a thumb toward the room he shared with Sebastian. "I'm going to call it a night."

Unless you give me a reason not to, he didn't say. But he might as well have.

"Sure," I said, forcing a smile. "Go ahead. I'll see you tomorrow."

110110

As soon as I'd finished unpacking I checked my e-mail on the observatory's Wi-Fi, but Alison still hadn't replied to the message I'd sent her. Maybe she needed more time to think about it, but I had a bad feeling my honesty had only made things worse.

I brushed aside the curtain and gazed out into the darkness—just in time to be dazzled by an enormous flash of lightning that silhouetted the pine trees and lit up the whole surface of the lake. The crash that followed was so loud it rattled the window. I grabbed my wash kit and retreated to the bathroom.

By the time I got back, the rain was pattering more softly and the thunder had subsided to an old man's grumble in the distance. I put on my pajamas and climbed into bed, pulling the covers around me. But I wasn't tired enough to sleep, and I couldn't relax. My brain was too busy thinking about Alison and feeling guilty about lying to Milo and worrying about what would happen tomorrow.

I stretched and flopped in all directions, trying to get comfortable, until finally I couldn't stand to lie in bed one second longer. I got up, pulled on a zippered sweatshirt, and walked out.

The dining room and kitchen were dark. But from the lounge beyond came the dim flicker of the TV, and the music and laughter of some late-night show. Wrapping the sweatshirt around me, I padded over—and there on the sofa, with long legs stretched out and the remote in hand, lay Sebastian.

"Hey, *Dr. Ashton*," I said. "Shouldn't you be in bed?"

"Did I wake you?" He swung his legs around, muting the volume as the show went to commercials. "Or are you regretting that afternoon nap?"

"Neither," I said. "I'm tormented by a guilty conscience. So I thought I'd come and join the club."

For six seconds Sebastian didn't say anything. Then he replied in a neutral tone, "I see."

I climbed into the armchair, pulling my knees up to my chest. "Tell me something," I said. "When you sent Alison and me back home, were you planning to wait a few hours and then come through the relay after her? Was that why you stayed behind, to take advantage of the time difference?"

"I had no opportunity to take advantage of anything," he replied, turning the remote over in his hands. "I knew time was moving faster for you than it was for us, but Mathis didn't give me the chance to calculate how long it had been before he let me go. I think he enjoyed the thought of keeping me in suspense—a petty revenge, perhaps, but more to his taste than murder."

I studied Sebastian's averted face. He was a good liar, but he still had a few tells if you knew where to look. Right now, though, he just looked tired.

"So what are you going to do if the transceiver works?" I asked.

"You mean if it doesn't work?"

"I mean what I said. Once the relay shuts down and you don't have to worry about it driving Alison crazy, are you going to talk to her? Or are you going to go on pretending you don't care?"

Sebastian switched off the TV and laid the remote gently on the table. "After all she's suffered because of me, don't you think she deserves better? Even if it was safe to go back to Sudbury, even if I could satisfy Deckard and settle the charges against me, it wouldn't be right to take advantage of Alison that way. I should never have let myself get so close to her in the first place."

Privately I agreed, but that horse had left the stable a long time ago and there was no calling it back now. "So you're going to do what you think is best for her, whether she likes it or not?" I shook my head. "Sorry, but you're not nearly old enough to be Alison's dad. And if you say one more time that she's too young and fragile to make her own decisions, I swear I will punch you in the face."

"Why?" Sebastian asked. "You saw that e-mail. You know the state she's in, and you know who's to blame—"

"I'm as guilty as you are," I interrupted. "Or more so. Because you've been out of her life for six months, but I could have been there for her, and I wasn't. I told myself it would be easier to lie to everyone else if I didn't keep reminding myself of the truth and that Alison needed to deal with things in her own way. So I shut her down, and then I abandoned her. Just like you did."

"If that's supposed to make me feel better," began Sebastian, but I cut him off.

"This isn't about you. The point is that Alison had every reason to doubt her own sanity, after what we put her through. But until Deckard came around and messed with her head and until she saw that ridiculous website about Meridian, she was doing okay. She's been through a lot worse than this and survived, so . . ." I shifted myself into a cross-legged position, tucking my cold feet beneath my thighs. "I don't see any reason why you shouldn't go and talk to her, once all this is over. Unless you're afraid she'll never forgive you."

"I'm not afraid of that."

No, he wasn't. He was expecting it. I puffed out a frustrated breath. "Fine. Do what you want. But you still owe her an explanation, when all this is over."

Sebastian raked a hand through his hair, silvery roots glimmering in the semidarkness. For several seconds he was quiet. Then he said, "Has she written back to you yet?"

He was trying to catch me off-guard, startle me into giving something away. But I was used to Sebastian's party tricks, and I wasn't surprised. "Not yet."

"What did you tell her?"

"What do you think?" I asked. "I told her the truth. I told her she wasn't crazy. I told her she was right about all of it, and

Meridian was just a fairy tale you made up for Milo." I paused to let that sink in, then went on more briskly, "Speaking of which, have you taken that website down yet? Because I know you didn't expect Alison to find it, but I think it's done enough damage already."

"I deleted it as soon as I saw her e-mail," said Sebastian. "I'd forgotten about Sanjay and his obsession with alien conspiracies. If I'd known he was still in touch . . . Anyway. It's gone now."

"Good."

"But if we're talking about the truth . . ." Sebastian leaned forward on his elbows, lacing his fingers together. "Have you told your parents yet? And what about Milo?"

The question was mild, but it set my teeth on edge. "My parents know as much as they need to know," I said. "They know I'm not normal, and I never was. They know I had a chip in my arm when they adopted me, and they know I was abducted and experimented on at least once. You think I need to add anything to that? How would it help them to know that I'm—"

The word caught in my throat. I tried to force it out, but it wouldn't budge. I shook my head and looked away.

"But they must have guessed at least some of the truth already," said Sebastian. "The technology that went into making that chip—into making *you*—is beyond anything this world has to offer, top secret experimental laboratories or not. Your doctor would have told them that the first time he examined you."

"Yes, of course," I snapped. "But there's a difference between 'Your baby was abducted by aliens' and 'Your baby *is* an alien.'"

There, I'd said it. The thing I'd known, or at least dreaded, as long as I could remember—until last summer, when my suspicions had been horribly confirmed. The secret Dr. Gervais had come close to finding out, even if she didn't realize it yet; the truth I couldn't confess to anybody, even the people who loved me most.

Alison knew, but only because she'd put the pieces together on her own. If she'd waited for me to tell her without prompting . . . well, she'd still be waiting.

"I don't know about that," said Sebastian calmly. "Some people are quite fond of aliens, at least in theory. Dr. Newman, for instance." He crossed his ankle up onto his left thigh and draped his arm over the back of the sofa, relaxed now that I was the one on the hot seat. "When I told him I'd spotted an anomalous object inside our solar system that might be an artificial wormhole and asked if he'd help me transmit a radio signal to those coordinates, he was positively delighted. He's been an active member of SETI for years."

That explained the warm welcome for "Dr. Ashton" and his two student assistants. "And let me guess," I said, remembering the well-worn equipment I'd seen in the control building. "You offered to give him the transceiver as payment."

"Well, one way or another, we're not going to need it after tomorrow. So it may as well be put to good use, don't you think?"

I rubbed my hands over my face, weariness creeping up on me. "I wonder if he'd be so eager to help," I said, "if he knew we were trying to close the wormhole and make sure nothing comes through it ever again."

"Yes. Well. Let's not find out, shall we?"

To anybody else, those words would have been a warning. But there was no need to remind me to be cautious of people in authority, no matter how friendly and well-intentioned they might seem. Mathis, Deckard, Dr. Gervais . . . they all had their reasons for wanting to get their hands on me, their own excuses for ignoring every attempt I made to resist them. Because when it came down to it, they all believed their lives, their goals, and their opinions were more important than mine. Why should Dr. Newman be any different?

"When you took that chip out of my arm," I said, rubbing the small scar above my elbow, "I thought I was safe. But I'm not, am I? Mathis could still send the relay after me if he knew where to look. And he still needs me back, if he's going to finish his experiment."

"I'm afraid so," said Sebastian. "Which was why I had to leave you, once I'd made sure Milo wasn't going to cause any problems. I wanted to keep the relay as far away from both you and Alison as possible, until I found a way to destroy it."

No wonder he'd looked so appalled when he'd realized I'd been keeping the relay in my bedroom. "So how much time do we still have, in theory?" I asked. "Shouldn't Mathis have made a move by now?"

"The problem is the time difference," said Sebastian. "Remember what I told you and Alison before I sent you home—the wormhole is temporally unstable. Mathis could have started programming the relay to search for you the instant I was out of the way, but on this end of the portal it could be days or weeks before the command gets through."

"Or hours," I said flatly. "And here we are at the butt end of nowhere, and you've got the relay in your luggage. I sure hope this plan of yours works."

Sebastian's mouth curled wryly. "So do I." He pushed himself to his feet and took a few steps, then paused and half turned. "Niki?"

I looked at him.

"I think you should tell Milo. Just in case."

"In case of what?" I asked, but Sebastian was already gone.

110111

Tap-tap.

I lifted my head groggily from the pillow, willing my bleary eyes to focus. The clock read 5:07 A.M., and I let out a groan. "This had better be good."

"I don't know about that," said Sebastian through the crack in the door, "but I'd say it's at least necessary. I've got the key to the control building. And I think it's time we installed that last component."

Meaning the relay, of course. And much as I resented being woken up after only three hours' sleep, I had to agree it was better to do the job when Dr. Newman and his staff weren't around to ask questions.

"Okay, okay," I mumbled. "I'm coming."

I dragged on some clothes and ran a comb through my hair, and by the time I'd finished I was more alert, if not exactly thrilled about it. It felt unreal to be getting up while the sky was dark, especially this late in the spring. But as I followed Sebastian down the steps to the parking lot, an enthusiastic chorus of birdsong assured me that dawn wasn't far away.

Milo was waiting by the truck, which shouldn't have surprised me as much as it did. He was the only one of us who'd had a decent night's sleep, for one thing, and he was used to getting up early. Though I still had to wonder why he'd made the effort . . . but maybe Sebastian had decided to bring him just for the look of the thing. Milo was supposed to be his assistant, after all.

So we piled in and drove to the antenna, and Sebastian opened up the control building. It was dark inside, but it didn't take long to find the lights, and soon I'd unwrapped the transceiver and popped open the hidden slot for the relay.

Now for the scary part. I hadn't touched the relay device in over three weeks—I hadn't even got close. What if it recognized me and beamed me straight back to Mathis?

And yet if I didn't take that risk, we'd never get anywhere. The transmitter part of the unit had more than enough power to send Sebastian's message through the wormhole, but no receiver on Earth could detect what was happening on the other side. Monitoring the relay was our only way to tell if the plan had worked. If the relay powered down completely and its automatic defense systems went offline—then we'd know its communications link to the space station had been severed, and Mathis could no longer find us. But without that, we'd never know if we'd succeeded in closing the wormhole or not.

Time to stop waffling, then, and get the job done. I pulled out a pair of rubber gloves from my tool kit, snapped them on, and held out my hand to Sebastian.

"It's been offline all this time," Sebastian said, as he took the dull metal sphere out of its case and passed it to me. "I don't think you need to worry."

"Well," I said as I eased the relay into its custom-built socket, "let's hope you're right." Gingerly I pulled out the metal probe, poised it above the top aperture, and began pushing it inside—

Tick.

"What was that?" asked Milo. He sounded alarmed. I couldn't blame him.

"It's not going in," I said distractedly, wiggling the probe around. It ought to reach right into the relay's quicksilver core; it was certainly long enough. But something was blocking its path.

A defense mechanism, to prevent unauthorized tampering? But I'd tinkered with the relay before with no difficulties, so what had changed now? I pulled out the probe, gripped the top half of the device, and tried twisting it open. It wouldn't budge.

Sebastian cleared his throat. "It wouldn't let me open it either," he said. "I suspect it'll only respond to a technician."

Milo looked surprised. "You don't know? I thought you helped design this thing."

"Before my time," said Sebastian. "I know how to use it, but that's all."

I looked down at my gloved right hand. Did I dare? My pulse was beating fast in my throat, but I reminded myself that I'd touched the device bare-handed before. I peeled off the glove and lowered my fingertips tentatively to the relay's surface. It warmed to my touch, as though in greeting.

Once again, I slid the probe through the top half of the casing, touched it to the core—and felt the faint tingle of connection. I'd done it. "Okay, Sebastian," I said, backing off and wiping my damp palms on my jeans, "we're good to go. Do you want to start up the transceiver and run some diagnostics now?"

"I can do that perfectly well on my own," said Sebastian, swinging his laptop bag off his shoulder, "so there's no reason to keep you. Why don't you and Milo walk back to the bunkhouse, and I'll see you at breakfast?"

I had an uncomfortable feeling that he was setting me up, probably hoping I'd take the advice he'd given me last night. Well, maybe it was for the best. Maybe it was time for me to stop keeping Milo at arm's length, and let him in.

111000

By the time Milo and I reached the bunkhouse the sky had lightened to the pale grey-blue of Alison's eyes, with a few white streaks of cloud along the horizon. The air was cool, and mist hung over the nearby lake.

"Too early for breakfast," said Milo. "Let's check out the beach." He jogged down the trail to the weed-dotted sand, scooped up a flat pebble, and flicked it out across the shallows. It skipped—once, twice, three times—and sank with a soft *bloop* beneath the surface.

There was a pair of Muskoka chairs by the shore, their cracked and flaking seats beaded with rain. I wiped one dry with my sleeve and lowered myself into it.

"Tough night?" Milo asked, picking up another handful of stones.

"Could have been better," I said. The morning was eerily quiet, our voices echoing in the stillness. From the other side of the lake came the lonely, warbling cry of a loon. "You?"

Milo sank three more pebbles one after another, then crunched up the beach and sat beside me. "Look," he said. "Can we skip the small talk? I'm not blind, Niki. I can see how worried you are. Whatever we're doing here, it's a lot more serious than you've been letting on."

My fingers tightened on the arms of the chair. I still wasn't ready for this conversation. But it had to happen sometime, and I couldn't put it off forever. "Yeah," I said quietly. "It is."

"I know there's some weird connection between you and the relay," Milo persisted, "and you didn't build the transceiver just because Sebastian needed it. This is more about you than him, isn't it? You're the one that Deckard and the people at Meridian really want. They only chased Sebastian because they thought he could lead them to you."

The treetops were glowing now, the mist over the lake swirling and lifting in tendrils as the sunlight burned it away. I nodded, not yet ready to speak.

"And I heard what you said to Barry about the transceiver—68 million kilometers." He was watching me closely now, unsmiling and intent. "This computer you're trying to shut down, the one that controls the relay—it isn't in some underground laboratory, is it? It's in space."

I nodded again.

"Why didn't you tell me about any of this?" Milo's voice rose. "Did you think I wouldn't help you? Did you think I'd be too scared to get involved if I knew how powerful Meridian really was?"

That was my cue to say it: *There is no Meridian.* To tell him about Dr. Gervais and Deckard on one hand and the wormhole and Mathis on the other, and to admit that everything I'd allowed him to believe about me was a lie.

But I couldn't do it. Because the first and most important

lesson my parents had drilled into me was that I should never tell anyone about the chip in my arm or my weird blood type or any of the other things that made me abnormal. I could talk to Sebastian and Alison about it, because they already knew—but when I opened my mouth to tell Milo, the words froze on my tongue. Especially *that* word, the one I couldn't speak even to my parents.

Alien.

"No," I blurted, hating the quaver in my voice and the way my eyes prickled when I said it. "Milo, you've been amazing, and I trust you as much as I trust anybody. I just didn't—I wasn't sure how to explain." And once Sebastian had started spinning his fairy tale about Meridian, I couldn't bring myself to contradict him. Especially once I'd seen how willing Milo was to believe it. "I figured that since you already knew I was in danger, the details weren't important. Just that you knew there was a risk, and you were still willing to help."

"Oh, yeah." His tone was bitter. "I've been a super big help on this trip." He smacked the arm of the chair and shoved himself back to his feet. "What am I doing here, anyway? Why did Sebastian ask me to come when it's obvious I can't make the slightest difference?"

It was a good question. At first I'd thought it was because Sebastian didn't like the idea of being cooped up in a truck with me for eight hours while I nagged him about Alison. But I'd already apologized for that before we left, yet he'd texted Milo and asked him to join us anyway. "Because it would look weird if he showed up with only one assistant?" I guessed. "Especially if that assistant is female?"

"Great, so I'm here to keep *Dr. Ashton* from looking like a perv. Nice to know." Milo scooped up a stick and flung it savagely into the lake. "But you've got to know there's more to it than that."

"Why?" I asked.

"Because he's been pushing the two of us together since the beginning, that's why. You should have seen the text messages he sent me the night after he ditched us at the café—about sticking close to you and making sure you had whatever you needed, and how he'd make it worth my while—"

"Are you trying to shock me?" I asked. "Am I supposed to feel horribly betrayed? Because if so, it's not working. I'm not surprised Sebastian made you that offer. But I also know that's not why you did it."

"Are you sure?" His voice was flat, his face turned to the lake. "I told you I needed money for university. And I'm going to need it even more once my mom finds out I'm going to Laurentian, because I'm pretty sure she's not going to pay for me to do the opposite of what she wants. You think you know all about me. But you're not the only one who can pretend, *Nicola*."

It was possible that there was something deeply twisted in my psyche, because the roughness in his voice and the shake in his clenched fists turned my insides to caramel. Except I wouldn't have felt that way if I'd thought, even for a second, that Milo meant it. He wasn't trying to hurt me; he didn't think I cared enough about him to be hurt. He was trying to protect himself.

"I don't know everything," I said, "but I know this much. You didn't hang around me for the money. You did it because you liked me and because you felt sorry for me and because you were curious about what was going on. And because you're a fundamentally decent and honorable guy, even if you are pretty frustrated with me and Sebastian right now."

"No kidding," he said, but the acid had gone out of his tone. "All I want is a straight answer, and neither one of you seems to know what that is."

I got up from the chair with difficulty—the seat was deep, and it hadn't been built for short people. I walked behind Milo and slid my arms under his, hooking my hands up around his shoulders. Then I leaned my cheek against the warmth of his back and said quietly, "I'm sorry. You deserve a better pretend girlfriend than me."

"I didn't know we were still pretend-dating," he said, trying to sound offhand. But I could feel his heartbeat quicken, and I knew I'd startled him.

"I don't know how to be anything but pretend," I replied, and it ached in me how true that really was. "But if I could be real, I'd be real for you."

He turned slowly, looking down into my face. He didn't kiss me, but I knew he wanted to. All I had to do was tilt my head up, raise my eyes to his, and it would happen. Mouth to mouth, skin on skin, an intimacy I might not even mind too much as long as he didn't slobber like Brendan. It would make Milo feel good and me less like a failure. If I couldn't give him the truth he deserved, at least I could give him this.

But I was tired of dishonesty, and kissing Milo now would be just another kind of manipulation. There was only one truth I could offer him right now, and I wasn't even sure he'd appreciate it. I bowed my head against his chest and drew a shuddering breath.

"I'm so scared, Milo," I whispered. "If the transceiver doesn't work—"

"It's okay," he said, his arms tightening protectively around me. "I'm here. I'm not going to let anybody hurt you."

As if he could stop the relay from beaming me back to Mathis, if it came to that. How could anyone stop a device that could turn itself invisible, move under its own power, and disintegrate anything that got in its way?

But Milo meant well. And it felt good to have someone solid and normal and uncomplicated to lean on, if only for a little while. So I closed my eyes and let him hold me, and I didn't say anything at all.

111001

We ate breakfast with Sebastian, Dr. Newman, and his staff—although Jacques was looking a little bleary and didn't say much, probably because he was nursing a cold. There was a lot of talk about gravitational microlensing and radar ranging and what it would take to prove that Sebastian's "anomalous object" was a wormhole, which made me glance uneasily at Milo. But he only looked blank for a moment before shrugging and reaching for another piece of toast.

"I knew Sebastian had talked them into helping him somehow," he said, when I caught up with him in the corridor afterward. "If they're happy to believe all that sci-fi stuff, I'm not going to argue with them. I could tell that guy Brian was skeptical, though."

"Skeptical is fine," I said. "I'm more worried about suspicious."

"I don't know why," said Milo. "It's not like you're beaming a death ray into Siberia. You're just sending a radio signal to switch off a computer on some satellite they probably don't even know exists."

Because it doesn't, I thought. But there was no point trying to say so after my failed attempt at honesty this morning. So I just smiled and headed for my room.

As I opened up my laptop to check my e-mail, it struck me that that incident by the lake wasn't the first time I'd been unable to go against my parents' orders. I'd thought I was stronger than that—no, I *knew* I was stronger. Sure, I respected Mom and Dad, but that shouldn't have stopped me from making my own decisions.

So what had stopped me in the hallway of the makerspace and kept me from confessing to Milo? It hadn't felt like fear or even guilt: it was more like a mental block. As though outright disobedience to the rules I'd been raised with simply didn't compute . . .

Then I spotted Alison's message in my inbox, and the thought vanished from my mind. Did she hate me for leaving her at Deckard's mercy? Was she angry that I'd known Sebastian was back and hadn't told her? Holding my breath, I clicked the e-mail open. *Thank you*, it read. *I can go on now. And yes, I forgive you.*

111010

The rest of the morning and the afternoon that followed passed both quickly and not nearly fast enough. First, Dr. Newman gave us a tour of the radio antenna—including a chance to walk right out onto its uptilted dish, which made me feel like a mosquito in a birdbath. Then we went back to the control building, where Brian, Jacques, and I started hooking up the new transceiver.

Strictly speaking, it wouldn't be my device that was sending the signal: that would be handled by the transmitter in the focus cabin of the antenna. Given a few extra hours, they could have winched the new transceiver up to replace it, but that would make it difficult or impossible for Sebastian to retrieve the relay on short notice. So he'd decided to route the signal through our unit to the observatory's unit instead, which caused a bit of head-scratching once Dr. Newman and his staff realized what we were doing.

Jacques was too stuffed up and semiconscious to care about anything but getting the job done, but there was a brief clash of wills between me and Brian, who was just as possessive about his equipment as I was about mine. We argued for a while about cabling and signal loss, but once Brian realized I'd built the new transceiver myself and knew what I was talking about, we came to a grudging agreement.

Meanwhile, Sebastian and Dr. Newman murmured to each other about azimuth and elevation and all the other calculations involved in directing the antenna. Milo sat in the corner with his laptop looking studious, but he had one earbud in, and when I sneaked a glance over his shoulder, he was reading up on the NBA playoffs.

We'd packed lunches before we left the bunkhouse, and since it was a beautiful day everybody went outside to eat them. But I could barely swallow a single bite. I went back to the control building, opened up the transceiver, and double-checked every circuit board, every wire. I ran my own set of diagnostics, including the incoming and outgoing feeds from the relay—something I hadn't dared to do when Brian was looking over my shoulder. Only when I was convinced that everything was in order did I back off and close it up again.

I'd dropped into a desk chair and was breathing into my hands, trying to get my nerves under control, when the others returned. Jacques wasn't with them—they'd taken pity on his wretched state, Sebastian said, and sent him back to the bunkhouse. But there wasn't much work left to do now anyway. Forty-five minutes later the radio telescope was in the correct position, the transceiver was online, and Sebastian's so-called experiment was ready to go.

"One minute fifty seconds and counting," he said, watching his computer screen. His fingers flashed over the keyboard, tapping out commands too quickly for me to read them. "Everyone ready?"

I got to my feet, moving closer to the console for a better view. I wanted to keep an eye on the spectrum analyzer, which would display our signal as it went out.

"One minute," Sebastian announced. I rubbed my goose-pimpled arms and tried not to shiver. Milo came up behind me and put a hand on my back, reassuring.

I wanted this to work. I *needed* it to work. Not that my troubles would be over if it did—I still had Deckard and GeneSystem to deal with. But it would be a colossal weight off my mind not to have to worry about Mathis anymore. To know that I still had a chance of making a life for myself in this world, instead of being snatched away to another one.

"Thirty seconds."

Milo's arm circled my waist, drawing me against him. I

covered his hand with mine as I mouthed the countdown, watching the seconds tick past one by one.

"Ten," said Sebastian. "Nine. Eight. Seven."

I could tell the drama was a little much for Brian, who glanced sourly at Sebastian as if to say, *Are you kidding me? We're not launching a spaceship here.* But Dr. Newman looked delighted as a boy on Christmas morning, and his voice joined Sebastian's on the final count:

"Three! Two! One . . . Mark!"

The spectrum analyzer spiked into peaks, and Brian yelped and snatched off his headset—this wasn't the signal he'd been prepared for. A noisy burst of what sounded like static but was actually Sebastian's quantum-encrypted transmission, rippling through the atmosphere and shooting out into the black emptiness of space. It softened to a hum, then faded away.

"You were expecting whale song?" asked Sebastian, as Brian shot him a glare. "My apologies."

"Now what?" said Milo.

"We wait," I told him and turned to Dr. Newman. "How long before the signal reaches the—uh—anomaly?"

"Just under five minutes," he said. He was frowning at the readings, obviously puzzled by the signal Sebastian had sent. "Of course, it'll take at least that much time again before we receive any kind of confirmation . . ."

Which made sense, because even the most powerful radio signal couldn't travel faster than the speed of light. But the relay's internal communication system was of a different order, and it shouldn't take nearly that long to find out if our plan had worked or not . . .

Except that the wormhole, as Sebastian had reminded me, was temporally unstable. So there was no telling how long it would be before we got a response. Feeling queasy, I detached myself from Milo and went to the window, staring up at the antenna as though I could see the radio waves bouncing off its parabolic reflector. Probably Alison could. I wished she were here.

When I focused on the glass, I could see Dr. Newman's faint reflection behind my left shoulder. He'd joined Brian by the spectrum analyzer, and the two of them were talking rapidly in low voices—no doubt trying to figure out what Sebastian was really up to. I was starting to have my doubts about whether we'd get away with this when Milo said quietly in my ear, "Look at Sebastian."

I turned around slowly, so as not to attract attention, and looked. He was sitting with his back to us, the screen of his laptop gripped in both hands. Lines of data were scrolling down the left side of the screen, and the waveform in the right—the one that monitored the relay—was oscillating wildly. Yet I'd never seen Sebastian so rigid or so utterly still. And when he slapped the laptop closed, yanked out the network cable and stood up, the face behind his smile was white as a dead man's.

"Excellent!" he said, too brightly. "I believe that's all we need for the moment. Thanks so much for your help." He seized Dr. Newman's hand and pumped it, then dragged me and Milo forward to do likewise. "Niki, would you have a look around and make sure we haven't left anything behind? Must dash—please excuse me—" And with that, he swung his laptop case over his shoulder and hurried out the door.

Milo and I looked at each other, and I could see my own

apprehension mirrored in his face. Whatever Sebastian had just found out, it couldn't be good. But there was no way to explain that to the observatory team. As far as their own readings were concerned, we couldn't know yet whether the experiment had succeeded or failed.

I could have murdered Sebastian for running out on us like this, but I couldn't afford to show it. Dr. Newman and Brian were suspicious enough already. All Milo and I could do was grab the relay and get out fast—and hope they didn't stop us and demand an explanation.

"Dr. Ashton's a little eccentric, you might have noticed," I said to the two scientists with an apologetic smile. "And I think, uh, there might also be a little bladder issue when he gets excited. Please don't take it personally."

Milo made a strangled noise, but I pinched his arm and he turned it into a cough. He pulled out his earbuds and started packing up his laptop. As soon as the others were distracted, I dropped to a crouch next to the transceiver and popped the hidden panel open. I thrust the relay into the pocket of my sweatshirt, resisting the instinct to fling it away from me and run. Then I picked up my tool kit and stood up again with all the professional calm I could muster.

"Thank you again," I said to Dr. Newman. "It's been very educational. I hope the new transceiver will be an asset to your work."

"Wait." The older man started forward. "What's going on?"

"Sorry!" I grabbed Milo's arm. "Can't explain now. Got to go. We'll call you."

Then I sprinted out the door and went after Sebastian.

When Milo and I burst into the parking lot, Sebastian was in the truck with the engine running, and a look of furious concentration on his face. "Hey!" I shouted. "Wait!" But he wrenched the wheel around and sped off without looking back.

I stopped and stared after the truck's plume of exhaust, unable to believe Sebastian had just ditched us. Then, angrily, I hefted my tool kit and started off in pursuit—but Milo stopped me.

"I know it's not too heavy for you," he said, reaching for the case. "But if I stuff it in my knapsack, we can run faster."

Fair enough. I let him have the kit and we started off again, pelting down the road in Sebastian's wake. Every now and then I glanced over my shoulder for signs of pursuit, but there were none. Probably Dr. Newman and Brian were too busy analyzing our data, trying to figure out what we knew that they didn't.

Ten minutes later, breathless and sweaty, Milo and I reached the bunkhouse. Sebastian had stopped the truck by the edge of the parking lot, but he hadn't gotten out. He'd shifted into the passenger seat and was hammering away at his laptop.

I slammed my fist against the window and yelled through the glass, "WHAT IS GOING ON?"

Sebastian flinched and set the computer aside. His eyes closed, as though he were praying for patience. Then he rolled down the window and said heavily, "I'm sorry, Niki. It didn't work."

Ice needled my stomach. "How do you know?" I demanded. "You got a signal through the relay? What was it?"

"Call it an error message," he said. "Or a fail-safe. Either way, we've been locked out."

I blew out my breath, slowly. Then I braced my arm along the top of the door and rested my forehead on it. "Does Mathis know?" I asked him.

Sebastian didn't reply.

"He does, doesn't he? You tried to hack into his system. He's going to trace that signal back to the relay, and when he does, he'll know—" Bile rose in my throat. I shoved myself away from the truck and whirled to run, but Milo flung out an arm and caught me.

"Hey," he said, gripping my shoulders. "I told you, we'll get through this together. There's got to be another way to stop him from finding you."

"You can't stop him," I said miserably. Even if the chip in my arm was gone, the relay still had my biodata on file. Eventually it would track me down, no matter how fast I ran or what obstacles I threw in its path. "Nobody can. We've lost, Milo."

"I don't believe that," said Milo. Then he grabbed the front pocket of my sweatshirt and shook it, and the relay dropped out into his hand. I tried to snatch it back, but he held me off with one arm, raising the silver sphere high with the other.

"What are you—" Sebastian began and then in rising alarm, "No! Don't—"

But Milo had already pushed me away and sprinted to the edge of the trees, where the blue lake glimmered between the branches. He leaned back with one leg raised, putting all his weight into it, and pitched the relay straight out over the water.

"There," he said, as he came panting back to join us. "If this Mathis guy wants to dive for it, he can go ahead."

I wanted to grab him and shake him until his bones rattled, but I couldn't bring myself to do it. It was my fault Milo didn't understand what kind of technology he was dealing with. And he'd turned away too soon to notice what I had—the flashing silver dot arcing toward the surface of the lake, then stopping abruptly in midair and winking out. The relay had gone invisible, and there would be no finding it now.

Not until it found me.

"You fool," said Sebastian in a low voice that was all the more terrifying for being so quiet. "You have no idea what you've just done."

"Really?" retorted Milo. "Then maybe you should explain it to me. Because as far as I could tell, the only *good* use for that relay was to help you send the signal to Mathis's computer or satellite or whatever. And you just told us that didn't work. So what's the point of carrying the thing around anymore, when all it can do is hurt Niki?"

Sebastian started to argue, but I cut him off. "Let it go," I said. "It's done now. If it comes after me, then it comes."

"But without being able to monitor it, we'll have no way of knowing—"

"I said, *leave it*," I snapped. "Who appointed you my Lord Protector, anyway? Because you've done a pretty crappy job of it so far. And I'm tired of being lectured and jerked around like this is all about you, when *I'm* the one with everything to lose." I nudged Milo, none too gently. "Come on, let's pack up. We're going home."

111100

As I stuffed clothes into my bag, I had an uneasy feeling that I'd pushed Sebastian too far. That when Milo and I got back outside, the truck would be gone. But when I came out of my room, Sebastian was waiting, his pack slung over his shoulder. He didn't speak or look at me, just stood there with his eyes on his battered loafers until Milo rejoined us. Then we all headed out to the truck.

I took the back seat, not feeling up to sharing my personal space with anyone at the moment. Sebastian gave Milo a hard look as he got in, but all he did was push the CB toward him and say, "Same as last night. Channel 23, every kilometer," before we drove off. As we sped toward the crossroads, I watched anxiously for the entrance gate, half expecting to find it shut and padlocked, and Dr. Newman waiting for us with folded arms. But the gate was wide open, and there were no other vehicles in sight.

The logging road was muddy from last night's rain, ruts slick and potholes brimming. We wallowed and bumped along with what seemed to me agonizing slowness, until the observatory sign and its yellow flashing beacon were lost to view. Soon after that, a narrow metal-grille bridge carried us over a set of churning rapids, but memory warned me that it was the last solid piece of construction we'd be seeing for a long time.

Overnight the swamps had risen even closer to the road, in places even washing right over it. I could hear water hissing through our wheel wells as Sebastian drove, and a muddy trickle crept along the floor beneath my seat. Milo sounded hoarser every time he picked up the CB, and Sebastian was muttering words under his breath that I didn't care to interpret. But nobody talked otherwise: we were all too focused on the road. It felt like decades in purgatory before we reached the gate out of the park and another six months until we left the gravel road behind and lurched onto paved highway again.

"Made it," I breathed, as the truck's laboring engine settled back into a steady roar. I hadn't thought either of the boys in the front seat would hear me, but Milo turned to look at me, his mouth set.

"All right," he said. "Explain to me what's going on with the relay," and then in true Canadian fashion he added, "*Please*."

"I . . . I don't know how," I said. "Sebastian—"

"Pull yourself together, Niki," said Sebastian, not taking his eyes off the road. "He's your boyfriend, not mine. Time to tell the truth for a change and see where it gets you."

As though I hadn't tried this morning to do exactly that, and failed. I had never hated Sebastian more than I did at that moment. But I sat up straighter and forced myself to try again.

"You were wrong about the wormhole," I said stiffly to Milo, wondering how much of the story I'd be able to get through before my tongue seized up on me. "It's real. Artificially generated and kept open by a steady influx of exotic matter from a machine on the other side. That's why we needed the transceiver to send a signal to those coordinates. To shut off the wormhole stabilizer."

"And we needed to do this," prompted Sebastian, "because . . . ?"

"If the wormhole closes," I stammered, "the relay won't be able to beam anything to or from Mathis's lab anymore. Because its sister relay and the computer that controls them both will be too far apart to communicate. And Sebastian, you're going to have to tell him the rest, because *I can't*."

Sebastian slanted a look at me in the rearview mirror, and I could see he was skeptical. But he said, "If you insist. What else do you want to know, Milo?"

"So if the wormhole is the shortcut from Point A to Point B," said Milo slowly, "then how far away is Point B?"

"There's no way to be certain," said Sebastian. "But at the best estimate, I'd say the two ends of the wormhole are at least a hundred light-years apart."

"Light-years—" Milo spluttered. "You can't be serious. How is that even—" He waved his hands in a vague, incoherent gesture. "You said the relay came from Meridian! I thought they were the ones who wanted Niki! Are you trying to tell me—"

"There is no Meridian!"

I hadn't meant to say it so loudly, much less yell it. But I couldn't bear to let this charade go on. I put my hands over my face and went on hollowly, "Sebastian made them up. And I went along with it. I lied to you. I'm sorry."

"Then . . ." Milo looked angry and more than a little nauseated. He turned on Sebastian. "That article on the website. *You* wrote that?"

Ahead of us the road sloped into a long descending curve, with a towering rock face on one side and a sheer ten-meter drop on the other. A lake lay at the bottom, dark blue and apparently inviting, but there were no boats on its surface, no cottages on its shores. No signs of life at all.

Just like Sebastian's eyes, watching mine in the mirror. Did he *want* me to hate him? I was beginning to wonder.

"Yes," I said. "He did. He created the whole website, just for you."

"Why?" asked Milo, hushed, and Sebastian answered,

"Because Niki needed someone to look out for her, and I needed to give you a story you could believe. At least until you were ready to hear the truth."

"What truth?" Milo spun around to me. "Niki, what is going on?"

If I didn't get the words out now, I never would. "I'm not—" I croaked. "I'm—" In desperation I tried to say *adopted*, but that was just as impossible. "I'm an—"

"Tell him," said Sebastian, low and firm. As though he had the right to give me an order. Or maybe he just wanted to make me so furious that I'd blurt out the truth without thinking about it at all.

Either way, it worked. "Alien!" I spat out and slumped back into my seat.

Milo froze. "What?"

"She is," said Sebastian, "as I am, a visitor from the other side of that wormhole." He paused, then added more briskly, "Though I came here the first time of my own free will, being young and stupid enough to think beaming myself to an unknown planet was a splendid idea. Whereas Niki was sent here as a baby by my old lab partner Mathis, who considered himself well rid of me and wanted someone more cooperative to experiment on. Does that answer your question?"

Milo took off his glasses and pinched the bridge of his nose. Then he gave a crackling laugh. "Well. That explains a lot."

"I'm sorry," I began, but he cut me off.

"Don't." He closed his eyes briefly, as though I'd given him a headache. Then he slid his glasses back on and looked at me. "Do you know what Deckard told me, when I accused him of being your stalker?"

I shook my head.

"He told me you were a pathological liar. He told me your parents were con artists who had made their money by manipulating people and that your family had Mafia connections. He told me you were good at making people like me feel sorry for you but that everything about you was fake. And he said I shouldn't get too attached to you, because you were the kind of person who'd abandon her friends in a second to save her own skin."

It was like looking at the truth through warped glass. But maybe that was how Deckard saw it. Maybe that was how Lara and Brendan and the others I'd left behind saw it too. I wanted to tell Milo that it wasn't like that, but why should he believe me? Why should he believe anything I said to him now?

"There's another thing you should know," Milo went on. "You know when Deckard got your cell number from Jon? It wasn't when he came into the store on Friday night and questioned everybody. He got it the next day, when Jon called him. Because Jon's aunt owns the Cakery, and he was working in the back when you and I came in together. So that was when he realized you'd been using him all along. Just like Deckard said."

The words wouldn't have stung so much if they hadn't been true. "How do you know that?" I asked. "Why would Jon tell you about—"

"He didn't. But when I got into work on Saturday, he grabbed me and said, 'Tell your girlfriend I hope she had fun making a fool out of me.' Once I remembered who his aunt was, it wasn't hard to do the math."

Sebastian was so quiet that he might have been invisible. This wasn't about him anymore, if it ever had been. This was between Milo and me.

"Alien, you say." Milo let out another humorless laugh. "I guess that explains the asexual thing? Don't want to get too close to the humans. Might get some kind of disease."

Sebastian's brows went up, and his eyes flicked questioningly to mine. *Asexual?*

"No," I said. "It has nothing to do with that. Milo—"

"Don't," he told me again. "I don't want to hear any more of what you think is the truth. I don't want to hear it even if it is the truth." He turned away and added quietly, "I just can't believe you've been lying to me all this time. I thought you were better than that."

Anger surged inside me. "Oh, yeah? Well, I guess it's easy for you to judge, seeing as you're such an expert on being honest with the people you care about. When were you planning to tell your mom your plans for September again?"

I waited, but Milo didn't speak. He just sat there with his back to me, shoulders stiff and his head unnaturally straight. Then he screwed his earbuds in and turned up his music so loud I could make out the lyrics from the back seat.

I knew, then, that I'd lost him.

111101

By the time we reached the gas station half an hour later, the silence had become toxic. Sebastian pulled up in front of the pumps and got out without saying a word. Milo disappeared around the side of the building, presumably looking for the washroom. I climbed the wooden steps to the convenience store and looked for something to fill the aching hole inside me, but the thought of putting anything sugary, salty, or chemically enhanced in my mouth made me sick. I wandered through the aisles, staring blindly at one shelf after another, until Sebastian came up behind me and said, "Never mind. We'll get something to eat in North Bay."

He pulled two water bottles from the fridge and went off to pay the cashier. I took out my phone and looked at it. There was reception here, so I could call my parents if I wanted. But I didn't have the heart to talk to them right now. I felt as though a single word of rebuke or kindness would break me.

So I texted:

–Heading home. See you around 11. Love you.

Then I shut off the phone.

When I followed Sebastian outside, the truck was parked by the edge of the road, with the tank filled and the cab empty. The tarp that had covered our baggage was loose, one corner flapping in the breeze, and Milo's pack was gone.

"Where is he?" I asked, whirling to look for him—but Sebastian put a hand on my shoulder.

"He's not coming with us," he said.

"But—"

"I know. But he can find his own way home from here, and maybe it's for the best." Sebastian sighed. "Though I'd hoped this would turn out differently."

So had I. I'd hoped that Milo would understand why I'd lied to him, that he'd give me a second chance. But he'd reacted just the way I feared my parents would, if I ever told them. Shock, disappointment and, finally, rejection. I pressed my fingertips against my eyes, warding off the sting of tears. Then I opened the door to the truck's front seat and climbed in.

"All right then," I said in a cool, brittle voice that hardly seemed my own. "Alien road trip it is. Let's go."

1 1 1 1 1 0

We stopped only once after that, for coffee and sandwiches. Sebastian drove fast and decisively, as though he were as impatient to get home as I was—except, I reminded myself, he didn't really have a home. And the closest thing he had to a family, on this planet anyway, was me.

Not that we were blood relatives, or at least I hoped not. We certainly looked nothing alike. But then, I had no idea who my biological parents were, except that one of them had been a technician. Or so Faraday thought. But what did that mean?

"Just what it sounds like," said Sebastian, when I asked him. He glanced over his shoulder, making sure the eighteen-wheeler lumbering up behind us wasn't too close, and merged into the fast lane. We were on the 400 now, heading south toward Toronto, and the traffic was flowing smoothly: with luck I'd be home in under two hours. "Technicians are bred to excel at building and repairing equipment. When a scientist or some other senior member of the Meritocracy requires a particular piece of machinery, the engineers design it and the technicians make it to their specifications."

Like I'd done for Sebastian, with the transceiver. "What if they decide to build it differently?" I asked. "Or get their own ideas about how to make it run better?"

"That doesn't happen," said Sebastian. "Or if it ever has, the Meritocracy made sure to quash the story—and probably the technicians involved—before anyone else found out. Technicians aren't bred for initiative. They're bred for dedication, endurance, and doglike obedience to their superiors. When there's a crisis, you can always tell who the technicians are, because they're the ones running *toward* the danger instead of away from it."

That description wasn't entirely me, thank God. But even so, parts of it hit uncomfortably close to home. "Doglike obedience," I echoed, making a face. "What a lovely way to describe it. Is that how my birth mother ended up pregnant? Because some engineer slapped his thigh and whistled, and she came running?"

"Possibly," said Sebastian. "But it could have been your mother who was the engineer, and it's also possible that your biological parents' affair was mutual. I don't mean that technicians have no will or initiative of their own. Only that they find it difficult to disobey a direct order."

One simple phrase, so casually spoken—and yet it hit me with the force of a bullet. No wonder I'd worked so hard to please my parents and do whatever they told me. No wonder I'd needed Milo to carry me into the makerspace that first time and choked up when I'd tried to tell him my secret. I had enough engineer in me to disagree with my parents and even argue with them at times, but when it came down to it I was still a good little technician inside.

And Sebastian was a scientist, which meant he outranked me. Was that why I'd gone along with his plan so readily? I'd grumbled at him and acted like I was doing him a favor, all the while telling myself I was building the transceiver for my own sake rather than his. But deep down I'd suspected—no, I'd *known*—that his idea wasn't going to work. Yet I hadn't tried to come up with an alternative.

Was any part of myself my own? Or was I just dancing to the tune of my manipulated DNA , and all the so-called choices I'd made in my life were an illusion?

"Tori?" said Sebastian. "Are you all right?"

As though he cared. As though it mattered, now. I thought about Milo, hitchhiking home from the middle of nowhere because he couldn't stand to be with me one minute longer. I thought about my parents, waiting anxiously for a daughter who was so much more than they'd expected and so much less than they deserved. And when I thought of telling them about the relay, I wanted to fling the door open and hurl myself into the oncoming traffic.

But I had to tell them something. Rightly or wrongly, they cared about me. And if I vanished again without warning or explanation, it would kill them.

"The relay," I said to Sebastian. "Do you think it followed us, after we left the observatory? Could it catch up to us now?"

Sebastian shifted restlessly, flexing his back and shoulders. "Well, it doesn't have to follow the road, so it can move faster and more directly than we can. But its scanning range isn't great enough to detect you at more than twenty kilometers' distance, which could slow it down considerably." He checked the rearview mirror and changed lanes again. "On the other hand, it did go into stealth mode after Milo threw it away. So it could be hiding anywhere right now. The back of the truck, for instance."

The idea made me shudder, but it only took me a second to dismiss it. Mathis wanted to locate me and beam me back to his lab as soon as possible. So if the relay was following me that closely, I'd be gone already . . .

But I wasn't.

Hope kindled inside me. Without a quicksilver chip in my arm telling the relay where to find me, it would have to scan in every direction to pick up my trail—and that would take time. Enough time, perhaps, that I could come up with a new and better way to protect myself. My own plan and no one else's, a plan that would actually work. I took a sip of my tepid coffee and felt the knot in my stomach loosen a little.

Sebastian hadn't relaxed, though. If anything he seemed to be getting more uptight with every kilometer. His hands were knotted around the steering wheel, and he kept hunching his shoulders as though they hurt him.

"Do you want me to drive?" I asked.

"You have your license?"

"Not yet, but I know what I'm doing. I won't tell if you won't."

Sebastian's mouth twitched. "Thank you. But I'll be fine."

And now he looked even more unhappy than before. Was it the shame of having his plan to stop Mathis fall to pieces? The disappointment of losing Milo? Fear for Alison's safety, now that the relay was out of his control?

Or was there something else on his mind that I didn't know about?

"Come on, Faraday," I said. "I know we're not exactly best friends, but I'm willing to call a truce if you are. What's going on?"

I made my voice gentle, even put a hand on his shoulder, but it didn't help. Sebastian flinched away from my touch as though I'd stung him. "Stop that."

So my charms were as wasted on him as his were on me. Well, nobody could say I hadn't tried. I sat back, folding my arms, and we drove the rest of the way home in cold silence.

I'd thought Sebastian was going to drop me off at my house. But when we reached the corner of Ross Street he turned the opposite way, into the graveyard. "What are you doing?" I asked.

"I think it'll be better to let you off here. For discretion's sake." He drove slowly up the cemetery lane and braked under a spreading maple, then jumped out, leaving the engine running. I was opening the passenger door to get out when he came around the back of the truck to meet me, carrying my bag.

I took it, ignoring the hand he offered, and climbed down onto the pavement. My legs felt weak from sitting so long, and I flexed them to get the circulation working. "It's been a trip," I said dryly. "Thanks."

Sebastian stood still, looking down at me. In the moonlight his face looked grey, and his eyes were tired and sad. "I'm sorry," he said. "I never wanted it to end this way." And he held his hand out for me to shake.

I sighed. Swinging the duffel bag to my left hand, I reached out with my right—

And Sebastian's fingers clamped around my wrist like a manacle. Before I could even cry out, he whipped his left hand out of his pocket and slapped something onto the inside of my forearm.

There was no pain. Only a millisecond of cold numbness, and the electric buzz of terror as I realized what it meant. I yanked my hand from Sebastian's and turned it over—to see the last shining drop of quicksilver, tiny as a pinhead, vanish under the surface of my skin.

I screamed, clawing at my arm in a desperate attempt to dig the stuff out. But my nails were too short, and it was too late. I could feel the liquid metal squirming into its preprogrammed shape, tendrils branching off in every direction as it tapped into nerves and muscles, arteries and veins. Learning my body's secrets, so it could transmit that information back to the relay—and to Mathis.

My knees buckled, and I crashed to the pavement. I hunched beneath the maple, sobbing and clutching my right hand to my chest. There was a chip inside me and the relay knew where I was and there was nothing I could do to protect myself now, nowhere in the world where I would be safe—

"I don't know how much time you have left," said Sebastian, so quietly I could barely hear him. "I hope it's enough. Good-bye, Tori."

Then he climbed back into his truck and drove away.

INTERLUDE: Deterministic Jitter

(A slight movement of a transmission signal in time or phase that can cause errors and loss of synchronization, and is reproducible under controlled conditions)

(3.1)

"So that's it?" I asked in disbelief, as Sebastian turned off the quantum impulse generator, and its low throb of power died down. "We're just giving up?"

We were standing in the main control room of the spacelab, where Sebastian, Alison, and I had first met Mathis nearly five hours ago. Only it was just Sebastian and me at the moment, because Alison was resting in another room, and we'd locked Mathis up in his quarters so he couldn't interfere with our attempt to escape.

An attempt which had, apparently, failed.

Sebastian braced his hands on the console and bowed his

head as though it was too heavy for him. "You built that generator perfectly, Tori," he said. "Thanks to you, we can open a wormhole again. The problem is, there's no way to tell whether it's the right wormhole to get you home. I thought I could compensate for the loss of the long-range sensors, but . . ." His shoulders slumped. "It's not going to work. I'm sorry."

A laugh broke out of me, so sharp it hurt my throat. "Sorry? You think that's going to make me feel better about being stuck here for the rest of my life?"

"No." Sebastian's long face was sober. "But right now, it's the only thing I can give you."

I couldn't look at him anymore. Swiping angrily at my eyes, I spun around and walked to the center of the room. Above me the domed viewscreen displayed a dazzling view of the stars, clearer and brighter than I'd ever seen them on Earth, but all the constellations were unfamiliar. Maybe I'd get used to that eventually, but I didn't want to.

I wanted to go home.

"I should talk to Alison," Sebastian murmured, sounding almost as lost as I felt. Then he walked out.

I sank onto one of the benches, numb to the core. I knew Sebastian was right about the long-range sensors, but part of me still couldn't believe it was over. I'd worked so hard to build that wormhole generator, reaching deep into myself to draw on instincts I'd barely known I had, and when it was done, I'd felt like a technological goddess. But it had all been for nothing in the end.

I stared at the floor for a few seconds, and then I got up again. I'd already had more than my share of emotional outbursts today, and I didn't have enough energy left for another one. I walked back to the console where Sebastian had been working, and looked at the cluster of touch panels and windows he'd left behind.

Most of the readouts were impossible for me to decipher, since they were in whatever language people spoke here. But in the top left-hand corner were a couple of tiny, colorful rectangles with moving shapes inside them. I touched the closest one and dragged it, and it expanded to show me a view of the room where Alison had been resting. She wasn't lying down now, though. She was sitting up, leaning against Sebastian as he sat on the bed beside her and told her the bad news.

I touched the window again and gave it a flick upward, splashing it onto the viewscreen in front of me. It expanded to fill the whole panel. Now the two of them looked almost as big as I was, the picture so clear and lifelike that I felt like I could have reached right into it and tapped Sebastian's shoulder or brushed back the tangled strands of Alison's hair. But if they knew I was watching, they gave no sign of it.

". . . Even if we could rig up a replacement," Sebastian was saying, his arm around Alison's waist, "it would take days to calibrate. Days we don't have. I'm sorry."

Alison didn't say anything. She just gazed at the wall until Sebastian said again, "I'm sorry," and then she turned to him and hid her face against his chest.

Well, at least Sebastian had been straight with her, painful as the news must have been for her to hear. But then, she had told me that he'd never lied to her yet—though how he'd managed to pull that one off I couldn't imagine . . .

And now he was kissing Alison, and she was kissing him back. Not a gentle let-me-comfort-you kiss, either. It was the kind of kiss that looked like it was going to end up horizontal, and Sebastian didn't seem to have any reservations about going there.

So obviously my apathy toward sex wasn't an Alien Thing, any more than it had been a Chip-in-the-Arm thing. It was just me.

Well, if making out made Sebastian and Alison feel better, I wasn't going to interrupt. But the idea of watching it happen was a definite Do Not Want. I swiped the image back down onto the console and squeezed it as small as it would go. Then I pulled the second window on top of it and opened that one up instead.

Mathis was sitting on the sofa in his quarters, dabbing dried blood from his nose. He looked disheveled and slightly dazed, as though the sedative had only just worn off. "Serves you right," I said aloud, knowing he couldn't hear—

But as I spoke, he looked around. Apparently he could. And when he touched something on the arm of the sofa and his eyes focused on mine, I realized he could see me too.

My heart rate jumped twenty beats a minute, but I told myself it didn't matter. Mathis and I had changed places: now he was the prisoner, while I was the one in control. "Sleep well?" I asked tartly.

Mathis stood up, smoothing back his brassy hair and tugging his crumpled tunic back into place. "Astin. Where is he?"

"He's busy," I said. "And even if he wasn't, I don't think he has anything to say to you at the moment. I, on the other hand, have plenty." I leaned closer, hoping to intimidate him. "What were you planning to do with me, before Sebastian stopped you?"

"If you thought he'd really stopped me, little girl," said Mathis, walking forward until his head and shoulders filled the screen, "you wouldn't need to ask."

Little girl. That was a laugh, coming from someone who looked a lot closer to my age than he did to Sebastian's. Just a junior scientist with big ambitions, so desperate to make a name for himself that he'd been willing to torture a baby and beam her through a wormhole to get the results he wanted. And so scared of competition, apparently, that he'd faked a relay malfunction and left Sebastian stranded on Earth for fifteen years.

"I'm asking," I told him, "because we outnumber you three to one. And if I were you, I'd be rethinking my original plans and trying to negotiate."

Mathis twitched a half-smile. "I don't think so," he said. "Because if you were me, you'd remember that before long the military will be arriving to take over this station. And if I'm not there to greet their commander and speak up for you and Astin and the Earth girl, you'll be identified as rebel intruders and shot on sight."

With sinking dread, I realized he had a point. I hadn't thought of that. But I wasn't ready to give up yet.

"Sebastian can speak for himself," I said. "If he was such a brilliant student, I'm sure at least some of your fellow scientists remember his name. And after what you did to him, maybe you should be more worried about whether he'll speak up for you."

Mathis laughed. "You're a clever one," he said, but in the same superior tone as a trainer might say *good dog.* I clenched my fists behind my back, resisting the urge to reach through the screen and throttle him.

"You still haven't answered my question," I said.

"That's because I don't know all the details myself. My intent was to keep you in isolation until the shuttle arrived, then take you back to the planet and turn you over to the senior scientists. What happens to you after that . . ." He tipped his head to one side in a shrug-like gesture. "They may decide to question you and keep you for further study. They may want to do their own experiments on you—to see how you react to certain bacteria and toxins unique to our world, for instance."

I had a sudden, vivid image of being trapped in a glass cylinder, choking and clawing at my throat as green fumes swirled around me. Of being naked and bound to a table, writhing as red welts and blisters erupted all over my skin. And as I screamed for mercy, men and women in neat grey uniforms watched me from a professional distance and took notes.

"At the least," Mathis went on blithely, "they'll take blood and tissue samples for further study. Likely they'll do a full brain probe and some stimulus tests as well."

I'd thought talking to Mathis might make him reconsider his attitude toward me, especially now that he'd had a literal taste of his own medicine. I'd hoped that my first impression of him had been wrong and that somewhere behind that smug facade he still had some sense of compassion, or at least shame.

But nothing had changed. In Mathis's eyes, I was only a worthless half-breed slave, a piece of biological rubbish he'd picked up cheap and had every right to use as he pleased. And now I realized, with sick certainty, that his fellow scientists felt the same way.

"And after that?" I asked, though I already knew the answer.

"Oh," said Mathis, "if you're still alive by then, we'll probably terminate you."

PART FOUR: Manual Override

(The process by which an automated system is suspended, modified, or otherwise put under the operator's direct control)

Ten

"Niki! Sweetheart, what's wrong?"

I'd come into the house quietly, hoping to wash my dirt-smeared face and put on some makeup before I talked to my parents. I hadn't wanted them to see me like this. But Crackers burst into excited barks as soon as he caught my scent, and before I could bolt, my mother came flying out of the kitchen to meet me.

"You look like a ghost," she breathed, catching my face between her hands. "Oh, honey! Who did this to you? Are you hurt?"

"I'll live," I said roughly, ducking away from her. I kicked

256

off my shoes and went into the living room, throwing myself down on the sofa and dropping my forearm across my burning eyes. The arm with the quicksilver in it—the chip Sebastian had put there. But why had he done it? *Why?*

Mom took a hesitant step toward me. "Do you want me to get your father? Or—is there something we should talk about first?"

I heard the catch in her voice, and I knew what it meant: she was trying to be calm and reassuring, because she thought that was what I needed. But inside she was terrified.

"Mom," I said hollowly, "I haven't been assaulted." Or at least, not in the way she thought. "Milo and I broke up this afternoon. But he didn't even touch me. He just . . . left."

"Oh." She exhaled the word, sad and slow. "I'm sorry."

"It doesn't matter. There's a bigger problem." I made myself sit up again. "Mom, I have something to tell you and Dad, and I need to say it quickly. Because . . ." I swallowed. "I'm going to disappear soon, the way I did last summer. And this time, I won't be coming back."

Nine

In the end, telling my parents wasn't as hard as I'd thought. I was still in shock over Sebastian's betrayal, and my initial hysteria had given way to a numb, fuzzy state where nothing seemed entirely real. Even as I talked, I felt like I was floating above myself, surveying the scene in the living room as a detached observer. Noticing odd little details like the dead fly on the coffee table and the flecks of toothpaste in my father's beard— things I would have dismissed or overlooked in the past but which held a strange fascination for me now. Maybe because I knew that whatever I set my eyes on, I might well be seeing for the last time.

But I couldn't forget how I'd got here or why I was telling this story. I needed my parents to know not only what was about to happen to me but what kind of person their daughter really was. All the secrets I'd kept from them, all the lies I'd told. How I'd taken my mother's painstaking lessons in kindness and courtesy and turned them into an operating manual for the human race, treating people like machines because that was the only way I could understand them or make myself care. How every relationship I'd ever had was an illusion, including my relationship with them. Because I'd been genetically programmed to submit to whoever owned me, so the choices I'd made to respect and obey my parents hadn't been choices at all.

"I don't belong on this world," I said finally. "I was never meant to be part of it. I know you wanted me to get married and have a family of my own someday. But I don't think that's ever going to happen, even if I could stay." I gave a pained shrug. "I'm just too . . . alien."

Tears had welled up in Mom's eyes, and now they spilled over. She buried her face in her hands, and Dad put an arm around her. Neither one looked at me or spoke. I might as well have been dead to them already.

Well, wasn't that how I'd wanted it? Now they knew I wasn't Their Kind after all, they wouldn't mourn me any more than they should. Maybe they'd even adopt another child to replace me. A nice, ordinary child who could fill the empty space I'd left in their hearts and give them the grandchildren they longed for. And in the end, they'd come to believe that my going away had been the best thing for all of us.

Or at least I hoped so, and I'd done everything I could to make that possible. Because the only thing I hadn't told them, the one secret I'd kept to myself, was what Mathis planned to do to me when he got me back. They didn't know—they didn't need to know—that all I could look forward to was a few weeks or months of captivity, before even that pathetic excuse for a life was taken away.

I got up quietly and began to leave.

"Tori!" Dad sounded hoarse, and his voice broke on the second syllable. He heaved himself up from the sofa to intercept me. "Don't. Don't you go anywhere."

And with that he threw his arms around me and hugged me so hard I felt like my heart would crack. I stood wooden in his embrace, too stunned to speak—and then I felt Mom reaching around me from the other side, stroking back my hair and pressing a kiss to my temple.

"You're our daughter," she whispered. "Always. No matter where you came from. Don't leave us, sweetheart."

I bowed my head against Dad's chest, swallowing tears. I felt ashamed of myself for not giving them more credit, for not realizing that their love for me really was as deep and lasting as it seemed. That it had never been about me being Their Kind, only about me being *theirs*.

But knowing that only sharpened the pain inside me. Because it reminded me how much I depended on my parents and how much it would hurt to lose them.

And now, even worse, I knew how much it was going to hurt them to lose me.

Eight

Neither of my parents wanted to leave me alone that night, for fear that I'd be gone when they woke up in the morning. So we dragged pillows and blankets into the living room and made ourselves as comfortable as we could. None of us slept. We all knew that every hour we spent together could be the last.

Dad kept quizzing me about the relay, unable to believe there wasn't some way of avoiding it, or stopping it from getting to me. I had to explain that the device flew too rapidly for me to outrun it and that it could scan through solid walls, so there was nowhere I could hide. Especially now I had this chip in my arm, telling the relay my exact coordinates at any given moment.

"And you know what happened when Dr. Bowman tried to remove the chip last time," I said. "The seizures nearly killed me. If we try anything like that again, they probably will."

Dad scratched his beard, mouth twisting with frustration. "Then we need to go on the offensive. Track down the relay before it can get to you, and destroy it somehow—"

"We already tried that," I said. "It didn't work. Just leave it, Dad. Please."

I knew he was trying to give me a challenge, so I wouldn't feel so helpless. I knew he thought I was giving up too easily, and it worried him. But my last hope had died with Sebastian's inexplicable betrayal, and when I reached into the part of my mind that fixed things, I found nothing but a dull grey fog. Even the thought of working on a new project felt like a colossal burden, too miserable to even contemplate.

Maybe I'd feel better once I'd slept. But I doubted it.

By dawn we were all cross-eyed with exhaustion, but the relay hadn't come. So Dad took the day off work, and he and Mom spent the morning sleeping in shifts. Once we were all awake again we played board games, watched a movie, and ordered in pizza for dinner. But it was all wrong—we were trying too hard to make every moment count, and that just made everything stiff and awkward and horrible. And by nightfall it was obvious that we couldn't keep on like this much longer, or we'd all go crazy.

So at eleven o'clock I announced that I was going to bed and that I'd leave my door open and yell if anything happened. Then I turned off my light and pretended to be asleep until my parents stopped hovering and whispering to each other, and went off to sleep as well.

In the quietness of the night, I was aware of every sound. Even the background noises I usually ignored—the creaks as the floor settled, the rustling of branches outside, the soft click of Crackers's nails as he waddled over the kitchen tile—made my nerves stand on end. Sleep was impossible and my thoughts were a tangled mess anyway, so I dragged my laptop out of its case and flipped it open. I'd never get the chance to pay Sebastian back for what he'd done to me, but it might make me feel better to demand an explanation and tell him exactly what I thought of him . . .

Except, I realized as I stared at the blank screen, I didn't have the heart even for that. Partly because I felt like someone had run over my emotions with a steamroller, and anger took more energy than I had left to give. But also because the shock of Sebastian's betrayal *had* been such a shock, which made me realize how much I'd trusted him, even liked him, in spite of everything. I'd pestered him about Alison not because I really believed he was being cowardly or cruel but because I'd felt sure there must be some good explanation, and I couldn't understand why he wouldn't tell me. And even though I'd tested his patience any number of times, challenged him and insulted him and demanded answers he obviously wasn't ready to give, I'd never imagined he would sell me out to Mathis because of it . . .

A soft chime sounded from the speakers, and a message flashed up on my screen. *MILO HWANG is ONLINE.*

Pride told me to ignore it. But I was so relieved to see his name that my fingers moved before I could hold them back.

    —Glad you got home OK. Can we talk?

Seconds passed, as I waited for his reply. Then came the sound of a door slamming and another message: *MILO HWANG is OFFLINE.*

Despair roared through me like a tornado, hollowing me out inside. I shoved the laptop away, not even caring if it fell, and curled up in the deep, smothering darkness beneath the blankets.

Seven

The next morning I got up early—which wasn't hard, since I hadn't slept all night anyway. Mom and Dad were still in bed and showed no signs of stirring. I dressed with mechanical efficiency, not bothering to brush my hair or put on makeup. I boiled some water and made myself a packet of instant oatmeal, which tasted like glue and weighed in my stomach like cement. I scrawled a note on the whiteboard telling my parents I'd gone for a walk and would be back around seven. Then I clipped Crackers's leash onto his collar and took him outside.

The morning sky looked like a nursery ceiling, baby blue with scattered puffs of cloud. A few maple seeds helicoptered down to land on the sidewalk at my feet. As Crackers trotted happily beside me, pausing at intervals to lift a leg or sniff a fire hydrant, I tipped my head back to the sunlight and drew a slow, deliberate breath of fresh air. Relax, I told myself. Enjoy this while you can.

But it was no use. I felt estranged from the world around me, as though the flowers and the birdsong and the smell of wet grass were meant for someone else and there was no point in me even noticing them. Exhaustion pressed down on me like a giant, invisible hand, and every time I inhaled my ribs felt tighter. Soon every breath was an effort, and my feet dragged. I wasn't walking Crackers; he was walking me.

I barely noticed when we turned away from the road and into the quiet, tree-lined paths of the cemetery. We passed the maple where Sebastian had betrayed me two nights ago, and I didn't even break stride. I was sleepwalking through a dream that could turn in to a nightmare at any moment, and if I stopped moving, I'd fall down and never get up again.

But it wasn't like I had anywhere to go, either. I was simply waiting for the moment when I'd be ripped apart at the sub-atomic level, reduced to a few quintillion bits of information, and fired back through the wormhole to Mathis. And when that agony was over, I'd have nothing but more torment and humiliation to look forward to. So what was the point of walking or breathing or even living now?

A black squirrel bounded across our path, and Crackers yipped and started pulling at his leash. I stumbled after him while he chased the squirrel up a tree. Then I leaned against the trunk and closed my eyes. *Pull yourself together*, I told myself. *Stop being so pathetic and whiny and useless, and* do *something.*

But what? Sebastian had put a chip in my arm, and the relay was coming. There was nothing I could do to change my fate, except—

A mournful whistle sounded in the distance. I turned my head toward the railroad tracks, running straight along the edge of the cemetery, and my stomach clenched hard, then unfolded like a flower.

Do something.

All my life I'd been fixing problems. Well, this time I was the problem. So why not fix myself? Why wait for Mathis and his fellow scientists to end my life, when I could take myself out of the equation right now?

It would take courage—all the courage I had. I'd have to measure the distance with my eyes and time my movements precisely, and then I'd have to repress every instinct that told me to run away. But my body was a machine, and I was a technician. I could do this.

The train howled again, louder now. I could hear the screech of its wheels as it braked, slowing down to prepare for the gateless road crossing at the cemetery's far side. Down the ditch, up the gravel, and onto the rails; a moment of terror, an instant of blinding pain, and then oblivion. Even if the driver spotted me, I'd be dead long before he could stop or the relay could interfere. Let Mathis beam my body back and pick over the bones if he wanted, or leave it for Deckard and Dr. Gervais to play with. Either way, I wouldn't be around to see it.

But first, I'd need to do something with Crackers. I led him to a nearby pine and looped his leash around one of the lower branches. Then I knelt down and tousled his soft ears one last time.

"Good doggie," I told him. "Sit."

He plopped down obligingly at the foot of the tree, watching me with innocent, liquid eyes. I kissed his nose, gave him a reassuring pat, and walked away.

The train's wheels were a heavy clack in the near distance. I thrust my way into the underbrush by the edge of the cemetery, keeping low so I wouldn't be seen. The driver would be looking ahead to the crossing, but I wasn't about to take any chances.

And now I could see the engine emerging from beneath the Second Street bridge, the north entrance into the cemetery. My legs felt rubbery and my head thick, but I crept down into the ditch and crouched there, counting seconds and measuring speed as the long chain of boxcars and tanker cars approached. Thirty kilometers per hour. Five hundred meters per minute. Eight point three meters per second.

Three hundred meters away.

Fear not, for I am with you, Mrs. Park's text had told me. Did that apply to someone who was committing suicide? Did it even count as suicide if you knew you were going to die anyway?

Two hundred and fifty.

Be not dismayed, for I am your God.

I wanted to believe that, but how could I? Whoever that verse had been written for, whatever had made Mrs. Park write it out so painstakingly and surround it with handmade flowers, it had nothing to do with me. I was a freak from another planet, a genetic mistake, and when I died that would be the end of it.

Or at least I hoped so. Because after all the lies I'd told and the people I'd hurt with them—people like Milo and Alison and Lara and even Jon—I didn't feel ready to face any kind of judgment right now.

"Forgive me," I whispered, to all of them. To my parents. To the universe, if anyone out there was listening.

Two hundred.

I will strengthen you.

A hundred and fifty. Eighteen seconds left.

Yes, I will help you.

"Help me," I breathed, as my trembling hands knotted into fists. "Help me do this."

Fifteen seconds.

Adrenaline sizzled into me. I kicked off the bottom of the ditch, flung myself onto the tracks and rolled over. The rail felt like ice on the back of my neck.

Ten seconds.

Crackers started keening, a high-pitched whine of distress. The pine branch rustled—he must be struggling with all the strength in his little sausage body. But I'd knotted his leash tight. It would hold.

The engine sounded a deafening blast, and the brakes let out another shriek. The rail was vibrating so hard my teeth rattled. I shut my eyes and tilted my head back, baring my throat to the wheels.

Seven. Six. Five—

Then came a loud *crack*, and my eyes snapped open. Crackers came pelting into the culvert with the snapped pine branch bouncing in his wake and launched himself at me like a caramel-colored rocket. He leaped onto my chest and began licking my face, deaf and blind to the train pounding toward us—

And with a scream of despair I grabbed Crackers, jack-knifed upright, and threw myself off the rails.

We crashed into the ditch together, Crackers squirming in my too-tight grip. The engine thundered past, showering us with bits of gravel, and as dampness seeped into my sock I was dimly aware I'd lost a shoe. But the boxcars were still grinding and rattling by above me, and I didn't dare move.

Crackers wriggled out of my arms and I cried out, afraid he'd bolt under the train. But he leapt in the opposite direction, the pine branch whipping across my body as he galloped away. He barked at me from the top of the ditch, urging me to follow, but I didn't have the strength. I could only lie there, stunned and spent, until the last whistle sounded and the end of the train clacked away into the distance. Then I crawled up the slope, floundered through the bushes, and collapsed onto the cemetery lawn.

Only a few minutes ago I'd felt cut off from the world. Now it all came rushing in on me, sights and sounds and smells all demanding my attention. The scent of crushed grass in my nostrils, salty blood on my lips. Crackers yipping excitedly, thrilled with himself for rescuing his pet human. The shudder of footfalls on the turf as Milo raced toward me, shouting my name.

This was why I'd come here, to this place, at this time. This was why I hadn't tied Crackers up more securely, even if I hadn't let myself think about what I was doing. Because deep down, in spite of everything, I loved my life and didn't want to lose it. And I'd wanted to see Milo again, even if only to say good-bye.

"Oh God," he breathed, dropping to his knees beside me and lifting me into his arms. "Oh God, Niki. *Why?*"

He'd seen the train go past. He'd seen Crackers running toward him, the broken branch tangled at the end of his leash. He'd seen me crawl out of the ditch. He knew what I'd almost done, and there was no way I could deny it.

So, in broken and gasping words, I told him everything.

When I was finished, Milo bowed his head, dark hair falling over his glasses. Then he pulled me closer, into the warmth of his body. "I had no idea," he said. "I'd never have left you alone with Sebastian if I knew—Niki, I'm sorry."

Still, it was selfish of me, maybe, not to pull away. Not to remind him that I'd be leaving soon and we'd never see each other again, and besides, I could never want him the same way he wanted me. But it felt so good to have him hold me that I didn't care. I dropped my face against his chest, brow pressed to the hard line of his collarbone, and closed my eyes.

"I'm not ready to die," I whispered. "I want to stay here and live, and make things, and be free. But I don't know how."

Milo cupped my chin in his hand, brushed my hair back, and kissed my forehead. Then he took my right arm and lifted it to the light.

"Show me," he said.

Reluctantly I let go of him and guided his fingers to the place where the quicksilver had wormed beneath my skin. Ten centimeters above the wrist, deep in the flesh of my forearm, where no one but Alison could see it.

"And we can't cut it out?"

I shook my head. There was a device that could dissolve quicksilver—Sebastian had used it on me last summer—but we'd left it on the other side of the wormhole. The only one who could disable the chip without killing me now was Mathis.

"Then . . ." He bit his lip. "Can we trick it somehow? Make it think it's got you, when . . ." He trailed off, then added with sudden savagery, "Or we could kill Sebastian. How he could do that, after everything you did for him . . ."

"It wasn't about me," I said wearily. That much, at least, I'd figured out. "It was for Alison. He wanted the wormhole closed to protect her."

"From what?" demanded Milo. "Aren't you the one this Mathis guy wanted all along? Why would he bother with some random Earth girl who had nothing to do with his experiment in the first place?"

"I don't know," I said. "Maybe he only threatened her to force Sebastian to betray me." And Sebastian had pretended to give in, thinking he could double-cross Mathis and destroy the relay or close the wormhole first. Only that plan hadn't worked, so he'd had no choice but to go through with the bargain. "Or maybe he found out about Alison's synesthesia, which is pretty incredible. A lot of scientists would give their right hand to—"

I will uphold you with my righteous right hand.

My breath caught in my throat, and my heart stuttered. I froze, the rest of the sentence forgotten, as a new and terrible idea blazed like a comet across my mind.

Could I really do something so enormous, so outrageous, so utterly appalling? It would take every bit of skill and determination I possessed. I'd have to confess some of my deepest secrets to people I wasn't even sure I could trust and put myself totally at their mercy. And even if I could get them all to cooperate, even if I had enough time to track down the necessary parts and build the device I needed, there was no guarantee my plan would work. I might end up hurting myself, traumatizing the people who loved me, and even beaming myself through the wormhole prematurely, with nothing to show for it.

But as much as the idea scared me, it was *my* idea. And though it might be the end of every dream I'd ever had and every ambition I'd ever treasured, it also felt like hope.

"What is it?" asked Milo. "You look like you're about to throw up."

"Alison," I said, struggling to my feet. "I need to call her. Right away."

Six

When I plunged through the front door fifteen minutes later, filthy and wild-eyed with Crackers barking hysterically at my heels, my parents nearly had a heart attack at the breakfast table. The next thirty seconds were total chaos, all of us talking at once and getting louder with every word. But eventually I got them to understand that I was okay, at least for the moment, and that I had a plan.

"But you have to let me do this on my own," I pleaded. "I need you not to ask questions or try to get involved. Because if you interfere, I won't be able to do it. And I *have* to do it. There's no other way."

Dad looked baffled, but Mom clapped her hands over her mouth. She'd seen it in my face—not the details of what I meant to do but the enormity of it. She knew I was about to do something that couldn't be undone and that whether I failed or succeeded, my life would never be the same again.

"Oh, honey," she whispered. "Are you sure?"

"Yes," I said, and turned to my dad. "So do I have your

permission? Will you trust me on this and promise you won't try to stop me?"

Every second I had left was precious, but I didn't dare rush him. I had to let him think it over and come to his own conclusion. But when he lifted his head and his sober brown eyes met mine, I knew the answer before he even spoke.

"You don't have to ask," he said. "You're not a child anymore. Do what you think is best."

My heart swelled. I threw my arms around him and kissed his cheek, then turned to embrace my mother. She clung tightly to me for three seconds, then kissed me and let me go.

"I love you," I told them. "I'll be back—I hope."

Then I bolted downstairs for my tool kit and parts bin, grabbed my phone from my bedroom, and dashed out. I was halfway down the driveway before I realized the bus wouldn't be fast enough and was about to drop everything and call for a taxi when Dad appeared in the doorway, holding up Mom's car keys.

"Drive carefully," he said. "Don't blow up the makerspace. Or yourself."

I hesitated. I wasn't surprised he knew where I was going, but how could he have guessed what I was about to do? I opened my mouth to explain—but Dad shook his head.

"Don't tell me." His smile was sad and tender. "It's probably better if I don't know. Love you, pumpkin."

Then he tossed me the keys and shut the door.

Five

I drove to the Sunrise Café, bought an enormous coffee, and spent the next hour contacting everybody I needed to help me

271

carry out my plan. I'd already talked to Alison, but I texted to confirm that she'd caught the early bus out of Sudbury and was on her way. I touched base briefly with Milo, to see how he was getting along with the worst research project ever. I called Barry, asking him to meet me at the makerspace right away. Then, last and hardest of all, I wrote to Sebastian.

Anyone else, even my past self, would have told me I was insane. If Sebastian had betrayed me to Mathis once, what made me think he wouldn't do it again? But right before he put the chip in my arm, he'd said that he was sorry and that he'd never wanted things to turn out this way. And when I thought back over everything that he'd done and said since the night he beamed into my bedroom, I believed him.

–This is your last chance as well as mine.
If you want to help me stop Mathis, you know
where to find me.

Then I packed up and drove off to meet Barry with my heart galloping all over my rib cage.

Not that our phone call had gone badly: Barry had seemed willing enough, if somewhat puzzled by my urgency. But my plan could so easily fall to pieces if even one person refused to cooperate, and I was afraid of how he'd react when I told him what I meant to do.

The answer, as it turned out, was something close to hysteria. He paced around the corridor outside the makerspace, waving his arms as he raved about unprotected electrical equipment and enclosed spaces and how he'd lose his membership if even the tiniest thing went wrong and how could I even ask—

"I'm asking you," I said with desperate calm, "because this

is the only place I know of that has all the equipment I need. And nothing that belongs to the makerspace will get damaged, I promise."

"You're right it won't," said Barry. "Because you're not going to do it here."

"Just listen," I urged him. "If I wire up a timed detonator with a kill switch, the EMP bomb won't go off until it's well out of range of the makerspace, or else we can stop the countdown before it happens. And to make absolutely certain that I don't wreck any of the equipment, I'll set it up in the woodshop and take everything electronic or explosive out of the room first. But I *have* to do this, Barry."

He gave a skeptical snort. "Look, there's no question that flux compression generators are cool. A lot of makers would love to build one, me included. But it's hardly a matter of life and death—"

"Yes, it is," I told him.

I'd been hoping I wouldn't have to tell Barry my whole story, especially since I knew how unbelievable it would sound. But I'd sworn to myself that I'd do whatever it took.

"I know I'm just some teenage girl you just met a couple of weeks ago," I went on quickly, before he could interrupt. "I know that right now I look like I just crawled out of an unmarked grave, and what I'm asking you to do sounds crazy. But I mean it, Barry. If I don't get that EMP bomb built and send it off fast, *I am going to die.*"

For a second, Barry looked shaken. But then he folded his arms. "Why should I believe that?" he asked. "It doesn't make any sense, for one thing, and you've lied to me before. All that stuff about having to build a transceiver for your dad's birthday—"

"I had good reason to lie," I retorted. "If I'd turned up at your Open House and said, 'Hey, there's an evil alien scientist who wants to abduct me, I need to build a deep-space radio transceiver to shut him down,' would you have listened to me?"

And there it was, in all its bald and uncompromising glory. The truth that would set me free—or destroy everything. I held my breath and waited.

Two deep furrows grew between Barry's caterpillar eyebrows. He stared at me for a full ten seconds, chewing his lip. Finally, he said, "So you're saying the transceiver didn't work?"

I shook my head.

"What'd you use for the antenna?"

"The Magnus Lake Radio Telescope," I said. "If you don't believe me, call Dr. Newman at the Observatory and ask if he's ever met a girl named Niki Johnson. Ask him if there's any chance that anomaly where we sent the signal could be an artificial wormhole."

Barry's scowl deepened, and I feared the worst. But then he sighed and reached into his pocket. "Len's never going to go for this," he said, "and Shawn's going to have an aneurysm. But at least we can get started before they show up."

Then he flashed his key card at the scanner, and the door clicked open.

When I first told Barry about my plan, I'd staked my life on the conviction that inside every maker, no matter how sober and responsible he or she might seem on the surface, is a big goofy kid who loves the idea of blowing stuff up. I was sure that Barry had at least some idea what a flux compression generator was and that if I could get past his initial reservations he might even enjoy helping me build one.

And I was right. As I opened up my box of tools and components and started scribbling a list of the additional parts I'd need to make an EMP bomb, he kept breaking in with comments like, "Oh, I know where to get you that capacitor," and "I saw a reflector that size over at Steve's last week." And by the time I'd told him the rest of my story—or as much of it as he really needed to know—he'd stopped questioning whether I could pull this off without frying all the electronics in the makerspace and started trying to figure out how to convince the other members to let me do it.

"So you believe me now?" I asked, as I handed Barry my shopping list and the cash I'd taken out of my bank account that morning. He'd already offered to drive around town and get me the parts I needed, and I'd accepted because he knew the local electronics and hardware dealers a lot better than I did. "Or are you just keeping the crazy girl distracted until the police show up?"

It was only half a joke. That was what had happened to Alison when she'd told her mother the truth, after all.

But Barry shook his head. "I don't think you're crazy," he said. "A bit paranoid, maybe. But I wouldn't bet my life on that, so I'm sure as hell not going to bet yours. Back soon." He tucked the list into his pocket and headed out.

Soon in this case turned out to be two hours and thirty-seven minutes, but I made good use of the time. Since it was the middle of the week, Shawn was at school and most of the other makerspace regulars were at their day jobs, so I was able to focus on my work without interruption. By the time Barry returned I'd finished the timer and the kill switch and was ready to start putting the main part of my EMP bomb together.

The flux compression generator. A single-use explosive device that would generate an intense electromagnetic pulse, capable of knocking out any equipment within a ten-meter range.

Like the wormhole stabilizer in Mathis's spacelab, for instance.

"I can't see how it's going to work at that size," said Barry as I squinted down the two lengths of metal pipe he'd brought me, one slightly narrower in diameter than the other. "And you'll need some explosive for that inner tube—"

"Don't worry," I said, rummaging in the bag and pulling out a coil of copper wire and a large box of safety matches. "I've got it covered. Thanks, Barry."

At two o'clock I was still absorbed in putting the device together, the lunch Barry had brought me sitting unheeded by my elbow, when my phone clanked. It was Milo.

—Bus from Sudbury just got in. See you soon.

—Great.

I replied, then hesitated and thumbed in another line:

—Best boyfriend ever.

Not exactly a declaration of undying love, but I couldn't afford to get emotional right now, and I knew Milo would understand.

Then I went back to work. I could hear Barry grunting and snipping wire in the background as he built a Faraday cage around the laser cutter, the only piece of vulnerable equipment in the makerspace that was too big for us to move. More minutes passed, until a familiar deep, quiet voice snapped me out of my distraction:

"I won't insult you by trying to justify myself. But if you still want my help, I'm here."

He'd always had a knack for dramatic timing, but this time Sebastian had outdone himself. I pushed up my safety goggles and studied him closely, searching for any hint that I might not be able to trust him after all, that the shame in his eyes and the self-loathing twist to his mouth weren't real. Then I put down my wire stripper and slid out of my seat.

"Come with me," I said, and led him into the woodshop.

F o u r

"No," said Sebastian faintly, when I'd finished telling him my plan. He shook his head and repeated, "Tori, *no*."

"Why not?" I demanded. "I did everything you asked, when it was your plan. Don't tell me you're too gutless to do the same for me. Or do you think I don't know what I'm doing?"

"Of course not." He put a hand over his eyes. "I don't doubt your capability. Or your courage. But there's no way this is going to work."

"Why not?" I asked. "When Alison broke my nose it was a good three seconds before the relay activated, so there should be enough time for you and Milo to move. And when it took me, it took my clothes and shoes as well, so if I strap the device to my arm—"

"That's not what I'm talking about," said Sebastian. "You're right about how the relay operates. But you'd need an extraordinarily sophisticated device just to detect its presence, let alone the exact instant when it starts to beam you away."

"That's not your problem," I said irritably. "I know all that and I've got it covered, so stop micromanaging me. All I want to know is, are you going to help me or not?"

277

Sebastian's throat moved convulsively as he swallowed. "There has to be another way."

"Yeah, well," I said, "I'm pretty sure that was what you were hoping when you made that devil's bargain with Mathis. But there wasn't, was there? Not in the end."

He was silent.

"Let me tell you what I think," I said, glancing at the doorway as Barry staggered past with the 3-D printer. "I think you thought you'd never have to choose between my life and Alison's. I think that all along, you were planning to double-cross Mathis and save us both. But when I got obnoxious, there was always the temptation to just put the quicksilver in my arm and be done with it, wasn't there? That's why you pushed me and Milo together. So there'd be somebody to protect me and make it harder for you to give in."

Which explained what he'd done at the gas station, on the way back from Algonquin. All Milo had wanted was a few minutes alone to get his head together, but when he'd come out of the washroom, his knapsack was sitting on the pavement and the truck was gone. Because by then, Sebastian knew he was going to have to betray me.

"It doesn't matter what I was trying to do." Sebastian's voice was rough. "All that matters is that I failed. And you're going to fail too, at a horrible cost to yourself, and I don't want any part of it."

"Too bad," I said. "Whether you knew it or not, you signed up for this when you shook my hand two nights ago. You put that chip in my arm. It's your responsibility to help me take it out."

"You'd rather do this than take your chances with Mathis?

Even if I told you he'd promised to make sure you were treated well and not terminated?"

I made a scoffing noise. "You think he's going to keep that promise? Your so-called best friend who left you stranded for years on an alien planet? The same guy who threatened to kill Alison if you didn't—"

"It was my fault." Sebastian sounded tired. "I should have remembered Mathis had access to the station's security system from his room—that he'd heard us talking about Alison's sensitivity to exotic matter, and the effect that the wormhole and the relay had on her synesthesia. He didn't threaten to kill her, Tori. He threatened to drive her insane."

There was a long silence. Beyond the vinyl-strip curtain in the doorway, a shadow moved and then went still.

"Oh, I see," I said. "So Mathis isn't a murderer, just a sadist? That makes me feel so much better."

"Tori—"

"Stop calling me that." I stalked around him, deliberately not looking at the line of power tools ranged along the countertop. "I don't want to know what lies Mathis told you or whatever excuses you made to yourself before you sold me out. I know I'm just a mongrel alien freak who was never meant to live on this planet in the first place, but there are at least two people in this world who love me and don't want me to go. I've got a couple of amazing friends willing to put everything on the line for me, and even Barry has been working hard all day to help me out. If you're too scared or squeamish to get your hands dirty, that's your decision. But you'll have to live with it for the rest of your life."

He didn't reply. I set my jaw and marched toward the door—

"Wait."

Thank God. For a minute, I'd thought I'd lost him.

"Why me?" Sebastian asked unevenly. "Why trust me with something this important, after all I've done?"

Because I understood him now, better than I ever had before. In a way, I even felt sorry for him. But I wasn't about to say so; that would be too much like letting him off the hook.

"Because you care enough to want to help me," I said, "but not enough to let the fear of hurting me hold you back. And because you'd do anything to redeem yourself, if you only believed that you could."

Sebastian gave a broken-sounding laugh. "This isn't redemption," he said. "It's more like retribution."

I shrugged, though inside I was anything but indifferent. "Call it whatever you want. But you may as well do it, because you're going to hate yourself either way."

Please, I added silently. For both our sakes.

For one last moment Sebastian stood without moving. Then he walked toward me, his dark blue eyes like bruises in the whiteness of his face. He said, "Do you forgive me, lady?"

I knew a little Elizabethan history too. Or at least I'd seen the movie. "It's my arm we're talking about, not my head," I said, speaking tartly to hide my relief. "But if you want to be all melodramatic about it, then yes. I do."

One corner of Sebastian's long mouth turned up. Then, before I realized what he was doing, he put an arm around my shoulders and gave me a hug.

"Just one thing," I told him, squirming out of his grip. "You have to *swear* to me that you'll carry through with this, whatever happens. And that you won't try to talk me out of my plan—any part of it—again."

"I promise," he said, sounding surprised. I glared at him, and he amended, "I swear."

"Good," I said, as I swept the vinyl strips aside and strode out into the lounge. Sebastian followed—and stopped, dismay dawning on his face. Because that was when he saw who'd been standing by the door all this time.

It hadn't been Barry—he was down the other end of the hallway. It hadn't been Milo, who was sitting on the sofa. It was a tall, slim girl with reddish hair spilling over her shoulders, and rain-grey eyes that looked too full of sadness to ever be happy again.

"Hello, Faraday," said Alison quietly.

Three

I'd been anticipating this reunion for a long time. In fact, before I'd left the Parks' house on Sunday morning, I'd asked Milo if he'd be willing to pick up Alison from the bus station while Sebastian and I were gone and bring her to meet the two of us when we returned. I'd envisioned the look on Sebastian's face when he saw her, the guilt and shame he'd feel, and at the time it had seemed like a fair punishment for the way he'd treated her.

But that was before I'd remembered that Sebastian had a very good reason to stay away from Alison, at least while he still had the relay on him. And definitely before I'd figured out that Mathis had forced him to choose between the freedom of an alien girl he barely knew and the sanity of the human girl he loved.

"Y-you . . ." I'd never heard Sebastian stammer before, and only once had I seen him this angry. "You brought Alison here on purpose? *She's* your relay detector?"

"It's not her fault," said Alison, with a tiny grimace as though she'd tasted something unpleasant. "I wanted to come. And didn't you just promise Tori you wouldn't argue?"

What it was costing her to stay calm with Sebastian right in front of her, I couldn't imagine. But though she looked tired and strained, she carried herself with a quiet dignity that made her seem older than the rest of us put together. She moved forward, holding out her arms to me, and before I knew it I was clinging to her and struggling not to ugly-cry all over her shirt. I hadn't realized until this moment how much I'd missed her.

"Is the relay close?" I choked, when I could speak. "Can you feel it?"

Alison pressed her lips together, visibly steeling herself. Then she said, "Show me your arm."

I unzipped my hoodie and struggled out of it, baring the T-shirt underneath. Then I held out my forearm, so she could see where the quicksilver had gone in.

Her face contorted and she flinched away from me, the same way she'd reacted to me the first day we were in school together. But back then I'd thought she was being rude and judgmental, and now I knew better. It was the chip that was bothering her, needling painfully at her senses in colors only she could hear.

"It's close," she said. She turned, her gaze following an invisible line from my arm to the corner of the ceiling. "There."

"*What?*" Milo jumped up from the sofa. "Where? I don't see it."

"That's because it's camouflaged," said Sebastian. "It must have found Niki the same night I put the chip in her arm, and it's been following her ever since."

Of course it had. How could I have ever believed otherwise? That was what the relay had been doing for most of my life—bobbing invisibly after me, or floating above my head, or lurking behind the nearest wall. Monitoring my vital signs through the chip, watching for any illness or injury that might compromise the experiment. Ready to beam me back to Mathis the moment my life was in danger.

And yet I knew now that my guardian devil had a weakness, one I fully intended to exploit. Because this morning when I'd laid my neck across the railroad track, my heart slamming in my chest and every muscle in my body rigid with terror, the relay hadn't done a thing. Mathis hadn't programmed it to care about my mental state, and he hadn't known enough about this planet's various threats and dangers to teach the relay to anticipate them. So it could only register any life-threatening injuries after the fact.

Which meant I didn't have to wait until Mathis told the relay to fetch me, or rather, until the time difference between the two ends of the wormhole sorted itself out and allowed the order he'd already given to come through. I could trigger the relay myself at a time of my own choosing and maybe—just maybe—shut down the whole experiment for good.

"It doesn't matter," I said. "Let it stay there for now. I've got an EMP bomb to finish, and the other guys from the makerspace are going to show up any minute."

Sebastian gave me a sharp look. "Are they? How much do they know?"

"Barry knows half of the plan," I said. "The technical half. The others, nothing."

"Then leave them to me," Sebastian said. He swung his laptop bag over his shoulder and headed out into the corridor, carefully not looking at Alison as he passed.

Not that Alison noticed. She was massaging her temples, her eyes squeezed shut in pain. "The Noise," she murmured. "It's so *loud*."

"I'm sorry," I said. "But it's going to be another forty minutes at least before I'm done here. Milo, could you take Alison out for coffee? I'll text you when I'm ready." Without waiting for an answer, I ran up the ramp and sat down at the workbench. I was reaching for my wire stripper when I felt Milo's hand on my shoulder.

"I've got the stuff you wanted," he said. "And I talked to my mom, so I know what to do. But I'm not going to lie, I don't feel ready for this. How are you holding up?"

All at once I was acutely aware of the tool in my hand. The slight weight of the metal, the rubbery texture of the grips, and the pressure of its handles against my palm. How I could twist it in any direction I needed, pinch it tight, and pull the plastic sheath off the wire in one easy motion. How easy it was to take such simple tasks for granted, until you couldn't do them anymore.

I clenched my teeth and reached for another length of wire. "I can't talk right now," I told Milo shortly. "I have work to do."

Two

I'd finished the main part of the flux compression generator and was wiring it up to the capacitor when Sebastian came back.

"Curiously enough," he said, slinging a hip over the corner of the workbench, "there's been a gas leak in the building, so the makerspace is closed for the rest of the day. Or at least that's what I told everyone on the mailing list."

And here I'd been imagining a nightmare of liability waivers and impossible explanations. I should have known Sebastian would come up with a much more simple solution. "Thanks," I said. "But what about Barry?"

"We'll deal with that when the time comes," said Sebastian. "At the moment, he's having coffee with Milo and Alison—are you all right?"

My hands were shaking. I put down my needle-nose pliers and pressed my palms against the workbench, silently cursing my weakness. But in the back of my mind all I could hear was Milo saying, *I don't feel ready for this.*

"This has to work," I said. "I need it to work. And I've tested the prototype in my head and it works fine, but Barry says he's never heard of anybody making an EMP bomb this small before, and what if I'm wrong?"

"A crisis of confidence?" Sebastian sounded surprised. "That's not like you."

I gave a bitter laugh. "Yeah, well, maybe this is what happens when a technician gets above herself."

"You're not just a technician," said Sebastian. "You're more than that."

"I don't know why you think so." I picked up a battery pack and put it down again. "You're the one who told me technicians were genetically programmed for obedience. And look at me. I'm seventeen years old, and I can barely even disobey my parents."

"Maybe," Sebastian said. "Maybe you grew up thinking of them as your masters, however subconsciously, and it's a hard habit to unlearn. But you're hardly a mindless drone. You stood up to Mathis, back on the station. You even stood up to me."

I shook my head. "Talking tough is easy. But actions? My whole life I've dreamed of making something new and exciting, something that would change people's lives. But the only times I've ever actually built anything important was when you asked me. This—" I waved a hand at the half-finished device on the workbench— "this is mine. The whole plan is mine. And nobody thinks it's going to work, or wants me to do it." My voice dropped to a whisper. "Even I don't want to do it. But what choice do I have?"

Sebastian reached out and laid his hand on my arm, right where he'd put the chip. He left it there for two seconds. Then, without a word, he got up and walked away.

One

Even finished, the EMP bomb didn't look like much—more like a twelve-year-old's Science Fair project than a weapon. It had none of the sleek, deadly menace of a rocket or the compact muscle of bundled dynamite. But all the right parts were there, and eight seconds after I pressed the button, it was going to send out an electromagnetic pulse strong enough to fry every piece of equipment in Mathis's control room.

Or at least I hoped so, but there were no guarantees. So many of the components I'd seen back on the space station had used metals and minerals I'd never seen before. And quicksilver was the strangest and most unpredictable element of all.

"I still don't get how this is supposed to work," said Barry, craning over my shoulder. "I know you've got a timed detonator, so you don't have to be there when it goes off. But how are you going to trick this relay thing into beaming up the bomb instead of you?"

He said *beaming up* with a relish that made my skin creep— but then, I reminded myself, he only half believed the story I'd told him. He knew I was afraid of being abducted by a scientist who might or might not be an alien, but if there was actual teleportation involved, he'd believe it when he saw it.

Unfortunately, he wasn't going to get the chance. I glanced at Sebastian and Milo, who had just come up the ramp, and nodded.

"Hey!" Barry yelped, as Milo grabbed his arms and yanked them behind his back. "What are you doing?"

There was a loud rip as Sebastian tore off a length of duct tape and plastered it across Barry's mouth. "Sorry about the beard," he said. He wrapped another strip of tape around Barry's wrists and lashed them together with a cable tie, while Milo dropped to the floor to work on Barry's ankles.

"I'm sorry," I said, as Barry's eyes rolled wildly and his face turned red. "But I can't ask you to be part of this. And trust me, you don't want to see it." Then I stepped back, and let Sebastian and Milo carry him out.

Alison came up to me when they had gone, forehead creased and eyes pained with the effort of ignoring my Noise. "Are you ready?"

My insides shriveled up like match-lit paper. I pressed a hand to my stomach, but it didn't help. "No," I blurted. "I mean, everything else is. But I'm not."

Alison's expression softened. "I know what that's like."

She did too. Because back on the station last summer, after Sebastian told her our attempt to find the right wormhole had failed, she'd volunteered to stand in for the missing long-range sensors and use her synesthesia to get us home. She'd been scared to start with, but the first wormhole she looked into had nearly broken her—the sensations were so overwhelming, so excruciating, that she'd thought she was losing her mind. I'd begged her not to give up, and in the end she hadn't. But how she'd found the courage to put herself through that torment again and again, knowing each time how much it would hurt and what it would cost her, was something I'd never understood.

"How did you do it?" I asked her. "When you had to find our way home?"

Alison looked down at the floor. "It's hard to explain," she said. "I remember I got to the point where it was so bad, I couldn't fight anymore. I felt like I'd come to the end of myself, and there was nothing left of me that was worth holding onto, even if I could. So . . . I let go."

I frowned. "You mean you stopped caring what happened to you?"

"No. I mean I stopped trying to control it. Stopped thinking it was about me being strong enough or brave enough to save you and Sebastian, or even myself. Because I couldn't do it, not on my own. And once I accepted that, it was like this enormous burden had rolled off my shoulders. I realized that everything that was happening or had happened or was going to happen next—it wasn't *about* me. The universe was so much bigger than that. So everything was going to be okay, in the end."

I stared at her. She gave an apologetic shrug. "Sorry. That probably doesn't make much sense."

"Yeah," I said slowly. "It sounds like you had to be there."

But I did understand, a little. If I hadn't come to the end of myself this morning, I'd never have come up with a plan like this. And if I thought the whole thing depended on me, I'd never have the courage to go through with it.

Yet there was still so much that could go wrong. I couldn't test out the EMP bomb to make sure it would work. I couldn't be sure what range the relay's beam would cover when it activated or whether Alison would give me the signal in time. And if Sebastian or Milo froze up, even for a second . . .

I shook the thought away. I couldn't worry about those details right now. Either I was prepared to pick up this bomb and walk into the woodshop or I wasn't, and that was all that mattered. Whether I had the courage to go through with this plan even knowing it could fail, or whether I'd rather give up than risk hurting myself for nothing.

Unless—the hope flashed into my mind, and I clung to it—I didn't have to make that choice after all. "Are we sure the wormhole hasn't closed already?" I asked. "I've been assuming the relay would go dead if there was no signal, but—"

"It's still open," Alison told me. "If it had closed, my synesthesia wouldn't be this strong." She winced and backed away. "I'm sorry. You're just so loud."

When I'd asked her to look at my arm, she'd known how much the Noise would hurt her. She also knew what would happen to her synesthesia when the relay went off. Yet she'd chosen to help me despite the cost, despite the danger. Because she cared about me, even after all I'd done.

And knowing that, how could I turn back now?

I picked up the EMP bomb from the workbench, hefting it in both hands. "Go ahead," I said. "I'm right behind you."

Zero Hour

Draped in tarpaulins and paint-speckled plastic, the woodshop looked like an alien landscape. The smells of sawdust and grease mingled with the fumes of rubbing alcohol from Milo's first aid kit, and as I sat by the worktop with the EMP bomb lashed to my wrist, I felt oddly light-headed, as though I'd been drugged.

I hadn't, though. Medication didn't always mix well with my alien biology, and it was too risky to start experimenting now. Milo was in charge of the kill switch and the timed detonator gave me a little leeway, but I didn't want anything dulling my reflexes when I pressed that button.

I looked down at my forearm, where Alison had traced the outline of my chip—the lurking spider beneath my skin that only she could see. And it did resemble a spider, with the blob of quicksilver in the middle and sensor-tendrils branching out in all directions. But the "legs" were only a couple of centimeters long, so it shouldn't be hard for Sebastian to avoid them. Or so I hoped, because the alternative was a massive seizure.

The marker brushed my skin again, drawing a line ten centimeters below the elbow. Not Alison this time: she'd dropped the pen and fled, tears of pain glimmering in her eyelashes. It was Milo who held the marker now, his dark head bent so low that the glasses were sliding off his nose. His hand shook, the line wobbled, and he breathed a curse.

"It's okay," I said. "It's just a guideline."

He pushed his glasses back into place and straightened up, his eyes haunted. "You're so calm," he said. "How can you be so calm?"

I didn't feel calm. My stomach was seething like an active volcano, and sweat trickled down my spine. But if I didn't keep it together, Milo and the others would fall apart too. And I couldn't afford that. I needed him. I needed all of them.

My free hand gripped the detonator, thumb hovering over the button. The strap that bound the EMP bomb to my wrist was too tight, blood throbbing beneath my reddened skin. I concentrated on my breathing—in through the nose, out through the mouth—while Sebastian worked quietly behind my back and Milo wrapped the tourniquet around my upper forearm. I was going to get through this. I was not going to panic. I was not . . .

A muffled clank sounded from the other room, unexpected but familiar. It took me two dazed seconds to realize that it was my phone, tucked inside my discarded hoodie. Someone had sent me a text—and since pretty much everyone else who'd ever texted me was here, it had to be one of my parents.

"I'll get it," said Milo. He ducked through the strip curtain and returned, frowning at the screen.

"What did they say?" I asked.

He shook his head, and set the phone aside. "Never mind. It can wait."

"No, it can't," I said. "That was my dad, wasn't it? What's the message?"

"Look, you don't need this right now. Let's just—"

"Tell me!" I shouted.

Milo closed his eyes, as though I'd exhausted him. Then he picked up the phone and turned it toward me.

It wasn't from Dad. It was my mother.

—DECKARD WAS HERE. I'VE CALLED DAD.

HE'S COMING TO GET YOU.

As though running could save me now, from Deckard or anyone else. And the thought of Dad barging into the maker-space, finding me like this, was unbearable.

"Lock the door," I said to Alison, but Sebastian spoke before she could move: "It's locked." He crouched in front of me, laying a steadying hand on my shoulder. "I won't let Deckard hurt you," he said. "Don't worry about him."

"I'm not," I said thickly.

He gave me a penetrating look. Then he stood up. "I've taken the guides off," he said, "and cleaned the blade. I'll need you to lift your elbow."

My hand felt slick on the detonator. I flexed my fingers, willing the cramped muscles to relax. "All right," I said, and a cool metal plate slid underneath my forearm as Sebastian pushed the saw into position.

A sliding compound miter saw, to be exact—also known as a chop saw. It consisted of a large circular blade suspended vertically over a metal platform, with a slit through its center so the blade could be fully lowered. The blade was designed with a hand grip at the top, so the operator could pull it down with as much strength as necessary to make a clean cut through the wood or metal below.

Or in this case, through the flesh and bone of a scared alien girl who might or might not survive the operation but either way would never use her right hand again.

My righteous right hand, Mrs. Park's Bible verse had said. I was fairly well ambidextrous, but even so, I depended on that hand for so many things. Without it, what kind of maker would I be? Not very righteous, I suspected. I'd be slow. Clumsy. Dependent on other people's help. No doubt I'd learn to compensate eventually, but I'd never forget what I'd lost.

"Wait," said Milo. "I have to tighten the tourniquet." He bent over me, pulled the strap snug, and twisted the pin until my arm throbbed in protest. "Okay, I think it's good."

I looked down at the sleek, professional-looking band, clearly designed for the purpose. "You got this from your mom?" I asked.

"Yeah. I told her I had to do a presentation on emergency medicine for health class." He straightened up, his eyes avoiding mine. "She was thrilled. Drove back to work and borrowed a whole bunch of stuff."

"Tori." Sebastian spoke quietly. "We'd better get started." He looked over his shoulder at Alison. "Ready?"

Alison was breathing hard, freckles stark against the whiteness of her face. She'd pressed herself against the opposite wall, as far away from my Noise as she could get, and she looked ready to faint at any minute. But she nodded.

Milo moved behind me, wrapping his arms around my waist and holding me tight. He said huskily, "I've got you. Try to relax."

"Just don't forget to let go of me afterward, okay? If it takes me, and you're too close—"

Milo bowed his head, silky hair brushing my cheek. His lips moved softly against the nape of my neck as he whispered, "I know."

He didn't want to watch what Sebastian was about to do. I didn't blame him. I clenched my right hand around the strap of the EMP bomb and poised my left thumb over the detonator. My throat ached, and my mouth felt dry. Any second now, it would begin.

"*Niki!*" Dad's voice echoed from the corridor outside, muffled but frantic. He was knocking on the door—no, pounding on it, with those big bear's paws of his. But it was a heavy steel door with a deadlock, and it wasn't going anywhere. "Niki, open the door!"

Sebastian looked at me for confirmation. I replied in a harsh whisper:

"Do it."

The saw buzzed to life, its whine escalating to a scream. Alison shrank back, covering her ears. Sebastian's lips moved, inaudible but clear: "God have mercy."

And the spinning blade came down.

The pain was white-hot, searing, breathtaking. It bit through my skin and ground straight down to the bone; it strangled the yell that had bubbled up in my throat and turned my insides to slurry. As the saw ground to a halt in mid-cut, Sebastian shaking with the effort of holding it steady, I felt darkness whirling in from the edges of my vision—

No!

I fought for consciousness with all my remaining strength, clinging to my own agony like a lifeline. I had to stay alert until the chip in my arm registered that my life was in danger, until the relay came zooming through the doorway to rescue me, until the instant I heard Alison cry out—

"NOW!"

Sebastian's hand jerked down. The slice of hot steel through my forearm gave way to a sickening rush of cold air, and the weight of the EMP bomb dropped away. My left thumb shook and slipped around the detonator, groping for the button. Where was it? I could feel the chip in my arm vibrating, and I knew I had only nanoseconds left—

All at once I was yanked backward, breath crushed out of me by the force of Milo's arms. The detonator tumbled out of my hand as I went flying away from the workbench, speechless with pain and the shock of failure—

I crashed to the floor with Milo beneath me. His head smacked the concrete with a sickening *crack*, and he went limp. Panicked, I scrabbled to get off him as my ears roared and my skin began to tingle—

"No! No, Tori, stop!"

Alison's face swam into my vision, blurred and distorted by tears. She grabbed my shoulders, sobs breaking like mad laughter from her lips. "It's done," she gasped. "It's over."

The saw whined to a halt, leaving only a deafening silence. I was shaking uncontrollably, my right arm numb to the shoulder, and when I tried to speak, no sound came out. Weakness swept through me, and the room spun sideways as I fell—

CLANG.

It sounded like the biggest gong I'd ever heard, a deafening reverberation that shocked my mind blank and turned my muscles to water. I heard Alison scream, and then a black hole opened up in front of me and sucked me in.

PART FIVE: Regenerative Feedback

(The increase in signal strength that occurs when part of the output energy returns to the input signal and reinforces it)

Phase I

It seemed like only a minute before I fought my way back to consciousness. But when I opened my eyes, everything had changed.

I was lying on a bed in a darkened room, with tubes and wires hooked to me everywhere and a monitor bleeping softly above my head. Light slanted through the half-open door, and sounds drifted in: the rubbery squeak of shoes on tile, the rattle of a wheeled cart, the distant ring of a telephone . . .

A hospital. I was in a hospital.

Terror stabbed into me. I grabbed at the bedrail, trying to push myself up, but my hand passed through it like a ghost.

I fell awkwardly onto my bandaged elbow, dull pain radiating up to my shoulder as my other hand flailed for support. Only when I'd steadied myself and got my breath back did I realize why I'd fallen.

My right hand and half my forearm were missing. There was nothing there now but a temporary prosthetic—a thick stump of padding that started five centimeters below the elbow joint and ended in a rounded knob where my wrist used to be.

And yet I could have sworn I had fingers. I could flex them open, curl them shut—I could even feel my nails digging into my palm. How could an illusion seem so real?

A sob trembled against my lips, but I swallowed it back. I had no time for self-pity. I had to pull these tubes out of my body, find my clothes, and get out of here fast, before—

Then something stirred in the chair by the foot of the bed, and a sleepy voice murmured, "Tori?"

I froze. "Mom?"

"Oh, thank God!" She leaped up and rushed to me. "I was afraid you'd never wake up!"

"Who brought me here?" I asked. "And when?"

"Your father drove you," she said. "Eight hours ago. You'd lost a lot of blood, sweetheart, and none of us knew how to fix what you'd done to yourself—he had no choice."

No wonder I felt so weak. "I can't be in a hospital," I said. "I have to get out of here."

"It's all right," she said, smoothing my hair back and kissing my forehead. "Just rest. Your friend Sebastian said he'd look after everything."

How? By hacking into the hospital's server and altering my medical records? I didn't doubt he could do it, but that wouldn't erase the memories of all the doctors and nurses who'd worked on me since I came in. And it definitely wouldn't stop Deckard and the people at GeneSystem from finding me.

"He asked me to give you this," my mother added softly and pressed something into my upturned palm.

My fingers closed around a sphere of brushed metal. I lifted it to eye level, turning it in all directions. It gave no light, no warmth, not even the slightest vibration. And when I put it down on my lap and tried to twist it open, the top half refused to move.

The relay was dead. And I was here, alive.

"Oh, honey," said Mom, touching my wet cheek. "Let me get you a Kleenex. And then I'll call Dad—they must be finished splinting his hand by now."

"His hand?" I took the tissue she offered and clumsily wiped my eyes. "What did he do to it?"

"Broke three bones, trying to get to you. We didn't realize at first—we were so afraid you wouldn't make it through surgery, and then . . ."

So they'd operated on me while I was unconscious. I had a feeling I'd be better off not knowing the details. "I'm sorry," I said. "I didn't want him to get hurt."

"Shh." She squeezed my good hand. "Don't worry about that. He'll be fine."

Phase II

After all the pain, stress, and emotion of the day before, not to mention the nurses checking on me every half hour all night, I slept badly and woke far too early the next morning. My parents had gone home to sleep at my insistence, so there was nobody I could talk to, and eating breakfast one-handed was frustrating, especially when I flipped my bagel off the tray and it landed jam-side down on the blankets. But by eight o'clock they'd taken most of the tubes out, and by nine they told me I could get up and walk around a little if I wanted.

I was shuffling down the corridor with my IV stand beside me and my injured arm in a sling, trying to ignore the cramping in a wrist I no longer had, when I heard footsteps coming up behind me. Automatically I stepped aside to let the nurse pass, but then a voice said, "Niki?" and I turned.

It was Alison.

She looked pale and nervous, a magazine twisted into a tight spiral between her hands. But when our eyes met she gave a little smile. "You look amazing."

"Don't you need a barf bucket for a lie that big?" I asked, and she laughed.

"I said *amazing*, not *beautiful*." She gestured back the way she'd come. "Do you want to go to the lounge? It's not far."

I looked down at my hospital gown and old-lady slippers. One of the nurses had helped me put on some pajama pants, and tied the gown up in back. But I still felt half-naked. "Is there anybody else in there?"

"No. The TV's off." The tone of her voice said, *Thank God for that*. "Come on. I bought you some coffee."

The lounge was a few meters behind us, down a short hallway: a cozy, sunlit space with plump chairs, plenty of tables, and a wall of windows overlooking the street four stories below. I lowered myself into a seat across from Alison, took the coffee she handed me, and breathed the fragrant steam until I felt human again. Or as human as I'd ever be, anyway.

"So what happened back at the makerspace?" I asked between sips. "I thought I'd screwed everything up."

"You didn't," she said. "You hit the detonator at exactly the right moment. Milo pulled you out of range, and I tried to reassure you, but you were in shock, and you fought us. You didn't realize the relay had already beamed your arm—and the bomb—away."

That was what I'd banked my life on. The relay's beam had a limited range, so it couldn't disintegrate two separate objects at once, and I'd guessed that the part of me with the chip in it would take priority. Though I'd also known it would quickly recognize the error and try to correct it, which was why I'd panicked when I couldn't get away from Milo fast enough. Because if my EMP bomb didn't go off and the relay came after the rest of me, there'd be no escape.

But Alison was still talking, and I didn't want to interrupt. "When I looked up, I saw the relay hovering over us," she said, "swiveling from side to side like it was confused. Then it just . . . dropped." She spread her hands in a final gesture. "It hit the floor so hard the whole room turned blazing orange, like the worst migraine I'd ever had. But when the pain cleared and the taste in my mouth went away, I felt better. More than better. I felt *normal*, for the first time in ages." She closed her eyes, savoring the memory. "That was when I knew the wormhole had finally closed."

So that was the *clang* I'd heard just before I blacked out. No wonder Alison had screamed. "What about Barry?" I asked. "Please tell me he's not still tied up at the makerspace."

"Your dad found him on the way in," she said. "That was why he was so anxious to get to you—he thought Deckard had done it. We let Barry go before we took you to the hospital."

"We?"

"Your dad and I," she said. "Faraday stayed at the makerspace with Milo." She turned the curled magazine facedown on her lap and made a half-hearted attempt at smoothing it out. "I haven't seen either one of them since."

Dad had told me last night that Milo had a mild concussion and that Sebastian had taken him home to rest. I also knew that at some point Sebastian had talked to Mom and given her the relay. So I wasn't worried, but I was surprised. "Then where did you sleep last night?" I asked.

"In your room," she said. "Your dog is adorable, by the way. I don't usually like dogs, but I'd adopt yours in a—"

She stopped, staring at someone behind me. I sighed and twisted in my chair. "Look, Sebastian," I began, but the words died in my mouth.

It wasn't Sebastian. It was Deckard.

"Good morning," he said in his soft voice. "Hope I'm not interrupting anything."

Rage boiled up in me, too hot for fear. How dare he come after me now, after what I'd just been through? "This is a hospital," I snapped. "I am a patient. I'm calling security."

"Wait." He held up his hands. "Just hear me out. I'm not here to cause you trouble."

I ignored him, looking around and under the chair in all directions. Where was the button? There had to be a call button around here—

"Tori." Alison's voice was quiet. "He's telling the truth."

"I came to tell you there's no need to run from me anymore," Deckard interrupted, as I drew breath to yell for help.

"You and your parents are no longer part of my investigations, on behalf of GeneSystem or otherwise. And Dr. Gervais has agreed not to make any further attempts to contact you."

"Agreed with whom?" I asked, but Deckard only gave a thin smile.

"I'm not at liberty to disclose that information," he said. He tipped his head to me, two fingers raised as though touching an invisible cap. "Good-bye, Ms. Beaugrand. Enjoy your freedom." His eyes flicked to my right arm, cradled in its sling. "Such as it is."

Then he walked out.

Alison and I traded glances. "I don't get it," I said. "Why would GeneSystem hire Deckard to hunt me down and then call him off as soon as he succeeded? What kind of game are they playing?"

"I don't think it's a game," she replied, looking troubled. "I can't taste lies as well as I used to, but I know that wasn't one. Or at least he believed he was telling the truth when he said it."

So either Deckard had found the answers he'd been looking for and GeneSystem had decided they weren't interested in studying my weird biology after all—both of which seemed unlikely to say the least—or someone had convinced them to leave me alone. Someone who was either powerful and threatening enough to scare them away or who could offer them something they wanted even more than they wanted me . . .

Just rest, murmured Mom's voice in my memory. *Your friend Sebastian said he'd look after everything.*

I sat up, clutching the arm of the chair. "Alison," I said. "I need to use your phone."

I texted badly, my left thumb clumsy on the keypad. Don't you dare leave without saying good-bye. Get up here and talk to me right now. I'm in Room 408.

But as usual, Sebastian didn't answer. And as I watched Alison gazing ruefully at the curled-up *MAKE* Magazine on her lap, I wondered if Deckard had warned him that she was here. Should I tell her what I'd guessed about the deal Sebastian had made with GeneSystem? Or would it only cause her more pain?

"I'm sorry," I said finally, giving back the phone. "I guess he's gone."

Alison took it silently and put it in her purse. Her eyes were dry, but I'd never seen anyone look so sad.

"Thanks for the magazine," I ventured after a minute. "Or the paper telescope. Whatever."

She gave a sheepish smile. "I don't like hospitals. Sorry." She touched the crumpled magazine. "I'll get you a new one."

Sunlight filtered through the windows behind her, and dust motes glimmered in a reddish halo around her head. Saint Alison of the Perpetual Disappointment, pray for us. "You don't owe me anything," I said. "You've already done more than I had any right to ask. If my plan hadn't worked . . ."

I didn't need to finish the sentence, because we both knew what would have happened. At best, Alison would have suffered through two or three weeks of hellish sensory overload, fighting for her sanity every second. At worst, Mathis would have beamed her through the wormhole right after me.

"Let's not even think about that," Alison said. "It's bad enough that it *did* work." She looked out the window and added, "That's probably how Faraday feels about it too."

"That explains why he might not want to see me," I said. Though it hardly excused him, in my opinion. If I could deal with losing my arm, there was no reason he couldn't get over being the one who'd cut it off. "It doesn't explain him avoiding you."

"No?" She raised her teacup, hiding her expression. "Well, maybe not."

We sat together quietly for a few minutes, finishing our drinks. Then my bladder twinged a protest, so I struggled to my feet. "Back in a sec," I said and pushed my IV stand out into the hallway.

And there was Sebastian, leaning against the wall outside my room with his arms folded and his long legs crossed at the ankles. As though he'd been waiting for a while.

"Hey," I said, and he glanced at me in surprise.

"I thought you were in the washroom," he said.

"No, the lounge." I jerked a thumb over my shoulder. "I'm doing a washroom run now, but it won't take long. Why don't you sit down and make yourself uncomfortable?"

His mouth twisted ruefully, but he didn't protest. He stepped around me, heading down the corridor and into the room beyond.

I listened for the intake of breath, the sudden stop—but it never came. And when I peered into the lounge, I saw Sebastian pull out the chair I'd vacated and sit down across from Alison, folding his hands deliberately on the table between them. As though he'd known she'd be there all along.

Well, of course he had. I'd texted him using Alison's phone. I could still use a washroom, but it wasn't unbearable yet. Carefully I lifted my IV stand off the tile so it wouldn't squeak. Then I backed against the wall and listened.

"Deckard was here a few minutes ago," said Alison. She sounded calm—a lot calmer than I would have been in her place. "Did you know?"

He couldn't lie to her, so he didn't try. "Yes."

"I thought so." The chair creaked as she shifted position. "How did you get him to drop the case?"

"Does it matter? The important thing is that he did."

"Yes, but he wasn't only looking for Tori, was he? He was searching for you as well. The Sudbury police—"

"The charges are minor," said Sebastian, "and easily settled. I'm not worried."

Alison was silent. Then she said, "You haven't asked me to forgive you."

"No."

"You don't think I can?"

"I don't think you should."

"Why not? Do you think I don't understand why you did it? Do you think I believe you ever wanted to hurt me, or Tori either?"

"That's irrelevant." Sebastian sounded tired. "Whatever my intentions, my actions were unforgivable. I betrayed your trust and hers, and you both paid a terrible price." The chair made a scraping noise as he pushed it back. I risked a glance around the corner, in case he was getting up to leave—but no, he'd walked to the window instead.

"I thought you'd be happier not knowing I'd come back, or

that you were in danger," Sebastian continued, his eyes on the traffic. "I thought I could handle Mathis on my own, or at least with some help from Tori. I was wrong."

Alison made a pitying noise. "You should taste what you sound like. All purple and bitter, like old-fashioned cocoa. All right, you made a mistake. Call it a sin, even, if *mistake* isn't a strong enough word. But if you hadn't put that chip in Tori's arm, she wouldn't be here now. The relay would just have kept scanning until it found her, and then it would have beamed her back to Mathis. All of her."

"We don't know that for certain. There might have been a better solution, if I'd had the wits to think of it. And I should never have pretended to cooperate with Mathis in the first place. If I'd stood up to him, maybe even killed him—"

"Don't." She got up and moved to his side. "You're not a murderer. And you did the best you could at the time. Not necessarily the best thing of all, but either way, it's *done*. And Tori's forgiven you, so don't try to tell me I can't."

"Alison—"

"No, you listen. You told me back at Pine Hills that I wasn't crazy, and on the station you told me I was stronger than I gave myself credit for. You believed in me, when I'd lost all faith in myself. Well . . . I believe in you now."

Sebastian said nothing.

"I'm not blind, Faraday." Her voice was quiet but firm. "I know you're not perfect. I knew that even before all this happened." She put a hand on his shoulder. "But I also know that you love me. And that's why you've been trying so hard to push me away."

He stepped sideways, out of her reach. "I have nothing to

offer you, Alison," he said. "Every bad thing that's happened to you in the past ten months is my fault. If I hadn't asked Mathis to send me to Earth the first time—"

"Faraday, you were barely thirteen, and you had no idea what was going to happen! How can you blame yourself for that?"

"I wasn't that young when I met you. I was old enough to pose as a graduate student. Old enough to know better than to use you the way I did."

Alison threw up her hands, and I ducked out of sight as she paced back to the table and tossed her empty cup into the bin. "Fine. I give up. Be miserable and lonely, if that's what you think you deserve. But it's not going to make Tori's arm better. It won't erase a single black mark from your record or balance out some cosmic scale of justice in your favor. It's just going to make you miserable and lonely. And I don't see the point."

"Not now, perhaps." His footsteps moved across the floor. "But you will. Good-bye."

I'd had enough. I grabbed my IV stand and stepped out to block his path. "You weren't even going to tell her," I accused. "Did you think she'd figure out the truth or were you expecting me to break the bad news?"

Sebastian didn't look surprised to see me, only resigned. "There's nothing to tell at this point," he said. "I don't know how it's going to play out."

"I do," I said. "What do you think I've been running from all this time? Being poked and prodded and bled and studied under a microscope, and branded as an alien freak for the rest of my life. You think it's going to be any different for you?"

Alison gripped the back of her chair. "What are you saying? That he—"

"I made a bargain with Deckard," Sebastian answered reluctantly. "I told him I had all the same anomalies in my genetic makeup as Tori did. And that I'd answer all his questions, and let GeneSystem do as many tests on me as they wanted, if he promised to leave her alone."

And that was why I couldn't hate Sebastian anymore, even if I'd been stubborn enough to try. Because he'd paid for putting that chip in my arm twice over, and there was no punishment I could think of that was worse than what he'd done to himself.

"You're going to tell them you're an alien," Alison breathed. "After all the years you spent hiding, making sure no one ever found out—"

"That was when I thought I'd been trapped on Earth by mistake," said Sebastian, "and that my real home was on the other side of the wormhole, with people like Mathis." He shook his head. "I've been there and back again. I'd rather stay here."

"As a guinea pig for a bunch of primitive genetic hacks?" I asked. "What kind of life is that?"

"They're scientists, Tori, not monsters," Sebastian replied patiently. "I don't think they're going to put me in a cage. I see no reason we can't work together—I'm a scientist too, after all. But even if that hope turns out to be naive, I have no job, no friends, and no family. If I disappear, no one will miss me." His eyes flicked to Alison. "Or they shouldn't."

"I don't agree." Alison's voice shook, but she kept her head high. "I think it would be a good thing if the people at GeneSystem knew there was at least one person who would care if you disappeared."

"More than one," I said, before Sebastian could speak. "Four people, if you add me and my parents. I think Milo probably counts too. And if you say anything more about being unfit to clean our mildew-infested grout or whatever, I'm going to smack you upside the head with my prosthetic."

Sebastian's mouth twitched, and then he started to laugh. But after a few seconds it sounded more like a cough, and he rubbed his sleeve across his eyes before turning away. "Thank you," he said. "I'll keep that in mind." He took a deep breath, then looked at Alison. "I apologize," he told her. "I misjudged you, in so many ways. But I still think you'd be wiser choosing something—somebody—else."

Alison lowered her eyes. "You're probably right."

Sebastian nodded. He moved toward the door.

"But," Alison called after him, "I made that choice a long time ago. Maybe you thought leaving me alone for three years, or five, would make a difference. But I always knew you'd come back to me someday. Because you didn't close the wormhole as soon as Tori and I were gone, like you were supposed to. You left it open."

I opened my mouth to correct her, but then I thought better of it. Maybe it was Mathis's fault that Sebastian hadn't closed the wormhole right away, but then again, maybe it wasn't. And Alison might have forgotten the time difference between Earth and the space station, but if Sebastian didn't think it worth reminding her, that was his business.

"I have to go," Sebastian said distractedly. "I told Deckard I'd follow him back to Sudbury."

Alison's shoulders slumped, and she began to sit down— but then Sebastian cleared his throat and spoke again. "Though there's room in the truck, if you'd like a ride home. Because . . . it's been good to talk to you. Very good."

Alison drew a slow breath. Then she whispered, "*Sebastian.*"

The way she said his name, and the way he looked at her when she said it, made me suddenly want to be somewhere else. Anywhere else. I backed up into the corridor, but not before I saw Alison and Sebastian leap together like two high-powered magnets, and their mouths met so hard and hungrily that I could tell this kiss would be going on for quite some time.

I tiptoed away with my IV stand and left them to it.

Phase IV

"Seriously?" said Milo, when I told him the story seven hours later. We were sitting together in the courtyard at the hospital's back entrance, inside a half-rusted pavilion littered with cigarette butts and old wads of gum. Between that and the traffic roaring by in the near distance, it was about the least picturesque spot ever. But I'd been pacing the corridors all day, and right now I was just glad to be outside.

"Yeah," I said, leaning back and stretching out my pajama-clad legs. I'd traded my hospital gown for a tank top and zippered sweatshirt my mom had brought me, so I didn't feel half-naked anymore. And though my arm still throbbed, the pain wasn't as distracting as it had been. "It was like watching an emotional grenade go off."

"Wow," Milo said. "Sebastian and Alison kissing? I can't even picture it."

Lucky him. "So what did you tell your mom?" I asked, to change the subject. "About your concussion?"

"Told her I'd slipped in the science lab and clocked myself

on one of the desks," he said. "So now I'm supposed to take it easy for a few days. No running, no biking, and no contact sports. The only reason I'm here right now is because she thinks I had to go to work early for a meeting."

Obviously my new policy of forthrightness and honesty had its limitations. I might have stopped lying to the people I cared about, but that just meant they had to tell more lies on my behalf.

"But I did tell her the truth about one thing," said Milo, as though he'd guessed what I was thinking. "I told her I wasn't going to medical school, even if my marks were good enough. That I'd applied for phys ed at Laurentian, and been accepted."

"Just like that? How did she take it?"

"About as well as I expected. But she didn't kick me out of the house, so that's something." He flicked a bottle cap off the bench, sending it skittering across the walkway into the shrubbery. "How do you feel?"

The sling was chafing the back of my neck. I wriggled out of it and laid my bandaged arm across my lap. "Alive," I said. "And glad it's over."

"You think it is?"

"I know it is," I told him. Even if the EMP bomb hadn't knocked out the space station's life support systems, Mathis no longer had the equipment to open another wormhole, let alone keep it open for more than a nanosecond before it collapsed.

Milo slid his fingers under his glasses and covered his eyes. "Okay," he said roughly. "Good to know," and it took me a minute to realize that he wasn't just tired or fighting a headache. He was crying.

I didn't have to ask why. What I'd put him through yesterday had hit him hard, not just physically but emotionally. In a day or two, when the initial shock wore off and the enormity of what I'd done to myself came crashing in, I'd probably be a wreck myself. But right now I only felt sorry for Milo.

"You were incredible," I whispered, sliding my good arm around his back and leaning my head on his shoulder. "I could never have made it without you."

He gulped a laugh, reached for my right hand—and I felt him shudder as he realized it wasn't there. For a second I thought he was going to pull away from me, but he didn't. He hesitated for one second, and then he drew his hand back and let it drop to his thigh instead.

His thigh, not mine. That was the difference between him and Brendan.

"I've had better dates," Milo said, clearing his throat. "Next time, can we just go out for cake again instead?"

I smiled, but briefly. "Do you want there to be a next time?" I asked.

Milo was quiet. Then he said, "Three days ago, I would have said no. But when I found you in the cemetery and saw how terrified you were, and yet so incredibly brave . . ." He laid his head against mine, soft hair brushing my cheek. "I realized that if I didn't try to make this work, I'd regret it for the rest of my life. Because I'm never going to meet anyone else like you."

"Alien, asexual, and missing a limb?" I pulled back, sweeping the bangs from my eyes. "I'm not seeing the selling point here."

"You're not *that* alien," said Milo impatiently. "Sebastian thinks his ancestors—your ancestors—started here on Earth, but they went through a dimensional rift or something." He touched my bandaged arm. "And I don't care about the hand, except for your sake. Knowing you, you'll find a way to be equally amazing without it."

I'd already started thinking about that. Imagining new prosthetic designs specially suited to the work I loved best, with delicate pincers that could grip solder and twist wire, and magnetic tips to hold tiny screws in place. Interchangeable tools I could snap on easily and almost as quickly as other makers could pick up a wire stripper or a pair of pliers. Maybe there were prostheses like that already—but if not, nobody was going to stop me from making one.

"That's two out of three," I said. "But it's still a pretty big three, don't you think?"

He looked at me, and I could see the uncertainty in his eyes. "Maybe," he said. "I don't know how this is going to work, or if it's going to work out at all. But so far, the good parts of being with you . . . have been pretty good. And I'm ready to keep trying if you are."

I gazed at Milo, studying every detail of his face, reminding myself of all the things I liked about him. Everything he'd done to prove that I could trust him and that he liked me as I really was. Then, gathering courage, I leaned forward and kissed him.

It wasn't a long kiss. It wasn't full of passion, like Sebastian's and Alison's had been. But it wasn't sloppy and disgusting like the way Brendan used to kiss me, either. It was tentative and hopeful and surprisingly sweet, and I didn't mind it at all.

When I drew back Milo's eyes looked slightly glazed, as though I'd dazzled him. He blinked, adjusted his glasses, and said, "So . . . was that real? Or was that pretending?"

I put my good hand in his. "Let's call it an experiment in progress," I said.

ACKNOWLEDGMENTS

This book would never have come into being without the help of many friends and acquaintances who gave up their time to read and critique the manuscript, to share their technical expertise, and to support me in countless other ways.

My first draft beta-reading team of Peter Anderson, Erin Bow, and Deva Fagan read each chapter in process and cheered me on, for which I am deeply grateful. Erin also told me about hackerspaces, which became a major plot element in the book. Jen J. Danna helped me with some crucial brainstorming in the early stages. Claudia Gray and Maggie Stiefvater offered moral support and sensible advice to help me over the hurdles. Kate Johnston, Liz Barr, and Brittany Harrison said heartening things about the first draft, while Tessa Gratton gave me excellent suggestions about how to improve it (bless you, Tessa!).

I am also indebted to the experts who generously shared their knowledge with me and helped me make the technical parts of the story more accurate. Dr. Calvin W. Johnston of San Diego State University advised me on quantum cryptography and helped me brainstorm some crucial aspects of the plot. Dallas Kasaboski shared his engineering knowledge and experience of visiting the Algonquin Radio Observatory. I also received great help and inspiration from the members of the Electro Tech online forum, including JimB, RadioRon, duffy,

BobW, and especially CowboyBob aka Paul Hadley, who went the extra mile to give me technical advice at the last minute. Jason Black also provided expert consultation in the final stages. Any scientific or technical errors that remain in the final draft are entirely my own fault.

The people Niki meets at her local makerspace and at the Magnus Lake Radio Telescope are all fictional, but both settings are based on real locations. I enjoyed my visits to Kwartzlab Makerspace (www.kwartzlab.ca) in Waterloo, Ontario, as well as the opportunity to tour the Algonquin Radio Observatory (www.arocanada.com) under the guidance of Dr. Brendan Quine, Dr. Caroline Roberts, and Catherine Tsouvaltsidis.

Emma Fissenden answered my questions about grocery store procedures, and Nick Bohner cheerfully corrected me in matters of trucks and teen vernacular. The Korean (askakorean.blogspot.com) put my concerns about Milo's name to rest, while S. Jae-Jones read over the manuscript for authenticity and suggested a couple of useful changes.

Finally, I am grateful to my faithful and long-suffering editors, Rebecca Frazer and Andrew Karre; to my wonderful agent, Josh Adams, and UK co-agent, Caroline Walsh; and to all the other members of the publishing team at Orchard Books UK and Carolrhoda Lab/Lerner Publishing Group. Thank you for believing in this book, and in me.

ABOUT THE AUTHOR

R. J. Anderson (known to her friends as Rebecca) was born in Uganda, raised in Ontario, went to school in New Jersey, and has spent much of her life dreaming of other worlds entirely.

She is the author of several books for young readers, including *Ultraviolet*, the Andre Norton Award-nominated companion novel to *Quicksilver*.

Visit Rebecca online at www.rj-anderson.com.